DEMONS AND DREAMS

By
Gerald Thompson

Finger Lakes Publishing

LIMA, NY

Gerald Thompson / Finger Lakes Publishing
1854 Eastwood Dr
Lima, NY 14485
www.demonsanddreams.com
www.geraldthompson.com

Publisher's Note: This is a work of fiction. Names, characters, places, and incidents are a product of the author's imagination. Locales and public names are sometimes used for atmospheric purposes. Any resemblance to actual people, living or dead, or to businesses, companies, events, institutions, or locales is completely coincidental.

Book Layout © 2021 BookDesignTemplates.com

Demons and Dreams / Gerald Thompson. -- 1st ed.
ISBN 978-1-7359287-0-8

To my patient wife, Lorrie,
for putting up with me for all these years.

Finally, be strong in the Lord and in his mighty power. Put on the full armor of God, so that you can take your stand against the devil's schemes. For our struggle is not against flesh and blood, but against the rulers, against the authorities, against the powers of this dark world and against the spiritual forces of evil in the heavenly realms. ...

Ephesians 6:10-18

Table of Contents

Chapter 1

Caleb

Friday, Early Morning

"Caleb, WAKE UP!"

Startled and confused, I struggled to open my eyes, but they refused to budge. I tried to raise my arm to clear them, but it remained frozen. I tried the other limb, and it too lay immobile. *Don't panic, Caleb.* Confused by the paralysis, I focused on the fingers of my right hand. The joints cracked as I slowly flexed my fingers. It didn't hurt, but they also didn't want to move. The more I bent them, the looser they got. My elbow snapped as I lifted my forearm. My shoulder protested as I reached and rubbed my eyes.

A blood-curdling scream broke the silence. I froze as deep chuckles echoed around me.

With urgency, I pried open my eyes. Veins of light flickered like candles and danced across the domed ceiling high above. My neck resisted when I looked left and again, right. With every joint cracking, I strained to sit up. Once vertical, I studied my surroundings.

The dim light revealed row upon row of beds with humanoid lumps lying on them. Mysterious beings wove their way through the cots while others floated above. I shook my head and blinked before looking again. It was hard to tell. The half-light and distance made it difficult to see.

I looked toward the bed on my right. A pajama-clad woman lay there without a blanket to cover her. An aisle separated us. The bare mattress rested on a three-foot-high grubby white metal frame. It looked like something you slept on at camp. As I watched, she smiled, sighed, and rolled away from me.

I turned to see what was on the other side. I scrambled backward and fell on the floor. Every joint made a sound like twisting bubble wrap. I crept to my knees and peered over the top of the mattress. A man lay on his back, and his legs thrashed wildly. A creature perched on the man's torso and held on as the man bucked. One of its arms dug into his head, and the other reached into his chest. The man's legs stopped, and his back arched as silent screams erupted from his open mouth. Pain and anguish painted his face. I gasped, and the creature turned its head towards me. A toothy grin split the ghastly mask as flames of sadistic pleasure danced in its eyes. The scent of decay assailed my nose.

Its eyes narrowed; it growled, "Go back to sleep, huu-maan."

I jumped up and fell flat on my face as my feet slipped on the glass-like floor. Blood gushed from my nose and left a trail down my shirt as I got up and ran. I dropped to the ground and rolled under several beds. When I found myself in another aisle, I crouched and tried to hide. I repeated this process a couple more times. Out of breath, I squatted between two beds and rested. Slowly, I lifted my head and looked for pursuit. I discovered none and returned to the floor.

What was that thing? It had bright red eyes, a human-like face with a pointy chin, and a mouth full of tiny sharp teeth. Sprigs of coarse hair sprouted from its head attached to its scrawny neck. Burnt red blotches mottled the crimson skin of its hairless body. Its muscular arms and legs looked too long for its build. The naked creature's gender remained a mystery.

Using my sleeve, I wiped the dripping blood from my nose. What a mess! Blood all over my shirt. I rubbed my hands on my pants and left trails of burgundy on them. The stains annoyed and disgusted me, but I put those thoughts aside for now.

Like a periscope, I lifted my head high enough to look around. I crouched in the middle of a sea of beds. Dull light still rippled in fluctuating waves across the high domed ceiling, providing dim illumination. A distant scream, followed by baritone laughter, echoed off the cavernous walls. I studied the ceiling far above. It must be hundreds of feet high. I couldn't see an end to this ocean of beds. Every bed I saw had a sleeper on it.

Off to my left, through the gloom, I saw a rectangular structure. To my right, I saw nothing but beds. Behind me, the aisle stretched into the twilight, and before me, a broad walkway crossed my path. Crawling on my hands and knees, I crept to the opening between the last two beds. I looked up and down the central aisle. Seeing no one else, I stooped low and ran toward the building. When I reached it, my burning legs forced me to rest. It was farther away than it looked. My heart pounded in my ears. With my back against the wall, I slowly slid down until I sat on the floor and waited to catch my breath.

Jumbled thoughts and a myriad of questions flooded my mind. I closed my eyes. *Calm down and think, Caleb.* My breath slowed; I opened my eyes and surveyed the surroundings once more. The half-light made it hard to see. Shadows continued weaving amongst and above the sleepers. Occasionally, a cry reached my ears, followed by a chorus of deep laughter. I didn't know which disturbed me more, the terrified shrieks or the sadistic mirth.

As I clambered to my feet, I stepped away from the wall and turned to examine the structure. I faced the short side of the rectangular building, perhaps fifty feet wide, standing about ten feet tall. *Why is this building here?* There was no other structure as far as I could see.

Broken ceramic tiles peppered the wall's surface, and many of them lay shattered on the floor. In the middle of the wall, an open doorway beckoned me. My foot kicked a piece of the broken tile, and it skittered across the ground. As I stepped through the opening, something materialized before me.

I fell backward and landed hard. I crab-scrambled away from the apparition. As I retreated, the monster faded from sight. What was that thing? It was similar to the other beast. Its crimson eyes bored into mine while the blood-red lips smacked as if I were a tasty morsel. The thing stank of death. *Why didn't it attack?*

A seed of a thought germinated in my mind, and it grew into a scary realization. These creatures are demons. They only lacked the horns and a forked tail.

I'm dead, and this is Hell! I collapsed on the floor as my fear and emotions poured through my eyes. *How can this be?* I just fell asleep on the couch! A pool of tears collected beneath me, and my chest hurt.

Eventually, my brain re-engaged. *This doesn't feel like Hell.* There are no flames or physical torment, comfortable temperature, and a bunch of beds with people sleeping on them.

Perplexed, I sat and drew my handkerchief from my pocket. I wiped my eyes and blew my nose. Dried blood and mucous stained the cloth. *Would a dead person need to blow their nose?*

With renewed hope, I stood. My legs wobbled a bit and steadied after a few seconds. I still didn't know what to do next. *Am I dreaming?* I slapped myself hard. *Ow! Ok, I'm awake.* If I'm not dreaming and not dead, where am I? No answers came to my mind. While contemplating my next step, a compulsion to enter the room grew within me. It felt like someone stood behind me and pushed me toward the opening. I panicked.

A voice spoke, "Trust me." My head whipped around, looking for the source of those words.

The force behind me strengthened. I planted my feet on the smooth floor, yet I steadily moved toward the demon doorway. I tried to turn around and run, but it was like a bulldozer pushed me. I leaned back against the force behind me, and my sneakers squeaked as I tried to brace myself on the smooth floor. With my arms straight out, I waited for the inevitable. With every inch I slid, my terror grew. My outstretched hands caught the door jamb as I locked my elbows to keep from entering the room. The constant push overpowered my strength and broke my grip. I stumbled over the threshold into the chamber.

The demon reappeared. It stood my height. Our eyes locked, and a toothy grin spread across its face. Saliva dribbled from the corner of its mouth as it chuckled and took a step towards me. Warm urine ran down my legs and pooled on the floor. It laughed even louder and took another step. "Are you scared, Huu-maan?" it asked. "You're suppooosed to be asleeeep." It smacked its lips, and another drop of saliva escaped its mouth. It took a third, slow step relishing my terror. "I don't think they'll miss you. They'll just wonder why you died in your sleep."

A new compulsion grabbed my vocal cords, and I shouted, "Jesus is my Savior! Jesus is my Savior!" I covered my head, closed my eyes, and waited for the attack.

When nothing happened, I cracked one eye open. The demon had retreated several steps and glowered at me. I opened the other eye as I straightened up. The beast just stood there. *Why isn't it attacking?*

Pulse racing, I peered at the beast then glanced around the room. My eyes flicked back to the creature; then, I dared a second glance about me. To my left, about two feet away, stood a stainless-steel table piled with an assortment of parts and junk.

"Pick up the tube," commanded the voice in my head. I didn't question it this time.

On top of this heap rested a black plastic tube about two feet long. It could have been a vacuum cleaner attachment. As I reached for it, a glimmer of white light crawled along its surface. My right hand grasped the thick end of the tube, and I heard myself say, "The Sword of the Spirit, which is the Word of God."

11

The plastic tube became a silver sword that hummed with a pulsing white aura. I stared at the blade. It shone brightly in this dark place. The sword was light in weight but solid. A tingling sensation flowed into my hand, spread up my arm to my neck, and scripture burst upon my consciousness. I felt like I could quote the whole Bible. No, I knew I could quote the entire Bible.

I staggered under the intense feelings and power. I lifted the sword closer to my face with renewed confidence, and I ran my left hand along the flat part of the blade. It felt warm and glass smooth. Stupidly, I ran my left thumb along the top edge. Sharper than a razor, the sword slid through the skin. I jerked my hand away and examined it. Instead of blood dripping from the wound, I found a severe, inch-long burn.

A low growl reminded me that I was not alone. I lifted the sword as I turned toward the sound, and the sword vibrated as if it looked forward to striking this monster. The demon took a wrestler's position: knees bent, elbows up. Inch long claws tipped each finger. I mirrored its stance. Ribbons of light rippled up and down the blade. The demon scowled as a deep-throated growl replaced its mocking laughter. Its eyes darted back and forth between the weapon and me as I quaked under its gaze and tightened my grip on the hilt. The metal felt pliable like clay in my hand. We circled each other, and I wondered who would make the first move. The beast approached the doorway. Suddenly, it turned and dove, disappearing as it passed over the threshold. Stunned, I lowered the sword.

Puzzled, I stood there. *What just happened? Why didn't it attack?* Relief replaced fear. I didn't understand what happened. I thought I was dead. Holding the sword in front of me, I walked over and looked out the doorway to see if the demon was out amongst the beds. I didn't see it so I turned and re-entered the building.

The same dingy, white tiles covered the interior walls. *Now what?* I peered into the gloom and felt compelled to go deeper into the room.

I didn't fight it this time. The sword's aura provided illumination. A long row of steel tables faded into the darkness down the center of the room. The closest one held the different vacuum cleaner parts and other junk. The other tables I saw contained nothing. Beds lined the walls, and the closest ones appeared empty. The dim light made it impossible to see what lay at the far end. I cautiously moved down the aisle.

As I crept forward, I could see one bed with a human-shaped lump on it. I jumped. A high-pitched scream bounced off the walls, and the person on the bed convulsed. I inched closer, sword ready. A small demon sat on a women's chest with both hands embedded in her skull. The creature screamed, sounding like a little girl, "Mmmooommmyyy." It cackled. It hadn't noticed me. I looked at the sword and then the little monster. I stepped forward. The light from the sword reached the demon causing it to turn its head in my direction. I swung. As the blade struck, surprise crossed its face just before it became vapor and dissipated. Alarmed, I spun around a couple of times, looking for the demon. *Where'd it go? Did I kill it?*

A low moan rose from behind me, and I turned my attention to the occupant of the bed. The woman no longer thrashed. For better light, I held the sword near her face. Tears pooled in her eyes and overflowed onto the mattress. A sob escaped her throat. I bent down and whispered in her ear, "Wake up. The demon's dead." She didn't stir.

I put a hand on her shoulder and gently shook her as I whispered, "In the name of Jesus, awake."

Her eyelids burst open, complete with panic. They darted about until they met mine. Even in the dim light, her green eyes sparkled. She struggled to sit. Her joints cracked as mine did. I tried to help her, but she turned away, causing a rapid popping sound. I stepped back to give her room. She placed her feet on the floor, and her knees buckled. She caught the bed frame and tried again. With more confidence, she let go of the bed and faced me.

"Go," I pointed toward the exit. "See if you can find a way out. Remember, Jesus will save and protect you." *Why did I say that?*

Wordlessly, she scanned my body from toe to head. Her eyes bore into mine as if she examined my soul. I pointed to the door again. She turned and left the way I came. I continued down the row of beds until I reached the end of the room.

I found neither people nor demons. I did pass about thirty tables and discovered a doorway. I stepped through it and found myself in the original cavern. I sighed. *Now, what do I do?*

Another bed sat by the door with a man lying on it. He looked the same as the other sleepers. No, not quite the same. The other sleepers had a faint glow about them. It was hard to notice until it was absent. He still breathed, but there was no inner spark. No spirit. Spiritually dead, but not physically dead. How odd and how sad, I thought.

I turned to continue my exploration and banged into a muscular wall of blood-red flesh. My eyes traveled upward. A demon towered over me; its foul breath and saliva rained down. I jumped back in terror. The sword clattered to the floor. Its clawed hand reached for me; evil red eyes filled my vision.

"Jesus is my Savior!"

Chapter 2

Caleb

Friday, Early Morning

"Jesus is my Savior!" I yelled, rolled off the couch, and smashed my nose on the dingy gray linoleum. Blood gushed and stained the floor, a brilliant crimson. Cursing, I jumped up and raced for the kitchen sink while blood splattered on my shirt. Several paper towels later, the bleeding stopped.

As I washed my face, I remembered that awful place and relief flooded my mind. *It's a dream!* A choked laugh escaped my throat as I dried my face, and I dropped into a kitchen chair. I reached for a napkin on the table and blew my nose again to remove the remaining blood.

What a nightmare: sight, sound, touch, smell, and fear. Never had a dream taken over my senses. It was so real. The receding adrenaline caused little spasms in my hands and arms.

Get a grip, Caleb. You're thirty years old, not five. You had a nightmare, nothing more.

I breathed a sigh of relief then laughed again. A dream, nothing but a dream. I can't wait to tell . . . Then the loneliness returned. There was no one to tell.

I had no close friends or relatives, just a few work acquaintances. A social cripple, that's what I was. I never knew what to say or how to behave when I met new people. As a teenager, I stuttered and looked at my feet, rarely lifting my head to look into their eyes. Bullies loved tormenting me. Though I no longer stuttered, I still had a hard time meeting people. Until I get to know them, I'm very uncomfortable.

Why was I like this? I blamed my father, and my father defined cruelty.

Mom wanted to name me "Caleb" after her daddy. Father protested until he looked up the name. It means "Dog" in Hebrew. Then he was all for it. Father relished telling me he had never wanted a kid; a dog is what he wanted, and that's what he got! He'd guffawed every time he said it.

Father whistled and patted his thigh whenever he wanted me to come to him. Most of the time, Father enjoyed mentally torturing me. When home, he watched TV and drank beer. I tried to hide in my room, but my old man usually wanted me nearby to fetch the next bottle. He subjected me to an endless stream of belittling insults. "Get me a beer, you mangy cur!" My only relief came when he passed out in his chair.

Sometimes his abuse became physical. I would do something that annoyed him; he would yell and punch me. He never hit me in the face. He didn't want any visible evidence of his abuse. However, he felt no such restrictions on my gut or butt.

If I made him furious, he ordered me to cut a switch off the pussy willow outback. I had to strip off the leaves and buds then give it to him on bended knee like a knight who presented the king his sword. He'd make me drop my pants, lean on the kitchen table, and "teach me a lesson about respect."

Fortunately, he only resorted to physical violence, maybe once a month. But this left me nervous the rest of the time because I never knew what might set him off. He'd accuse me of looking at him funny or mocking him, and then my backside suffered his wrath.

The only way to survive the onslaught of abuse was not to care about anything. Maybe I was depressed, I don't know. I went through the motions of life, but not the emotion. I was rarely angry, but I was also rarely happy. I take that back; the anger towards my father never showed on my face but simmered beneath.

I had no friends in high school. I interacted with people when I had to. I became a failure because I didn't care. My apathy doomed all of my college, women, and career efforts as I drifted through life.

I returned to the present, stood, and looked around my apartment. What a dream, so vivid! And why would I say, "Jesus is my Savior?" I hadn't been to church in over a decade and hadn't given Jesus much thought at all. Well, He got more thought during desperate times. My only recent exposure to Jesus had been the late-night television evangelists.

I shook my head, trying to untangle the thoughts and emotions that ran through my mind. *What day is it? Friday?* I pulled the curtain back and looked out the window. The daylight was brighter than I expected. I glanced at my watch and panicked. I had to get moving or be late for work, and I hadn't been tardy in three years. Falling asleep in one's work clothes did have its advantages. I went to the bathroom to wash up.

In the mirror stood a mess of a man. Blood covered much of the front of me. Wait a minute. There were bright red wet stains that mingled with darker dried blood. The sleeve mainly had old blood on it.

I didn't have time for this mystery. I stripped off the garment and tossed it in the bathtub to deal with it later. It took a few moments to wash my face, slap on some deodorant, and drag a toothbrush across my teeth. I grabbed a clean shirt out of the closet, slipped it on, and buttoned it as I trotted to the kitchen. Breakfast had to be coffee and a donut on the way to work. Ready to depart, I looked at my watch again. Four minutes, not bad. I think that's a new record.

Pausing, I surveyed my apartment one last time before heading out the door. I saw the red puddle on the floor. I'd forgotten to clean up the blood. I looked at my watch and back to the blood. I was going to be late, yet I needed to clean that . . .

"Aarrgg!" I ran to the kitchen sink, stripped some paper towels off the roll, and splashed cold water on half of them. I turned with dripping towels and leaped for the bloodstain. Landing on my knees, I attacked the blood with a circular motion. On a particularly vigorous scrub, my hand clipped an object just under the edge of the couch. Surprised, I paused, reached under, and pulled something out.

I dropped the object. It banged on the tile as I staggered backward.

Caleb

Friday Morning

There, on the floor, lay the black plastic tube from my nightmare. It appeared to be a rigid, plastic vacuum cleaner tube. It shared the same characteristics, such as color, length, and weight, but I don't own a vacuum cleaner. On a rare occasion, when I felt motivated to clean, I borrowed one from work. I supposed I looked silly, walking it down the sidewalk, but I didn't care. Besides, things can't move between dreams and reality. Still, it sure looked like the one I dreamt about last night.

I picked up the tube again to look at it closer. YYEEOOWW! A sharp pain shot through my hand, and I discovered an inch-long burn on my left thumb.

The tube rattled as it hit the floor again. My mind reeled; the bloody paper towels fell to the floor. I staggered for the door. It slammed behind me as I turned, shoved the key in the lock, and twisted it. Breathing hard, I ran down the hall and crashed through the outside door. I nearly knocked over some guy in a suit. A stream of profanity poured from his mouth as I mumbled apologies and joined the river of pedestrians as they flowed down the sidewalk.

This October day had dawned bright and brisk. I often relished these crisp, clear mornings, but not today. My thoughts and emotions churned as I hurried down the thoroughfare. The mystery of the black tube and the burn on my thumb haunted me.

I didn't have much; I owned no car, bike, or computer. I had an old TV in the corner of my room, a prepaid cell phone, and stacks of books. I spent a lot of time at the library, where I'd surf the web or read. While I never finished college and admit apathy was one of my companions, I'm not stupid. I just didn't care what happened to me or those around me.

It took twenty minutes to walk from my dumpy, first-floor studio apartment to Foe Financial Services. I wove through the sidewalk traffic with my head down, collar up, and rooted in thought. The FFS building dominated the Stanton skyline. A monument of steel and glass to Ichabod Manheim Foe, founder and CEO of Foe Financial Services. I'm one of a dozen cleaners.

Life had been hard. I floated from job to job, not caring about the work or myself. Three years ago, I lost my job again. To get by, I ate dinner at the City Mission Soup Kitchen for almost a month. Listening to a sermon was the only price of the meal. Different preachers spoke throughout the week. I paid attention to the passionate pastors full of fire and brimstone. Others rambled, and I tuned them out. One day the City Mission Pastor spoke, but he said something that made me realize I didn't have to live like this. I don't exactly remember the words. I prayed to God for the strength to change. I wanted to make a better life for myself. I resolved to do better. A week later, I got the job at Foe Financial. I worked hard but forgot all about the "with God" part.

My previous boss fired me due to chronic tardiness. I wasn't going to let that happen again. I vowed to be on time, no matter what kind of weather I had to plow through or how I felt. My floors met or exceeded my supervisor's expectations. The hard work paid off with positive reviews and regular raises. Also, my anemic self-esteem ballooned.

Glancing up, I saw my destination in the distance. Most of the downtown buildings were five to fifteen stories high, but not Foe Financial. It soared above the rest with thirty-five floors, and many people considered it an eyesore. The local news interviewed Ichabod Foe during the groundbreaking ceremony. When asked why his building needed to be so tall, Mr. Foe said, "I'm a big man, and I deserve a big building." I laughed when he said that. What a pompous jerk! Some people had more nonsense than sense.

My stomach rumbled; I lifted my head and looked around. I had walked right past the coffee shop. I stepped out of the main flow of pedestrian traffic and looked at my watch, trying to decide if there was time to go back. I glanced up.

I froze.

A man walked toward me and, on his left shoulder, sat a dark red shape. As he drew near, I could see the tiny body with gangly arms and legs. It was one of the demons from my dream. As the man passed by me, I saw the evil thing had its right hand stuck into the back of the man's skull. I stared at them. The imp's lips moved as if it whispered into the man's ear. As this odd couple moved out of sight, a woman approached me with a similar creature hitching a ride. Then I saw another demon, and another, then more. Dozens of monsters rode on dozens of shoulders or floated above the crowd.

The world spun. My legs became rubbery as if all the bones evaporated, and I fell back against the building. I pinched myself hard. Other than a sharp pain and a red welt on my forearm, everything remained the same.

No, no, no, no . . . How can this be? It was just a dream . . . A DREAM! Wasn't it?

Confusion filled my mind as I leaned against the wall. Breathing hard, I fought the panic and fear. Slowly, the panic subsided, but my legs still felt wobbly. I studied the passing crowd and tried to wrap my mind around what I saw. The demons ranged from the size of a baby to a full-grown man. Scattered amongst the morning crowd, I noticed different groups of people. I calmed down, focused, and analyzed what I saw.

About half the people looked as you'd expect. They had a faint spirit glow and no demon hitchhikers. One person had no aura at all. He walked, but he looked dead. How is that possible?

Several people had bright white auras. I sensed that they were the most alive of all the people. Two floating demons split to go around one of them, disgust on their faces.

The rest of the people looked like horses with diminutive jockeys. All the small creatures sat or stood on the shoulders of their "steeds." Other monsters floated a couple of feet above the heads of the tallest pedestrians. I only saw one walking amongst the people.

So far, no one, demon or human, paid any attention to me. The horrors didn't know I saw them.

I forgot about the coffee and donut and hurried to work. The entrance to my sanctuary came into view. A few more strides, and I'd be there.

An arm reached out, a hand grabbed my jacket, and yanked me off the sidewalk into a storefront doorway.

"Hey, what the . . ."

Whipping around to face my assailant and banged my nose again on someone's chest. I raised my head and searched his face. My first impression was the person was male, but the more I looked, the less I was sure. He had the bluest eyes, a Roman nose, and full red lips. Light brown hair flowed out of the hood covering his head. No blemish or wrinkle marred the smooth, lightly tanned skin. A big Adam's apple bobbed in his throat. I stepped back. I felt waves of heat, wait, not heat; power and majesty washed over me. I locked my legs because I felt a desire to kneel before him.

"Hello, Caleb." He said with a baritone voice.

"How do you kn . . . Who are you?"

The stranger furtively looked around. He stepped out from the doorway and looked up. Then he ducked back under and, with his rich voice, said, "Listen, Caleb, my time is short and my message urgent. I'm an angel, and God has sent me . . ."

"An angel? Wha . . . " fear bubbled up into my throat.

"Silence, Caleb, and listen. God gave me a message for you. You received a great gift last night. You can now see and interact with both the physical and the spiritual worlds."

"N-n-n-no." I stuttered as my legs gave way, and my butt hit the cement. I drew my knees up to my chest and hugged them.

"Hmm . . . I don't have time for . . . A more direct approach is needed," the angel muttered.

Louder, the deep voice, stated, "You might find this unpleasant, but I don't have time to mess around, and this will speed the process up."

The angel squatted down. His arm reached for my face. I thought he intended to grab it. Instead, I could feel each hot finger as they passed through my skin and into my skull.

"OOOWWW!" I cupped my head between my hands.

"Do not resist, and the pain will stop," the calm and baritone voice resonated inside my head. Images, thoughts, emotions, some mine, and some from the angel flew around inside my skull.

"Focus on my voice, Caleb. Follow it. The pain will decrease. My name is Ramiel."

I stood in the eye of a mental hurricane and faced the angel. Images and our memories whirled around us. I say "our memories" because I saw many places and people I had never experienced. I felt the angel's spirit supporting me like a warm hug. My panic and fear lessened. Internally, our conversation continued.

"Good. Now listen. You can see the spiritual condition of the people around you and the demons that torment them. Satan's minions are on the move. The city is at the tipping point where it will slide into depravity or rise to greatness. What's happening here has the potential to spread like cancer throughout the world. God has chosen you to be

His instrument to save the city and, in turn, the physical realm. In the days to come, there is a challenge, a task you must face. However, you must first secure the Armor of God. With the Armor of God, you will be able to battle the demons that hold this city hostage."

My mind exploded. Everything started swirling again.

"CALEB, FOCUS!"

The mental shout startled me, and I pushed the panic back down.

"There's more to God's message. Last night He gave you the Sword of the Spirit. You must gather the rest of the Armor of God before you can face the demons."

"You've gotta be kiddin', Angel! Look at me. I'm a loser."

"The name is Ramiel. Perhaps that is what you believe, but God knows differently." Ramiel replied. "Last night, you saw just a part of the dark side of the spirit realm. You were in a bubble, a Dream World, inserted between the physical and spiritual realities. The rules of reality are blended there. Items of dual-purpose can pass between both worlds, and the Sword of the Spirit exists in both realms. It appears as a simple plastic tube in the physical world, but it is a sword of immense power in the spirit world.

"While the citizens of Stanton sleep, the demons torment and tempt them. And when people are asleep, they exist in both places. Their spirit is in the Dream World while their body rests in the physical world. In the Dream World, since it is part of the spiritual realm, your spirit is "solid" and behaves much like your physical body." Did you hear the voice of God, and did you receive the Sword of the Spirit?"

"Yes . . . I mean . . . No. I mean . . . I don't know. There was a voice in my head, but I didn't know it was God. I only wanted out."

"Do you remember accepting Jesus as your Savior when you were seventeen?" the Ramiel asked, his words musical notes.

"Yes."

"Your prayer then was sincere. At that moment, the Holy Spirit took up residence in your body. To survive your father's abuse, you developed a mental shell and crawled inside. The Holy Spirit has been speaking to you since then, but you chose not to listen. Last night, God shattered that shell. When the Spirit spoke, this time, you heard."

"Maybe God spoke to me last night, but I don't know how to accomplish this task you're talkin' about."

I felt the fingers withdraw as they slid out of my skull, and I watch them recede from my face. "Depend on God and listen; you will know what to do when the time comes," Ramiel said as he faded from sight. I stared at the spot where the angel had stood just a moment ago.

Demons? Angels? God? This can't be real . . . Can it? This is a nightmare. I must be crazy. I stood up, filled with fear and confusion. The tornado of thoughts and emotions spinning in my brain slowed enough to realize I was late for work.

Stepping onto the sidewalk, I bumped into some guy in a suit, mumbled an apology, and stumbled the rest of the way to work. Bursting through the door, I clocked in twenty-five minutes late.

I walked to my locker, checked the schedule, and retrieved the cart with my cleaning supplies. My body went through the motions of work while my mind obsessed over the events of the morning. *Is this real, or am I still trapped in a nightmare? Did I hear God? What am I going to do?* I kept reliving the dream, the demons, and Ramiel's words.

The day passed in a blur. Four o'clock arrived; time to quit. I was no closer to a plan of action. I went to the office to get my paycheck.

"Caleb, you okay?"

"Uhm, yeah, I guess. Why?"

"You were late and have been out of it all day. That's not like you. You need help or somen'?"

"Naw, I didn't sleep well last night. Just tired," I mumbled. He handed me the paycheck, and I clocked out.

I returned to my locker and grabbed my coat. As I got ready to leave, fear and doubt seized my spirit. I plopped down on the bench in front of my locker. *What am I supposed to do? If He is God, isn't He all-powerful? Why does He need me?* Full of self-doubt, I closed my locker, took a deep breath, and walked out.

I marched home with my head down because I didn't want to see any demons. As I stood on the corner waiting for the light to change, a loud gurgle emanated from my abdomen. The person next to me turned their head and gave me an odd look. I missed breakfast and skipped lunch. I'll stop at Krantz's Deli. Ron Krantz and his family made the best subs in Stanton.

The deli stood on the opposite corner. I crossed at the signal light and approached the antique eight-foot-tall doors. Motion by the entrance caught my attention. Besides posters of this week's specials and community events, there were three pint-sized demons stuck to the windows peering inside. *Caleb, stay calm.* I held my breath, walked up to the door, and pulled it open.

As I crossed the threshold, I stepped out of a desert and into an oasis.

Bright, spiritual warmth hit me as I entered the shop. My mood brightened, and a grin broke out on my face. I examined the scene before me. Some patrons ordered dinner and others placed groceries into small baskets. The Krantz family stood behind the counter and served their customers with good cheer and friendly banter. Ron, his wife Judy, and adult children, Ben and Sue, emitted bright white auras. I never enjoyed standing in line so much. The spiritual hope and promise that filled the store watered my wilted soul.

The line moved too quickly. I just wanted to stand there and soak it all in, but I was next. Ron called from behind the counter, "What'll it be, Caleb?" I ordered a roast beef sub, chips, and a large coffee. Ron handed off the order to Ben while he reached for the coffee pot and poured it into a foam cup.

As he handed me the coffee, I asked, "Hey, Ron, can I ask you a personal question?"

"Sure, Caleb. What is it?"

"Do you and your family have a strong faith in God?"

"You're right. That's a personal question, but I don't mind answering. Yes, we do. Jesus Christ is our Lord and Savior. We like to think of Him working the counter with us," he replied with a smile. "Why do you ask?"

"I just wanted you to know that your faith shows. Thanks, Ron." I grabbed my tray of food and headed for a table.

While I ate my sandwich, I watched people stream in and out of the shop. Diminutive demons bobbed outside the doors of the deli. A man came in with a little imp on his shoulder and got in line. The creature appeared agitated. It whipped its head back and forth, eyes wide with panic. I leaned forward. Blisters boiled upon its skin, and little plumes of smoke escaped when they popped. Suddenly, the creature released its charge and made a beeline for the door. It passed through the glass, did a U-turn, plastered its face against the front window, and watched its human. After the demon had left him, the man's face broke into a huge smile. Outside was cold and dreary, while the inside was bright with physical and spiritual warmth. I lingered longer than usual, basking in the pleasant ambiance.

Another man grabbed his order and headed for the front door. As it opened, one of the little imps pounced on him like a cat on a mouse. The man's shoulders sagged as the demon inserted its hand into his skull. Sad . . . BUT not my problem.

My anger and fear reignited. *Why me?* Several people hovered looking for seats, so I decided to leave. I paused, hand on the door, and braced myself for the chill and the demons. The door swung open on well-oiled hinges; I rushed past the demons and turned down the street toward home. I locked my eyes on the pavement in a vain attempt to block out the monsters and the spiritual darkness surrounding me. A few minutes later, I reached my door, unlocked it, and entered the apartment. I closed and leaned against the door breathing a sigh of relief.

I looked around. Dishes stacked high in the sink, a table full of papers, clothes draped over chairs, and a plastic tube lying in the middle of the floor. *Sword of the Spirit. That's a good one! It's a plastic vacuum cleaner attachment!* I picked it up and gave it the once over, and it remained a plastic tube. "It sure doesn't look or feel like a sword," I said aloud. *I must be nuts!* I set the plastic cylinder down on my dinner table.

Three days of dishes filled the sink. I grabbed a scrubber, squirted some dish detergent, and tackled them. The dried-on food required extra elbow grease. I kept turning my head toward the plastic tube. *If this is the Sword of the Spirit, then why doesn't it look like a sword?* I thought back to the dream when the voice spoke in my mind.

I put down the scrubber and the pan and walked over to the table. Picking up the end of the tube, I said, "The Sword of the Spirit, which is the Word of God." In a blink of an eye, the plastic cylinder became the double-edged, shining sword. As it transformed, warmth and scripture flowed into my hand and up my arm to my brain.

I collapsed onto a kitchen chair and stared at the sword. Several moments had passed.

It was about two and a half feet long. "Aren't you a little short to be a mighty sword?" In an instant, the sword grew another foot. The sudden growth spurt caused me to grip the hilt harder, and as I squeezed, it molded to my grip. The guard expanded and extended to cover my right hand. I resisted the temptation of running a finger along the blade. I didn't need to learn that lesson twice. It only weighed a pound or two. That razor-sharp edge had no nicks or imperfections.

I saw words. Faint text embedded into the blade moved. The letters traveled up and down the length of the weapon. I held the sword flat across both hands and lifted it to my face. Small inscriptions peppered the surface. The text wasn't on the surface. It was part of the material of the blade! The words weren't in any language I recognized. While I examined them, they slowly shifted and changed. Some of the text faded, and new letters came to the forefront. Warm, adaptable, and full of ever-changing words. It seemed like the sword was alive.

Speaking to the weapon, I said, "According to Ramiel, I'm to seek the full Armor of God." *What is the Armor of God?* I don't know about spiritual things and hadn't been to church in years. I didn't own a Bible. Wait, churches have Bibles. *Where's the nearest church?*

Then I remembered. The City Mission Soup Kitchen was two streets over. I had met the pastor during my last bout of unemployment. It was that pastor who spoke and helped me to be serious about my job. He tried to get me to accept Jesus as my Savior. I told him I got Jesus as a teen, but he kept saying being saved and turning my life over to Him wasn't the same thing.

But what was his name? I think it was Bill . . . No . . . Bob . . . Pastor Bob, something. I can't wait, and I needed to visit him tonight.

Chapter 4

Bob

Friday Night

Mary, one of our long-time volunteers, cupped both her hands around mine.

"Thanks for singing and teaching tonight, Pastor Bennett. I know you spoke to their hearts."

"Thank you, Sister," I replied. *Not likely.* I mentally snorted.

Surrounded by a small troop of volunteers, I stepped back to let them out. "Good-byes" drifted back down the hall. A half-dozen folks from one of the local churches filed out of City Mission's front door.

I turned my attention to a pair of men and a woman waiting nearby.

"Brother Tim, Brother John, please go to the dormitory and get the clients settled in for the night.

"Sister Fran, it's eight o'clock. Please lock the doors to the dining room. I'm going to pray for a while in the sanctuary. I'll also secure those doors."

"Okay, Pastor Bob," replied the ever-cheerful Fran as she headed for the front door.

Nothing gets her down. Why am I stuck?

Deep in thought, I slowly walked to the sanctuary. Despair coursed through my veins. Any dreams and aspirations had withered long ago. *Oh, Lord! How long has it been? A year? More? I've lost track.* It's been a long time since I felt any purpose or joy.

Daily, I begged God for release. Release from this job. Release from the despair. Even release from this life. I ached to be done and to be with God. So far, He ignored all those prayers. God's voice used to whisper in my mind, but it had been quiet for a long time.

I hid my inner turmoil well. You'd see a smile on my face every Sunday service or evening at the Mission.

I said things like, "Hello Sister Claire, Brother Steve, how are you this fine day?" Or "Brother Tom, that was some heavenly singing this glorious morning."

My public façade didn't reflect how I felt inside. On those days when the despair slipped out, I said I was "tired" or "slept poorly."

I should've been proud of what I've accomplished with the City Mission. I've been the Senior Pastor of Stanton Community Church and overseer of the City Mission Soup Kitchen for the last ten years. Early in my ministry, hundreds of people came and accepted Jesus as their Savior. I poured myself into the Mission. It resulted in baskets full of spiritual fruit.

Lately nothing . . . Nobody saved . . . Nobody is spiritually growing—just a bunch of ungrateful moochers wanting free food. I've delivered hundreds of sermons to the homeless and needy. And now, I resented the very people I initially desired to serve.

When I first took the job, missionary zeal filled me. People said I was a fountain of energy, drive, and ambition. God and I planned to bring revival to Stanton. I was God's messenger. I pictured myself in the pulpit. One hand clutched the Bible and the other raised in worship to God. My cape blew in the breeze. I stood ready to battle the forces of evil in the world.

But it did not transpire as I envisioned. Initially, many accepted Christ as their Savior. As time passed, I prayed less as discouragement and doubt grew. I became two people. There was the mask I wore in public on Sunday and when ministering to the homeless. And the wreck of a man I became in private. *Why do I even try? I have failed. FIRE ME! God, why do you remain silent?*

I entered the sanctuary. It was a large room, with four sections of pews. A wide center aisle split the room, and we often had over fifteen hundred people on a Sunday morning. Our church consisted of and ministered to many ethnic groups and nationalities. I stood in the center and gazed upon the giant cross suspended in midair behind the podium. A realistic, life-size depiction of Christ hung from it. I fell to my knees and lay prostrate before the altar. Tears dropped on the carpet.

"Why have you forsaken me, God? I only desire to do your will. Each day, I reach out to teach people about Your Son. Each day I have little effect. I'm a failure, Lord."

I don't know how long I prayed. At times, I babbled, unable to form the words or sobbing.

Emotionally spent, I laid as a crumpled heap before the cross. I heard a footfall behind me.

Oh no. I forgot to lock the door. I rose to my feet, wiped the moisture from my cheeks. I turned. In the dim light, a silhouette of a man stalked down the center aisle. He held something in his right hand.

"C-can I help you?"

The stranger walked up to me and stared at the space above my head. He looked a bit rough, and his craggy face had seen its share of pain. Wait . . . I've seen his face before.

"Hey . . ." I ducked as the man stabbed the air above my head with what looked like a black tube.

Chapter 5

Caleb

Friday Night

The City Mission Soup Kitchen did more than prepare meals for the less fortunate. It also housed a church, a community thrift shop, and a dormitory for the city's homeless. The sign on the wall said, "Doors lock at 8:00 p.m." I pushed the light button on my cheap digital watch. 8:15.

I tugged on the dining hall's door handles, locked. I moved down the block to the church's doors, and the first door didn't budge. I moved to the next, and the hinges squeaked as the door opened. The nightlights guided me through the foyer. My footsteps seemed loud on the slate floor, and incense hung lightly in the air. I skulked into the sanctuary, feeling like an intruder.

"Failure . . ." came from somewhere in the front. In the soft light, a figure lay prostrate on the floor. Behind the altar, a single spotlight illuminated a crucified Jesus hanging from a wooden cross. I hesitated. Garbled words rose from the body before me. He's praying, and it felt wrong to interrupt.

I lifted my head to look at the cross again, and I noticed something hovering in the air. Silhouetted against the spotlight floated a small demon. The air between the man and imp shimmered like heat off the sunbaked pavement. I crept down the center aisle. As I drew closer to the wretched creature, I saw its pointy white teeth in the dark. A smile stretched from ear to ear. Its red eyes focused on its victim below. Once in a while, it twisted its hand like a puppeteer pulling the strings of a marionette.

With a thought, I transformed the tube into the Sword of the Spirit. Even though I expected the change, it still startled me. Its warmth and the way it molded to my hand felt like something alive. Scripture expanded and filled my mind. A slight vibration made its way up my arm as if the sword anticipated the coming battle. I walked forward, emboldened.

As I neared the altar, my steps faltered. I can't do this. I'm no warrior. Why bother? Nobody cares! A mental pit yawned before me, and I stopped in the middle of the aisle. Despair and hopelessness pressed down on my skin. I wanted to turn and run away.

Then I looked up at the demon. One arm pointed at the man below while the other towards me. Contempt and wicked glee covered the creature's face. It was having fun. Shimmering waves filled the air between me and the little monster.

Jesus, be my shield. With new resolve, I willed my feet to move. Stiff-legged but determined, I approached the altar. Hearing me, the man rose and spun to face me. It was Pastor Bob.

The demon floated about seven or eight feet above the floor. I swung the sword at it. It bobbed and danced just out of reach while it taunted me.

It stuck out its tongue. "Nyah, nyah human, you can't reach me," I stabbed at it. "Hey! You can see me!" Its raspy voice said as it bobbed above us. Foul taunts flowed from its mouth. I jabbed at it again. No good, the little beast fluttered just out of reach. I lowered the sword and glared at the demon as my mind sought a solution. I heard Pastor Bob's voice in the background peppering me with questions that I ignored. When I suggested it was too short, the sword elongated. Would different words give me a different weapon?

Pastor Bob was in the middle of one of his many questions when I barked at him, "Pastor, do you know any Scripture that talks about a spear?"

In a deep voice, Bob sputtered, "I demand to know . . ."

"In a minute, Pastor! Do you know any Scripture with a spear in it?"

"I-I c-can't think of any." He paused. "Wait. In Joel, it says, 'Beat your plowshares into swords, and your pruning hooks into spears.'"[1]

Pointing the sword at the demon, I repeated the scripture. As the word "spears" left my throat, a surge of energy rushed down my arm. The sword elongated and pierced the demon, and it disappeared in a puff of wispy smoke, just like in my dream. The sword had become a seven-foot-long lance. It still had a white aura and chrome-like shine. And even though it had grown three times its current length, it weighed the same.

Now I had a different problem. The sword was seven feet long. How do I return it to its original size? "Sword of the Spirit." My arm grew warm again, and it returned to its previous size and shape. Smiling, I turned to Pastor Bob.

"Are you okay?" I asked.

"Am I okay? Brother, you're the one swinging a plastic tube around. Who're you, and what're you doing here?"

"Pastor, I needed to see you. A lot of weird stuff has happened today. I'm desperate for help." The words rushed out of my mouth. He stared at me like I was nuts. We stood eye to eye, so he must have been about five feet ten inches tall. Although he had more girth around his waist and facial skin smoother and darker than mine, we had similar builds.

"Sorry, Pastor, let's start over. I'm Caleb Kincade, and I live nearby." I sat on a pew. Bob hesitated, then he too sat down, facing me.

"I've been to the Mission before for meals, so I know who you are. I have a story that you will not believe. And I might be crazy, but I need your help."

---

[1] Joel 3:10 NIV

He looked at me. When he didn't respond, I began my narrative. I went into detail about the dream and told him what happened to me that day: the demons, Ramiel's message, Krantz's deli. Bob's eyes focused on mine as he listened without interruption. I finished my story and waited. Bob turned toward the altar, leaned back in the pew, and stared at the ceiling. *Say something!* the suspense was killing me! A few moments later, he leaned forward, turned, and asked, "Please tell me again why you needed scripture about a spear?"

"A small demon hovered above your head. As I got closer, despair and hopelessness flooded my mind. It paralyzed me. Then I realized the little monster had filled my mind with those thoughts. I knew I had to kill it, so I attacked. But the sword was too short. The sword can change shape. Once I repeated the verse from Joel, it transformed into a spear and pierced the demon. When imp disappeared, the despair in my mind stopped."

Bob stood. "Brother, you know, all I can see is a plastic tube, and that tube never changed shape or color. Everything you said sounds pretty questionable."

I looked down at the sword in my hand. "You see a plastic tube and not a bright and shiny sword?"

"I only see a black plastic tube."

"But you're feelin' better, aren't you?"

"I feel like an enormous burden has lifted from my shoulders. How could you know that?" He smiled and sat back down.

"People with demons are covered with a shadow. A white aura surrounds those who believe Jesus is their Savior. The brighter the glow, the stronger their faith. Your aura was dim when I first saw you, but it has steadily brightened with the monster gone. The demon hitchhikers had either their hand in the person's heart or head or both. Also, none of those people had the aura of Christ. This monster circled above your head. I think they can influence God's people but can't touch them."

Pastor Bob countered, "When you first spoke, I thought you were a psycho with a plastic tube. I can't deny feeling better. I can feel my faith reviving like the hope of a new day. Part of me still thinks you're a nut, but for now, I'll accept your story." A weary smile crossed his face.

"I came here for another reason. Ramiel, the angel, said I needed to find the whole Armor of God. What is the Armor of God? I have the Sword of the Spirit. What am I looking for, and how do I find it? Can you help me?"

"Yes, at least with some of that," Bob stood and walked up to the altar. Standing behind the podium, Bob opened the enormous Bible resting there. I heard a click, and a small light illuminated the book. He turned the oversized pages to the back of the Bible.

"Ephesians 6, verses 10-18 describes the Armor of God."

"Finally, be strong in the Lord and in his mighty power. Put on the full armor of God so that you can take your stand against the devil's schemes. For our struggle is not against flesh and blood, but against the rulers, against the authorities, against the powers of this dark world and against the spiritual forces of evil in the heavenly realms. Therefore, put on the full armor of God, so that when the day of evil comes, you may be able to stand your ground, and after you have done everything, to stand. Stand firm then, with the belt of truth buckled around your waist, with the breastplate of righteousness in place, and with your feet fitted with the readiness that comes from the gospel of peace. In addition to all this, take up the shield of faith, with which you can extinguish all the flaming arrows of the evil one. Take the helmet of salvation and the sword of the Spirit, which is the word of God. And pray in the Spirit on all occasions with all kinds of prayers and requests. With this in mind, be alert and always keep on praying for all the saints."[2]

"Wow, please read that to me again?"

"I'll write it for you, Brother."

The Pastor pulled a notepad and a pen from below the altar and wrote on it. When he finished, he handed me the paper.

Belt of Truth

Breastplate of Righteousness

Feet fitted with the Gospel of Peace

Shield of Faith

Helmet of Salvation

Sword of the Spirit, which is the word of God

"God gave you the sword. Brother, do you have any ideas about finding the rest?"

"No. A voice woke me in the Dream World, I wandered to the sword's location, and the same voice said to pick up the tube. I don't know how or where to find the rest."

"Ephesians talked about praying in the Spirit. Brother, at some point in your life, did you asked for forgiveness of your sins and for Jesus to be your Savior?" questioned Pastor Bob.

"Yeah, when I was a teenager. While my prayer had been sincere, my commitment . . . let's just say my faith has been weak."

"Then the Holy Spirit already resides in you," he muttered as he turned and moved away from me.

Pastor Bob returned to the Bible and flipped forward a few pages. "Romans 8:26-27 states: 'In the same way, the Spirit helps us in our weakness. We do not know what we ought to pray for, but the Spirit himself intercedes for us with groans that words cannot express. And he who searches our hearts knows the mind of the Spirit because the Spirit intercedes for the saints in accordance with God's will.'"[3]

---

[2] Ephesians 6:10-18 ESV

"You must pray to God to find the rest of the armor," Bob concluded as he stepped down from the altar. He moved to the second row of pews and flipped down the kneeler. He knelt and motioned me to join him. "Kneel, close your eyes, and in your heart, talk to God. Tell Him you need His help."

Feeling awkward, I knelt next to Bob, his hand reassuringly resting on my shoulder. I said nothing audible, but my mind screamed, "God! I'm so lost. I know You placed this task before me. I don't know why. I'm scared. I've never done anything like this. I don't think I can do it. But . . . but . . . I'm willing. What do I do? Where to go? Please, God, I'm desperate and need you." Then spiritually, I collapsed before God and physically over the back of the pew in front of me. My eyes remained closed; tears dropped into the fabric below. My mind went blank. Time and my ability to think came to a stop.

An odd fluttering sensation built in my chest and a soft moan escaped my lips. I wiped the tears from my face and straightened up. I looked at my chest then at Bob with alarm. "Pastor, this will sound strange, but I feel like something is whirling around in my chest. It's like God has reached inside of me and flicked a game spinner." The whirling sensation slowed, stopped, and I felt a pull. I stood, and the Pastor followed.

"I know the direction. Will you come with me?"

Bob's brown eyes bored into mine. I returned his gaze and imagined the battle that waged in his mind. "Lord, I'm tired, and this guy might be insane." The seconds dragged by.

The decision, or perhaps resolve, flickered across his face.

"Brother, let me grab my jacket from my office. I also have to let the staff know that I'm leaving. I'll meet you at the front entrance in 3 or 4 minutes."

Bob trotted out the side door while I spun around and walked toward the foyer. The pull-on my chest remained steady and urgent. I

[3] Romans 8:26-27 NIV

paced back and forth. Every time I turned, the needle reversed direction like a compass always pointing north. *What's taking so long?* Bob returned, and I bolted through the door. The sharp October air slapped me in the face. The rain let up a couple of hours ago. Every surface had a film of water on it, and the number of light sources seemed magnified due to the many reflections. I stopped on the sidewalk, foot-tapping, and waited for Bob to lock the door. As soon as Bob's feet touched the cement, I turned and headed down the street. I barely noticed the puddles I marched through. Bob's loud footfalls followed me.

My internal compass pushed against my rib cage. It pointed towards a building on my left, but I knew that was not our destination. Since I could not go through the building, I walked down the street in the general direction that my inner needle pointed me. We walked briskly with my internal compass shifted more and more to the left.

The streets of downtown Stanton, New York, are like most urban areas. Islands of streetlight surrounded by darkness. Ambient illumination from other sources such as neon store signs, windows, and headlights from the passing cars gave us enough light to see where we were going. The streets were surprisingly empty. Stanton has about two hundred thousand residents, yet we saw only a couple of other souls as we marched down the sidewalk. Those people were too far away to tell if they were humans or demons.

I stubbed my toe hard on the raised edge of the sidewalk and swore. "Sorry, Pastor," I muttered.

"No problem, Brother, God will forgive you. I have used crude language in similar situations."

We hiked three blocks. My chest hurt as if the point of the spinner poked through ribs under my left arm. I stopped at the corner and turned left and, in my haste, almost tripped over a garbage can. I had to do a fancy little jig to dodge the obstacle. The pull shifted to the front of my chest. Pastor Bob asked a bunch of questions as we walked. I didn't pay much attention to what he said and grunted answers. He eventually stopped asking and kept pace with me.

We walked several more blocks. Following the needle commanded my full attention. It gradually swung to the left again as we approached an alley. We passed the alley opening, and the compass needle reversed to my back. I stopped, turned around, walked back a couple of steps, and stood at the entrance. The spinner centered in my chest again and pulled me into the opening. I looked at Bob. "This is it." The dark passage loomed before us. We cautiously entered, and the internal pull lessened with each step.

A bright light lit up the ground before us. Bob had grabbed a flashlight along with his jacket. Surprised, I looked at him. "Brother, I never go out after dark without a flashlight." He handed it to me, and we continued our journey. About thirty feet in, my feet stopped again as the needle swung to my right. In a nook between two buildings lay a refrigerator box on its side. A "door" of darkly stained material covered the carton's end, and flickering light seeped out the seams. A fit of coughing and a low moan escaped from the box.

"H-hello?" I whispered.

A weak, hoarse voice responded, "Yesss."

Dropping to my knees, I lifted the door-flap and crawled in halfway. The stench of an unwashed body and sickness assaulted my nose. Bob squeezed in next to me. A single candle provided light and heat. On the other side of the candle lay a dark heap of rags with a bright white aura. The pile moved, and I was able to discern an old face in the soft glow of the candlelight.

"I'm Caleb, and this is Bob. What I have to say might sound odd, but God led us here."

"Yes . . . I know," the old man responded weakly. "My name . . . Albert. Die . . . soon." A fit of coughing racked his frail body.

"Didn't want . . . die alone. God said . . . never alone." More hacking coughs. Albert wiped the drool from his mouth with his sleeve. I gagged when his bad breath surrounded me like a poison gas cloud.

"He said . . . not to . . . fear. But must . . . tell the story . . . give a gift."

Albert's labored breathing hurt my ears. His face twisted with pain, and I had to turn my head for a moment. Tears swelled in my eyes. I had never been with someone in the last moments of their life. I felt helpless in the face of Albert's suffering. Both of my parents died several years ago. I didn't see them die, although I wish I had been able to watch my father die. I hoped he suffered. But this is not the time nor place for such musings.

Albert continued, his voice low and gravely. "Year ago . . . the clinic said . . . lung cancer. Get treatment . . . or die. I'm old." Albert curled up into a ball with his hacking cough. It sounded like he might lose a lung. He dabbed his mouth. In the candlelight, I saw spots of dark crimson mixed with the mucous.

When the painful fit passed, he continued. "No money . . . No treatment . . . at City Mission met Jesus." Albert's back arched. The pain etched on his face. As it lessened, and he continued.

"Free hat . . . named it 'Helmet . . . of Salvation.'" Albert's laugh degenerated into another bout of gut-wrenching coughs.

"Heaven soon . . . Must give you . . . my hat."

He reached up, pulled the dirty knit cap off his head. As he touched the hat, a glimmer of light passed over it, and he handed it to me. I took the knit cap from him as his hand fell limply to the ground. Albert died.

I stared at the hat in my hand and caught movement out of the corner of my eye. I glanced at his body, and another figure knelt next to it. I blinked. The person was semi-transparent. I could see him and what was behind him.

"Albert?"

A new, younger-looking Albert had a big smile on his face. The apparition turned his head toward me. "Yes, Caleb, it is," the spirit replied.

"A-are y-you, Okay? Are you in pain?"

The apparition laughed. "I'm pain-free and alive like never before."

Albert's spirit peered at the cardboard wall to my left with a faraway look on his face. He faced me and spoke again. "Thank you, Caleb, for being here, but it's time for me to go. We'll meet again someday." He stood, his torso going through the top of the box, and walked through the carton to my left. I backed out to watch him go, and all I saw was his back as he passed through the wall of the building across the alley.

Dumbfounded, I knelt there, staring at the bricks. I turned my attention to the knit cap dangling from my hand. *Is this the Helmet of Salvation?* And as my thought finished, the knit hat transformed just like the sword. It became a bronze helmet surrounded by a white aura. The Helmet of Salvation looked like something a Roman Officer might wear. I put it on my head. Warmth flowed down my neck, and it molded to my head as the sword conformed to my hand. Nose and cheek guards expanded and protectively covered much of my face without obstructing my view. A new, thorough understanding of what salvation and the actual cost of it meant. My eyes moistened as I pondered this information. Several minutes passed before I took the helmet off, and with a thought, it became a simple hat once again.

I re-entered the box, closed Albert's eyes, blew out the candle, and backed out.

Wait! Where's Bob? I had forgotten about Bob.

I swung the flashlight up and down the alley and about fifteen feet away, huddled in the dark crouched Pastor Bob. I walked over to him. Bob squatted with his back against the brick building, and his forehead rested on his knees. His body shook as he gulped air. He was crying.

"Bob, what's the matter?" I asked, putting my hand on his shoulder. More sobs. I waited.

Several minutes passed. My attempts to comfort Bob felt weak and insufficient. Bob lifted his head and looked at me. In the glow of the flashlight, moisture glistened on his cheeks. Bob said, "Brother, he was saved at City Mission. During one of my sermons. MY SERMON! I had no idea. Hopelessness and despair made me blind. I thought the work made no difference because I was focused on ME. I didn't notice Albert. I wish I had known him. Lord, please forgive me." He buried his face in his hands again.

A few more minutes passed. I gently said, "Bob, there's nothing more to do here. Let's call 911."

A few more sniffles, and he said, "Yeah, you're right." He reached into his jacket pocket for his cell phone and made the call. Bob spoke into the phone. He gave his name, current address, and a few details.

"They said to wait on the street for an officer."

We exited the alley and waited on the main street for the police to arrive. Within a few minutes, a patrol car pulled up in front of us. The door opened, and a big, burly man got out.

"Are you Pastor Bob Bennett?"

"Yes, Sir," Bob replied."

"I'm Officer Hayes. You found the body of the homeless man?" He flipped through his notes, "Albert. What can you tell me?" A cargo van with "Coroner" in large reflective lettering pulled up next to the cop car. The driver and another got out and walked over to us.

The driver said, "Good evening. Please direct us to the body."

I pointed to the alley. "I'll show you."

The other coroner opened the back doors of the van and pulled a gurney out. He wheeled it in our direction. Resting on the stretcher sat a couple of portable, battery-powered spotlights. I turned, led them down the drive, and pointed to the cardboard box. One of them set up a portable work light that illuminated Albert's carton and more. The driver unsheathed a utility knife and sliced the box open, exposing Albert's body to the night air. Soon they gently lifted him out and set him onto the gurney. He looked even smaller and frailer.

"What happened here?" the driver asked.

"We were out walking and heard a cry from the alley. We decided to investigate."

"You know that was pretty stupid. You could've been mugged," the medic said.

"I know, but at the time, it seemed like a good idea. The man lived long enough to tell us his name was Albert. He had cancer and thought he was going to die. And before we could call you, he passed away."

"OK, thanks. We'll take it from here." I returned to Bob and the police officer.

Officer Hayes continued, " . . . and you don't know his last name?"

"No, but he said he'd been to the City Mission Soup Kitchen a year ago. I manage the Mission, but I didn't recognize him."

"Why were you out walking so late? It's pretty cold. Not exactly the best walking weather, plus you know it's dangerous to walk around this area at night." Officer Hayes said, his eyes bored into Bob's searching for the truth.

"I was counseling Caleb . . . ," Bob pointed in my direction.

Turning from Bob, he asked me, "What is your full name, please?"

"Caleb Kincade."

He returned to Bob, "Please continue."

"Caleb became agitated and said he needed to go for a walk. As you said, it's dangerous to walk around here at night. I decided to go with him figuring two would be safer than one."

The cop turned to me and asked, "Why were you so agitated, Mr. Kincade?"

Bob interrupted, "I'm sorry, but that is a private matter between client and counselor."

Officer Hayes must have been satisfied with that answer. He jotted a few more notes down. "And Albert never said what his last name was?"

The back doors of the coroner's van thudded closed. Both men hopped into the cab, the engine roared, and they pulled away. No lights or sirens, though. They didn't need to hurry.

"Like I already said, he didn't tell us his last name, only that he had been to the City Mission for dinners about a year ago. We make anybody wanting a meal register. Sometimes they give us their real name, and sometimes they don't. I can look over the sign-in sheets in the morning. May we leave now? It's late."

"You can go. Someone will stop by in the morning to see if you found Albert's last name."

"Thank you, Officer," I said, and we headed back to the church.

As we turned the corner, I looked around to make sure no one was watching. I stooped over and slid some garbage aside and picked up the Helmet of Salvation. I had hidden it while we waited for the police to arrive. I put it on my head again, and with a thought, transformed it and enjoyed the warm sensation that flowed down my neck.

"Is that the Helmet of Salvation?" Bob asked.

"Yes. As soon as I touched it and thought "Helmet of Salvation," it transformed into the helmet you see now."

"Caleb, remember, all I see is a dirty hat on your head."

"That's amazing. To me, it looks like a bronze helmet fit for a Roman officer."

"I also think we need to wash it as soon as possible. It stinks," commented Bob as we walked.

When we arrived at the church, Bob said, "It's late. You shouldn't be walking home alone tonight. I could find you a bed in the dormitory with the rest of the clients. However, there's a couch in the room behind the sanctuary. It's quieter and more private. Why don't you stay there for the night and in the morning we'll decide our next step? My apartment is behind the kitchen. I'm up early; just find me when you're ready."

Bob escorted me to the room with the sofa. He excused himself to go and get some sheets and a blanket. When he returned, he tossed them to me and said, "I'll be right back." I started to make my "bed." When he returned the second time, he brought two five-gallon buckets; one half-full of hot soapy water and the other with clean water.

"What's that for?"

"The Helmet of Salvation," he said. "I was serious about washing it. Can't you smell it?"

"Yeah, it reeks, but do ya think the water will hurt it?"

"Brother Caleb, it's the Helmet of Salvation, imbued with power from God to defend against evil. I'm pretty sure a little soap and water won't hurt it," Bob chuckled. With those final words, he relieved me of the hat, tossed it into the soapy bucket, and dunked it up and down. Then Bob repeated the process in the clean water. When he started ringing it out, I winced, expecting it to fall apart. Bob hung it over the edge of one of the shelves to dry.

Bob said, "I'm exhausted. Brother find me in the morning. I'm usually in my office."

"Okay . . . and Bob, thanks for believing me even though you can't see what I see."

Bob quietly responded, "No, it's I who should thank you. You rid me of the demon of despair and helped rekindle the faith I thought lost." Handing me a blanket, he said, "Good night, Brother," and left the room.

Chapter 6

Caleb

Saturday Morning

I woke up with a start. *Where am I? What time is it?* I rolled over, looking for my clock, and found myself in a strange room. After a moment, I remembered. I was in the backroom of Stanton Community Church. Then the flow of memories went from a trickle to a flood; Pastor Bob, vaporizing the demon, Albert dying, and the Helmet of Salvation. *Was it real?* It must be, here I am. I glanced at my watch, 8:05.

While my body ached from sleeping on the sofa, I felt mentally alert and ready to face the day. "I need to find Bob," I muttered to myself.

I opened the door and entered the sanctuary. The orderly rows of pews glowed with gold, red, aqua, and purple as sunlight streamed through the stained-glass windows. I just stood in awe of the beauty.

"Brother Caleb, isn't it glorious?" Pastor Bob remarked with a broad smile as he strode down the center aisle.

He continued, "When the founders built the church a century ago, it stood alone. The sun shone through the windows much of the day. It was a kaleidoscope of colors. Now, the surrounding buildings are taller, shading us much of the day. Because of a break between two buildings, the sun only comes through the windows for about thirty minutes. This time of the morning has always been my favorite place to pray and study God's word. But I stopped when the despair crept in." A tear threatened to roll down Bob's cheek. We stood for a moment marveling at the beauty while he regained his composure.

48

"So, what's the plan?" Bob inquired.

"I don't know. Last night, I knew what to do. Today, I don't know."

"May I make a suggestion, Brother?" Bob asked. "I've called the police to claim Albert's body if nobody else does. I want to give him a proper burial. The police said they were stopping by to ask more questions. Stay here, pray, and seek God's counsel. Come to the dining room when you're finished. It's through that door and at the end of the hall. We'll talk to the police when they arrive. How does that sound?"

"It's not much of a plan, but at least it's a plan," I said as Bob strode back up the center aisle. He stopped halfway and turned around. "I need a favor."

"Name it."

"Would you be willing to help serve lunch today? Two volunteers have called sick. I could use your hands."

"I'd be glad to," I replied, then I had a realization, "Uhm, Bob . . . I-I don't know how to pray. I mean, I did it last night, but I'm not sure I did it right."

Bob gave me a kind smile. "Brother Caleb, close your eyes and just talk to God inside your head or out loud." With that, he turned and left the sanctuary.

I sat in one of the pews bathed in a shaft of glorious color and warmth. I bowed my head and closed my eyes. "Dear Lord, during the last day, You have done a miracle in my life. My faith in Jesus and You have grown so much. I care about doing Your will. I don't understand why You chose me, and I don't know what to do. And even though I'm clueless, I'm willing to serve You. Please, Lord, what's the next step? I need Your guidance and wisdom."

Sitting . . . waiting . . . listening . . . my mind wandered. I wonder what we're having for lunch . . . I smell like dirty socks . . . I need a shower . . . FOCUS. "Please, Lord, I need to hear from you." More waiting, mental wandering, and nothing. No spinners, tugs, pulls, or urges manifested themselves inside or outside of my body. My stomach growled.

By now, the shafts of colored light had faded as the surrounding buildings shadowed the church. I guess I'll wait.

Chapter 7

Bob

Saturday Morning

Banging greeted me as I approached the front doors of the Mission. The old lock turned, and the hinges moaned as I opened the doors. A uniformed Policeman stood a few feet from me.

"I'm Officer Mendez. I'm looking for Pastor Bob Bennett."

"I'm Bob Bennett."

"I understand you found the body of the homeless man . . . ," he glanced at his notepad, "Albert, last night?"

"Yes, Sir"

"Did you have a chance to find his last name?"

"I think so. Everything is computerized and entered into a spreadsheet. It helps us keep track of how often and how long people use our services. I found three Alberts and was able to eliminate two. I believe his last name was Paxton, Albert Paxton. He hadn't been here for several months."

"Can you tell me anything else?"

"I can tell you what we served and how many meals the cooks prepared, but nothing about Albert. We only insist on a name, and even then, sometimes they lie."

Officer Mendez continued. "My Sergeant said you wanted to claim the body and give him a proper burial. Why would you do that for a homeless man?"

"I didn't know the man, but before he died, he told us that he had accepted Jesus as his Savior during one of his visits here. I feel an obligation and responsibility for him. If nobody else claims him, I will."

The Officer gave me a sharp look. His eyes bore into mine, trying to determine if I spoke the truth or not. I stood there and tried to look innocent. I squashed the urge to blab everything.

Caroline

Saturday Morning

"Mommy! You promised!" my precocious six-year-old Anna demanded. "You sai' we'd leave right, af'er brea'fast." as she stamped her tiny feet.

I sat on the chair in the kitchen. Anna stood between my knees, her blond hair hanging in those moist blue eyes while her little chin quivered. "Sweetie, yesterday it seemed like a good idea, but today it just seems silly." I noticed Anna had my hair and eyes, but she had her father's nose, jawline, and temperament.

"It's impor' ant, Mommy. I ha'f to give it to da man ta' day!"

I wiped the tear from her cheek with my thumb. *Why did I agree to this?* I met her watery eyes again. The ice in my heart melted.

"Okay."

Caroline, what've you gotten yourself into?

When I arrived home last night, Anna bounced into my arms and announced she had a "gift" to give to a man at a soup kitchen on Saturday.

"Great, we'll take it right after breakfast tomorrow." I boldly stated.

That was Friday. That was yesterday.

Yesterday I felt like a butterfly that emerged from the cocoon of darkness. I don't understand what happened, but I'm happy that it did.

Thursday night started like most nights for over a year. I'd fall asleep, and next, I heard Anna scream my name. It tore my soul as she desperately called out to me. I'd follow that cry until she stood before me. Behind her stood an ominous silhouette. I never saw any details.

Long, clawed fingers wrapped around each of her biceps and picked her up. The monster turned and strode into the darkness. I ran after them, but it felt like I moved through waist-deep molasses. As her screams faded, I'd struggle to follow, trip, and collapsed on the ground. I'd wake, sobbing into my pillow and drenched in sweat.

Like most dreams, the sharpness of the memory faded as the light of the day brightened.

But when I woke on Friday, something was different. I remembered the nightmare, but I felt different. It felt like the sun rose above my soul's horizon and burned away the mental fog and darkness. I felt alive, light as a balloon. Yesterday, I danced my way through the workday and raced home to be with Anna. Yesterday, I would have agreed to anything.

Today, reality and guilt assaulted me. Watching Anna eat her breakfast, I realized how I had neglected my sweet daughter, the only bit of color in my black and white life. I kept her fed and clothed, that is, if you count junk food and dirty clothes as care. I hadn't realized how dark my mind had been until the fog inexplicably lifted.

Tears threatened to spill from my eyes, and I grabbed a tissue from the box on the table. I loved her so much; nothing else mattered.

Other than Anna's babysitter, Grace, I had no real friends. Every day I struggled to get out of bed, feed Anna, and go to work.

"I need to take a shower and get dressed. When I'm ready, we'll go."

Sighing, I returned to the bedroom for some clothes, crossed the hall, and entered the bathroom. I turned on the shower. Steam filled the air as I undressed. Sliding the curtain aside, I stepped into the tub and relished the warmth that flowed over me.

Without Anna, my life had no meaning, and without Jack, I wouldn't have had Anna. That jerk. I loved him so much. He said he loved me. I didn't care that he was twenty-eight, and I was only eighteen when we met. He seemed so worldly and sophisticated. It was ten months before I figured out he had a wife and kid. I didn't care. I was in love. Why didn't he leave his wife as he promised? Oh, yeah, the time was never "right." Six years! I gave him six years of my life. The best six years that I'd never get back!

Tears mingled with the water running down my body.

And then I saw him and his wife at a coffee shop. He saw me, and his eyes got big for a moment. Then he turned away, and I became invisible. I realized this guy would never leave his wife. Just a gullible and pleasant distraction; that's all I was.

Love. I had it and wanted to give it to someone. Since I couldn't have all of Jack, I'd have a piece of him - a tiny bit. I threw my birth control pills away that day. We rendezvoused several more times. I should have won an Oscar for my performance. I don't know how long I could've kept up the false front. My disgust grew with every touch. Fortunately, I got pregnant in two months.

I watched the remaining water swirl down the drain as I twisted the faucets closed, kind of like my life. I grabbed a towel and dried off.

I relished the look on his face when I told him where to go. He couldn't believe his free ride was leaving. He yelled and called me names. I knew I had enough.

The blow dryer roared in the small bathroom. In the mirror, I noticed the dark roots of my hair.

And where did those nasty thoughts come from? "Failure," "lousy mother," "not good enough," whispered through my mind. And the nightmares, almost every night, those horrible dreams. Someone stole Anna, or someone chased or tortured me. You know, if it wasn't for Anna and Grace, I . . . would . . . would've. . .

The blow dryer clattered into the sink, and my hands caught the edge as my legs turned to rubber. Understanding and fear stared back at me from the mirror. I had walked the line between life and death for a long time.

Closing the toilet seat cover, I sat down and buried my face in my hands. Fresh tears squeezed between my fingers.

The pounding on the door startled me.

"Mommy, what's taking so long?"

I stood and reached for a tissue box on the back of the toilet to wipe my eyes and nose. "J-j-just a minute, S-sweetie, I'm getting dressed."

On went, the tee shirt and jeans followed by the comb made several trips through my hair, and the toothbrush raced around my mouth.

For the last three days, I had ridden an emotional roller coaster. Thursday: down, depressed. Friday: up, exhilarated. This morning: the ride ended, and I got off confused.

Yesterday, the euphoria lasted all day long, but I couldn't wait to finish work. I wanted to be with Anna so desperately that I rushed home in record time. I pounded on Grace's door, turned the knob, and raced into the room. I dropped to my knees and scooped Anna up into my arms. After rounds of hugs and kisses, Anna reached for a plastic bag lying on the floor behind her.

'Close your eyes, Mommy; I wanna show you sometin.'"

Amused, I did as requested. After a bit of rustling, I heard an excited, "Open your eyes!"

Again, I obeyed and draped between her two tiny hands hung a finger-thick, five-foot-long, dirty yellow rope.

"A yellow rope . . . that's interesting . . . Uhm, where'd you get it?"

"From the angel in the park."

Alarmed, "You mean a man gave it to you in the park?"

"No, Mommy, an angel! Me, 'n Grace, was sittin' on the bench feedin' bread to da pigeons. The angel walked up and put it on da bench. He said he was 'n angel 'n I had to help God bring da rope to da man at da soup ki'chen. And when I saw da man, I would know him."

Concerned, I looked up at Grace again.

"Did Grace see this "angel?""

Grace gave a little shrug. "We sat there feeding the pigeons as she said, and the next thing I knew, she had that rope in her hands with a story about the angel. She must have found it on the bench. I didn't see it when we sat down, but it must have been there. No one approached us."

Ookkaayy! Relieved, I stifled a chuckle. My good mood didn't care where she got the rope. If Anna wanted to give it to a man at the soup kitchen, I'd be willing to help her. I would have agreed to deliver a donkey to the President at that point.

That was Friday. Now Saturday morning had arrived, and I felt pretty foolish. I only knew of one soup kitchen, the City Mission Soup Kitchen. It's a twenty or thirty-minute walk, and I couldn't afford a cab today. Thankfully, I lived within walking distance of work; it had been a miracle that I found an apartment so cheap and close. Not having a car had its advantages, but it limited my options on when and where I could go.

I took one last look in the mirror. I wiped my eyes and attacked my hair with a brush. I put a smile on my face then I exited the bathroom.

With a defeated sigh, "Alright, Sweetie, let's go." Anna squealed with delight as I picked her up and plunked her down on a chair. I put her shoes on. Anna picked up the plastic bag with the yellow rope.

Earlier, the weatherman said it would start bright and sunny, then turn colder and rain as the front passed. I peeked out the window. As predicted, the sunny day had turned cloudy with light rain.

"Anna, please get our jackets. It's raining; we'll need to dress warmly."

She brought my coat. I put mine on then knelt to help Anna with the zipper on hers. She didn't care about the weather; a big smile adorned her face as she waited for the adventure to begin. In a few minutes, we had our coats on and hooded.

Anna waited as I closed and locked the door to our second-floor apartment. We walked down the stairs, opened the door, and rain pelted our faces. I pushed Anna back inside.

"Sweetie, are you sure we need to go now?"

"Yes, Mommy. We ha'f to go noowww."

"Okay, wait here." I ran back up the stairs, unlocked the door, and grabbed the umbrella from the closet. My feet clomped loudly on the stairs as I returned to Anna in less than a minute. Laying it on the ground, I crouched in front of her. I found the drawstrings and tightened Anna's hood. "Boop," I said as I playfully bopped the tip of her nose with my finger. After I had zipped her coat up to her chin, I did the same for mine. Lastly, I bent over and picked up and opened the umbrella. As I pushed the button on the handle, the umbrella whooshed open.

"Here we go," I said. Holding the umbrella as a shield, we left the warm building and walked briskly down the sidewalk. With every step, conditions worsened. Pieces of paper and other debris fluttered by while we leaned into the wind and pushed on. This is stupid. I examined Anna's face for defeat and found determination, so we trudged on. She clutched the bag with the rope. But this is important to Anna. We'll go find this "man," and hopefully, he won't laugh in her face. Steeling myself against the cold wind, we marched on.

Chapter 9

Caleb

Saturday Morning

I gave up praying—time to find Bob. I also need to put the Armor of God in something. Assuming it had six pieces, then I needed something. I returned to the back room, where I had slept, and discovered a box of black plastic garbage bags. I grabbed one and put the Sword of the Spirit and the dry Helmet of Salvation in it. Then I headed for the dining room. I heard voices down the corridor and followed them. I found Bob by the front door of the dining hall speaking with a police officer. That cop could be a linebacker.

Bob introduced us. "Officer Mendez, this is Caleb Kincade. He was with me last night when we found Albert."

"Good morning," I said and extended my hand to the policeman. His giant paw engulfed mine. I expected him to crush my hand, but he had a surprisingly gentle grip.

All business, Officer Mendez continued, "The coroner took a quick look at him this morning. He said he had been sick for some time, and there were some suspicious lumps that he thought might be tumors. He also indicated there was no foul play. I'm just here to get your statements to wrap things up," said Officer Mendez. He continued reading from his notes. "You were out walking, heard some noise from an alley, investigated, found Albert Paxton, he told you he had been to City Mission before, and you are willing to bury him if nobody claims him. Does that sum it up?"

"Yes, sir," Bob said.

He pulled a business card from his shirt pocket, wrote a number on the back, and handed it to Bob. "Call the number on the front if you think of anything else. In about a week, call the number on the back and ask about the body's status. They'll be able to help you from there."

Bob said, "Thank you, Officer."

"Thank you, gentlemen. We'll contact you if we have further questions," said Officer Mendez. He turned and headed back to his black and white patrol car.

We stood on the sidewalk and watched the patrol car leave. The glorious sun now hid behind a bank of clouds. Airborne dust and trash flew by as wet spots appeared on the sidewalk. We ducked back into the building.

I said, "I'm glad that's done."

"I agree. Did God tell you the next step?" Bob replied.

"No."

Bob said, "Then we wait. Let's go to my office."

We turned and headed down the hall to Bob's office, and I wondered. I wondered how he crammed so much stuff into a small space and why he didn't dump half of it. And I wondered where I would sit. Bob had stacked years of magazines, books, and papers on every flat surface. He took a pile off of one chair and placed it on top of the collection in the other chair. I sat down.

"Is the Armor of God in the bag?"

"Yeah," I replied.

"Take it out, Brother, and let's have a look," Bob directed.

I pulled the plastic tube and the knit hat from the bag. I set the cap on the desk, and I held the tube in my right hand. Then I thought, "Sword of the Spirit," and the sword transformed. Well, at least for me, it changed.

"Ok, it's done."

"Hmm, I only see a plastic tube. What do you see?" Bob asked.

With both hands, I held the Sword of the Spirit up before my eyes. "I see a two and a half foot long shiny silver sword surrounded by a white aura. It is warm to the touch. It molds to my hand when I squeeze the hilt, and it became a spear to stab the demon last night. It has words inside, not on the surface, of the blade. It's like I can see into the metal, and floating in there is text. The words are written in a language I don't recognize, and they're always moving and shifting positions. Some fade, others get more pronounced and then fade again."

Bob opened the Bible on his desk and said, "Ephesians 6 says ' . . . Sword of the Spirit, which is the word of God.' The Word of God is Scripture. Some think it is just the four Gospels; many believe it is the entire Bible. Most scholars agree you need to be knowledgeable in God's Word so you can speak its truth into other people's lives. The Word of God is the only answer to evil in this world. Evil cannot tolerate the presence of the truth. Evil will either flee or try to smother the Word of God."

Bob turned some more pages in his Bible. "Hebrews 4:12 says:

> 'For the word of God is living and active. Sharper than any double-edged sword, it penetrates even to dividing soul and spirit, joints and marrow; it judges the thoughts and attitudes of the heart.'[4]

Bob closed the Bible. "You understand that I can't see what you see. Assuming your description is accurate, it doesn't surprise me that the sword can change shape, and it feels alive. If it is the embodiment of God's Word, then it is alive."

Bob leaned back in his chair with his hands clasped behind his head. Talking to the ceiling, Bob continued, "The languages on the sword are probably Hebrew, Aramaic or Greek, which are the original languages the Scriptures were written in."

---

[4] Hebrews 4:12 NIV

He tipped his chair forward and looked intently at me. "Describe again what happened after you struck the demon."

"There was a brief sizzle sound, and the demon turned to a wisp of smoke or vapor."

"Fascinating. I need to think on that," Bob said. "What do you see when you look at the Helmet of Salvation?"

I reached for the knit hat, and, with a thought, it transformed into the Helmet of Salvation. "It is a brown metal; I think it's bronze. A metal flap covers the nose, and wings on each side wrap forward to cover half of the cheeks. There are words in the metal, much like the sword, but they don't move around. It is warm like the sword and molds to my head."

Bob looked at the ceiling again. *That must be how he does his thinking.*

The Pastor spoke, "In battle, the head is one of the most vulnerable places on the Roman Soldier. The helmet protected this vital area. It could keep the soldier from harm and allow him to continue fighting. Salvation is the deliverance from sin and evil. Jesus is our salvation, our deliverer from sin and evil. In the spirit realm, the helmet must either protect you directly from the blows of demons, or perhaps it guards your mind against their influence. Either way, it will help you with those spiritual battles."

Bob sighed. "I wish I could see what you see."

We sat there. Both lost in thought for a minute. "Without guidance from God, what do we do next?" I asked, subdued.

"We wait. You go help with the preparations for lunch. I'm giving the message today, and I need to put some final touches on it," Bob said, rubbing his hands together. You could see the excitement on his face.

"Ok, see ya later," I said and headed down the hall to the kitchen. I re-introduced myself to Fran, and she put me right to work. The Mission offered a sermon and a meal most days of the week.

Depending on the day, they had a hearty dinner or soup and sandwiches. Fran parked me in front of a stack of large soup cans and showed me how to open them and into which kettle to dump them. Then Fran handed me several pounds of cold cuts and instructed me in the fine art of Soup Kitchen Sandwich making. Fran redefined multitasking: she seemed to be everywhere. As we worked, Fran chatted amiably about the Mission.

She explained, "The City Mission Soup Kitchen began during the Great Depression in the 1930s. It is one of the oldest ministries to the poor in the state. Monday through Friday, at 6:30 PM, Bob or another volunteer begins the worship service by singing songs from the old hymnals. At about 7:00, they served dinner. Clients don't have to listen to the teaching. They wait in an area by the door, but those that listen get in line first. The customers took the leftovers "home."

"Saturdays are different. There's lunch, no dinner. Doors open at 11:00, worship at 11:30, then lunch at noon. Normally, there're enough volunteers, but not today for some reason," she observed.

"Following the message, the speaker blesses the food, and they line up to get their meal," Fran concluded.

About 11:00 a.m., a stream of people flowed into the teaching/dining area and found seats around the various size tables. The room was a jumble of round, square, and rectangular tables surrounded by an assortment of folding and stackable plastic chairs. A platform with a podium stood in the front with an old upright piano next to it.

The crowd mainly consisted of men, but there were a few women and children. It was getting crowded. The weather had turned nasty outside. Bob entered the room about 11:30, welcomed everyone, and invited them to pick up a hymnal. As I stood behind the counter, I listened to the people sing the old hymns. Fran disappeared from the kitchen and reappeared behind the old upright piano, where she banged away on the keys. The tunes tickled my memory. I recognized

"Amazing Grace." One or two others sounded familiar. I must have heard them in my youth.

With the hymns finished, Bob began to speak. His animated teaching held their attention. After a while, the people started to shift and fidget. You could tell his sermon ran into overtime, but Pastor Bob was on fire. He gave the gospel message with great zeal. Then Pastor Bob asked if anyone there would like to accept Jesus Christ as their Savior, four hands shot up. Two men and one woman with a child raised their hands. Bob asked them to join him upfront. The people shuffled forward, but the woman and child remained sitting. Bob gave thanks for the food. The chair legs scraped the floor as the clients stood and formed a line, and that was my cue to begin dishing out the meal.

Chapter 10

Caroline

Saturday Morning

"Are we almost there?" Anna's question dripped with anticipation.

Amazing. Even though Anna was cold and wet, excitement still bubbled from Anna. On the other hand, doubt and anxiety had their hold on me. "I think so, Sweetie." The rain came down heavier. Up ahead, the City Mission Soup Kitchen sign peeked between the raindrops.

"There it is, let's hurry." We moved our feet faster, and we soon arrived at the door. I stopped. *This is stupid. Even if the guy is here, he's going to think we're loony.* "Anna, are you sure you want to do this?"

"Yes, Mommy. The angel said so." She pulled my hand with her whole body toward the door.

A smiling older woman sat at a table by the door. "Welcome. You made it just in time. Have you been here before?" she asked.

"No."

"Please sign in and go find a seat. There is usually some in the front because nobody likes sitting that close to the pastor." She gave me a wink and continued. "And there's a short service that has just started. The Pastor will say a blessing over the food, and you will then be able to eat," she added.

"Oh, we're not here to eat," I said.

"Mommy, I'm starving," Anna stated. The woman gave me a polite smile.

"Names?"

"Caroline and Anna Sullivan," I said and quickly signed the paper. Feeling awkward, I grabbed Anna's hand and headed down the hall to the dining room. My senses came under attack as we entered the room. We walked into a wall of heat and humidity. The smell of cooked food and unwashed people made my nose crinkle as the odors collided.

I looked over the heads of the guests, searching for two open seats. I spotted a winding path to a couple of free chairs in the front. We waded through the crowd toward the empty seats. Most of the patrons were male, with a few women and children were sprinkled here and there. "Excuse me . . . pardon me . . . sorry about your foot." My face warmed with embarrassment as several heads turned in our direction. The gruff singing sounded surprisingly beautiful, not a tabernacle choir, but still pleasant to the ear.

Anna and I arrived at the seats. Old and well-worn hymnals lay scattered on the table. Just as we sat, the Pastor asked us to stand. We stood by our chairs and picked up a hymnal. A neighbor with a scruffy black beard and a missing tooth smiled and pointed to the song number. The pages rustled as I searched for the hymn. "A Mighty Fortress is Our God," read the title. We had just finished verse two. I opened my mouth to sing, and the words died in my throat. I stopped and listened.

Tears pooled in the corners of my eyes and ran down my cheeks. From deep within, memories welled to the surface.

Verse 3.
And though this world, with devils filled,
should threaten to undo us,

I found myself trapped in one of my frequent nightmares. Someone had taken Anna, and I chased the kidnapper through a dark forest following Anna's terrified screams. I yelled her name until my voice gave out. Her screams mixed with evil laughter faded in the distance. I tried to run fast, but it was like I was running through wet cement. With each step, it became harder and harder to pick up my feet. Exhaustion overwhelmed me. I tripped on a root and fell to the ground; my heart pounded, and my breath ragged. I couldn't get up. Anna's cries faded until I no longer heard them.

we will not fear, for God hath willed
his truth to triumph through us.

I screamed and sobbed as I beat the ground. I looked in the direction of the last cry, and the forest faded into a white mist. A voice whispered in my ear, "Awake, the demon is gone."

"What? What demon?"

Several moments passed, then the voice whispered again, "In the name of Jesus, awake." It felt like someone threw me a life preserver and pulled me to safety. The fog in my mind cleared, and I opened my eyes. My confused mind moved slowly, like molasses. *Where am I?* I sat up and looked around. A room lined with dirty white ceramic tiles filled my vision, and three sizeable stainless steel tables sat in the middle of the chamber. The place reminded me of a hospital, a very grimy hospital. I sat on some kind of bed.

The Prince of Darkness grim,
we tremble not for him;
his rage we can endure,
for lo, his doom is sure;
one little word shall fell him.

A man stepped into my line of sight. He held a sword surrounded by a pale white light, and I saw kindness and warmth in his brown eyes. His brown hair framed his rugged face. Everything seemed so surreal.

The man said, "Go, see if you can find a way out. Remember, Jesus will save and protect you."

That seemed like an odd thing to say. I had rejected Jesus a long time ago. Why would He save me now?

Verse 4.
That word above all earthly powers,
no thanks to them, abideth;

I did as the man said. With some trouble, I stood up and left through the door he indicated. Exiting the room, I met a sea of hospital beds similar to mine. Scared, I slowly walked down the central aisle and looked around. What I saw didn't make sense. Screams pierced the gloom, and foul shapes walked and floated among the bodies. Stopping to survey my surroundings, I examined the nearest bed. Panic exploded in my mind, and my joints locked. A man lay on his back. A small, gangly, limbed creature sat between his head and heart. One burnt red arm dug in his forehead, and the other clutched his heart. The man screamed. My screams mingled with his as I ran away. The beds stretched on and on in both directions while I searched for an exit.

the Spirit and the gifts are ours,
thru him who with us sideth.
Let goods and kindred go,
this mortal life also;

Out of breath, I stopped and wildly looked around. I turned and checked the aisle behind me and down both side aisles. "Am I going the right way?" I wondered aloud. I must come to a wall or something soon and turned to continue in the direction I was going. Inches from my face hovered a creature, the same kind of monster I just encountered. I jumped back. The thing floated in the air—about the size of a small monkey with large red eyes on its human-looking face. Sharp claws tipped its fingers and toes. Dark red and hairless, the creature opened its mouth, and a puff of foul breath escaped.

It rasped, "What are you doing awake? Back to your cot, human!"

the body they may kill;
God's truth abideth still;
his kingdom is forever.[5]

The terrible creature reached for me. I screamed, grabbed the small but muscular arm, and flung it. It wailed as it sailed out of sight. The ghoulish thing's cries faded as I watched it fly. I knew I had to leave before it came back with others. I ran down the aisle, hoping that I ran in the right direction. Many minutes passed, and I saw the row of beds end at a white wall. I looked left, then right, for some sign of an exit.

I twisted around and scanned the sea of beds for any monsters chasing me. I heard their cries in the distance, but the dim light made it impossible to see much. Their shouts grew louder.

I spun back around to face the wall again. This time I saw a thin blue outline of a doorway. Where did it come from? It wasn't there a moment ago. Above the arched door glowed blue words which read, "Come to me, all you who are weary and burdened, and I will give you rest."

I found no handle or knob to turn. With desperation, I placed my hand in the center of the door and pushed. It felt warm and smoother than glass, but nothing happened. I tried again and pushed with all my strength. Still, it didn't budge. A cry of anguish escaped my throat.

---

[5] A Mighty Fortress is Our God, Verses 3 & 4 by Martin Luther Public Domain

The monster's shouts sounded even closer now. My heart thudded rapidly in my chest, and sweat stung my eyes.

Wait! What did that man say? "Jesus will save and protect you." How can that be? I don't believe in Jesus.

Behind me, I heard a shout. "There's the human!"

Terror in my heart and panic in my mind, I did the only I could. I screamed, "Jesus save and protect me." I pushed against the center of the door, it swung outward, and I stumbled through it.

And . . . I woke in my bed with my nightgown soaked with sweat, and my lungs labored to catch my breath. What a dream! But I was awake and feeling great for the first time in a long time. But like most dreams, it faded quickly, the details forgotten until now.

Dazed, I came back to the present. The song had ended, and the Pastor spoke now. The words seemed to glow and hang in the air. Heaven. Hell. Sacrifice. Redemption. Forgiveness. Jesus. The Cross. Lord and Savior. Then the Pastor asked the question. "If you were to die tonight, do you know if your spirit is going to heaven?"

"No," I whispered with a sob.

The Pastor continued, "You need someone to accept your sin and replace it with His holiness. Jesus can do that for you. He can be your Savior. Are you ready to believe and accept Jesus to be your Savior? If you're ready, raise your hand."

I didn't fully understand what was happening to me. But I knew I no longer wanted to live as I had been. I needed help, and I needed God. I raised my hand.

"If you raised your hand, please come see me after I give thanks for the food."

The Pastor prayed, and I sat weak and emotionally drained. The pastor said, "Amen," and every chair scraped the floor as people rose to get their meal, except mine.

I sat there and cried.

"Mommy, what's wrong?" Anna sounded small and frightened. Through tears, I watched the Pastor speak with two other men. They bowed their heads and prayed. When they finished, he gave them each a small book.

I rejected Jesus years ago. Am I going to accept Him as my Lord and Savior based on some dream?

The Pastor held another book with "New Testament" stamped on the front. He came over and sat down next to me as tears refilled my eyes.

"I'm Pastor Bob. Would you like to receive Jesus as your Savior?" he kindly asked.

I nodded, unable to speak; the tears continued to escape my eyes.

"Pray with me, Sister. Repeat what I say," Pastor Bob said. He bowed his head and closed his eyes.

"Lord God, I have sinned against you. I repent, turning from those sins and seek your forgiveness . . . " the Pastor began.

I repeated, "Lord God, I have sinned against you. I repent, turning from those sins and seek your forgiveness . . . "

Then a soft voice beside me echoed the same line. Startled, I looked down at the top of Anna's bowed head. I took her hand in mine and closed my eyes again. As Bob prayed, Anna and I repeated each line.

"You are the mighty creator of Heaven and earth . . ."

"You sent your son, Jesus, to die on the cross . . ."

"You accepted His blood as payment for my sins . . ."

"So I may be forgiven and be adopted into the family of God. . ."

"Jesus, I ask you to be my Savior and to take charge of my life . . ."

"Help me to live a life pleasing and obedient to You for all eternity. . ."

"In Jesus' name, Amen."

We lifted our heads. Relief and emotion crashed over me like an ocean wave. Again, tears welled up in my eyes and ran down my cheeks, but this time, they were tears of joy and thankfulness.

Pastor Bob handed me the Bible. "Bless you, child," He said to me.

"And bless you too, little one," he said to Anna. "What're your names?"

"I'm Caroline Sullivan, and this is my daughter, Anna," I replied with a big smile as I wiped my cheeks dry.

"I'd like to talk with you sometime next week, Sister. Just to see how you're doing and if you have any questions. I suggest you read the Gospel of John, but I think you need to have some lunch for now. The line is almost finished. Just go over to the end, pick up a tray and let the server know what you want."

I took his hands in mine. "Thank you, Pastor." I turned to follow Anna, who had skipped over to the line. I followed and picked up two trays and handed one to Anna.

"Mommy, what's to eat?"

I looked down at the food choices. "I see salad, carrots, sandwiches and a sign that says 'Chicken Noodle Soup.'"

Anna reached for some carrots and moved down to the sandwiches. I picked up a bowl of salad and added some ranch dressing. Suddenly Anna squealed and pointed, "Mommy, there he is. There's da man I'm suppos' to give the rope to."

I looked where she pointed. Behind the counter stood a man serving sandwiches. A shock of auburn hair covered his head. He seemed to be about five feet, eight inches. He smiled at Anna and turned his head in my direction. Our eyes locked. His were brown and gentle, just like in my dream. Wait! Not possible! They were the same eyes that I saw in my dream. "You!" I squealed. The room spun, and all went dark.

Chapter 11

Caleb

Saturday Noon

"Caleb, make sure the sandwiches don't run out. It's okay to have extra; the clients will take any leftovers with them," Fran said. I had already made about sixty and had enough bread and lunch meat for about thirty more.

As Pastor Bob finished blessing the food, the group rose in unison and headed for the food. Dirty hair, clothes, and faces formed a neat and orderly line. Each person picked up a tray and patiently waited. I heard a few gruff, "'Scuse me" and "Sorry" as the line developed. I thought I had a rough life. I've been a client myself at the mission, but I now realized I hadn't hit bottom yet. These guys had. My eyes moistened, and I wiped my face on my forearm. I couldn't respond to the "thank you's" for several minutes. I could only nod my head.

When the crowd thinned a bit, I looked out over the room at the men and women wolfing down their meals. Upfront knelt Bob with head bowed and his hands on the shoulders of a woman and young girl. The woman's shoulders shook as she cried.

The last person in line accepted the sandwich I handed him. Then Bob and the two ladies stood. The mother and daughter both had bright new believer auras. The little girl came bounding over to the beginning of the food line. She said some things to her mother. Still wiping her eyes, the mother responded and lifted two trays from the stack, handing one to her daughter. The little girl stood on her tiptoes to reach a plate and added some carrots to it. She bounced over to where I stood and inspected the sandwiches. Then she looked up at me.

She squealed with delight pointing at me, "Mommy, there he is. There's da man I'm suppos' to give my rope to!" Her yell startled me, and I stood there unsure how to respond. I gave the young girl an awkward smile. Then I turned my head and had my first good look at the mother. She had the most stunning pair of green eyes. I couldn't believe it; this was the woman from my dream. Hers was the first demon I sliced in the white-tiled room. Our eyes locked.

She cried, "You!" And much to my surprise, her eyes rolled up into her head, and she collapsed onto the floor.

I rushed from behind the counter and called for Pastor Bob.

"Bob! Hey, Bob, this lady passed out," I shouted.

Her daughter knelt next to her mother and cried, "Mommy, Mommy, wake up!"

"Excuse me," Bob said as he gently pushed Anna out of the way. "Sister Caroline, Sister Caroline, come back to us," as Bob gently patted her cheek. In about a minute, moans escaped from her throat. Her eyes fluttered open, and she wore a dazed expression on her face.

Then panic appeared on her face.

"You. How. . .? You were in my dream! You woke me up," she sounded hysterical.

Bob whispered, "We need privacy." Then louder, he said, "Help me get her up, Caleb. Sister Fran, would you finish adding food to their trays and bring them to my office, please?"

Bob and I got on each side of her, we each grabbed an arm. We half shuffled down the hall to Bob's office. We sat her in the chair I had occupied earlier. The "whump" of a pile of papers hitting the floor startled me as Bob cleared the other chair for me. Anna sat on a stack of books next to Caroline's Chair. Concern on her face replaced the innocence that it wore earlier.

The lady still had a wild look in her eyes.

Gently Bob introduced us. "Sister Caroline, this is Caleb Kincade. Brother Caleb, this is Caroline and Anna. Caroline, you need to hear Caleb's story. I know this will be hard for you, but I believe he is speaking the truth. Brother Caleb, please begin."

I started my story by waking up inside the Dream World. I told them about the first demon I saw and my trip to the white tile structure. I explained how she screamed when the beast had its claws inside her head. Lastly, I told how the monster into a wisp when I struck it with the sword. The story took a while. She sat there very still and quiet. I wasn't sure if she even listened; she stared straight ahead. I kept going. I told her everything that had happened up until the moment she fainted. As I spoke, she relaxed. I paused the story when Fran arrived with the food. Each tray held a sandwich, a cup of soup, a carton of milk, and a cookie. Anna sat on the books and watched me while she ate while Caroline stared at the floor and ignored the food. I hoped I wasn't wasting my breath.

When I finished, Caroline snapped out of her reverie. "So is the Dream World real?" she asked.

"I think so. If I can see demons and the Armor of God in this world, then I have to believe the Dream World is equally real."

"I've been fighting depression for at least a couple of years. Have these monsters been tormenting me that long? I would hear whispers in my mind. Was that a demon?"

"Last Wednesday, I'd said that was impossible. Today, yes, I think a Demon of Depression tortured you, causing you to believe you were good for nothing and a bad mother."

Then Caroline told her story. The affair, her move to this city, Anna's birth, the struggles of a single mother, and her depression. She shared her version of the dream, about the demon and her escape from the nightmare and how she felt like life had meaning for the first time in years.

She continued, "The only reason we're here is that Anna said an angel told her to give the man at the soup kitchen a gift. Anna, where's the bag?" Caroline asked.

"Oh, I left it on the table. I'll get it," Anna said as she ran out of the room.

A few moments later, a shriek echoed down the hall and into the office. Anna screamed. "MMMOOOMMMMMYYY, da bag's gone!"

We erupted from our chairs and ran down the hall to the dining area. Anna sobbed. "I-I-It was here."

"What was in the bag, Anna?" Bob asked.

"A yellow rope," she replied.

Bob went to the front, flipped some switches, and grabbed a microphone. Most clients had left, but a few still lingered.

"Attention. Can I have everyone's attention, please? Did anybody pick up a bag with a yellow rope in it? Brother Tom, did you see anything? No. This is important. Any information will help."

"Past'r Bob, I saw Jed putting a yeller rope on fur a belt," said one of the clients.

"Is he still here?"

"No, he j'st walk'd out da door."

I bolted for the front door, Bob right behind me. The cold rain pelted us as we hit the sidewalk. Shielding our eyes, we both looked up and down the street.

"You go left; I'll go right," Bob commanded. "Jed is fiftyish and very short and stocky. He usually pushes a cart."

We took off in our respective directions, and I half-ran down the street and stopped at the corner. My head whipped back and forth and searched for Jed. Across the road to my right, I saw a short person pushing a cart. A demon stood on his shoulders with both hands in his head. I crossed the road, dodging cars, horns blaring.

I called, "Hey Jed. Wait. Stop! I need to talk to you."

The demon turned and glared at me. "Keep running, Jed. This man wants to hurt you." I heard the imp say.

I reached for the Sword of the Spirit and realized . . . I left it at the Mission. Oh no!

Jed had stopped and turned to face me. "Get 'way from me. I din't do nutin'." I saw the yellow rope holding his pants up. The demon had a smug look on his face.

"Demon, tell him to give me the rope."

"No . . . hey, you can see me!"

"Not only can I see you, but I can destroy you."

"There ain't a human alive that can hurt me," the imp bragged.

"Who 'r you talkin' to? You're crazy, man, ge' a'way frum me," Jed cried.

"Are you sure about that? Demon, tell him to give the rope to me."

"NO!" it yelled.

I had enough. I reached above Jed's head and grabbed each of the little monster's arms below the shoulders. The demon howled in pain; the red skin beneath my palms started to sizzle and smoke. It let go of Jed and batted at my arms.

I opened my hands, and the demon shot into the air. Handprints branded the monster's upper arms, and the beast howled again and rocketed out of sight. I examined my palms. I felt the demon's muscular flesh blistering where I touched it, but I hadn't felt any pain or even mild discomfort in my hands. The smell of burnt flesh hung in the air.

I turned my attention to Jed. "Are you okay?"

Jed had this glazed look in his eyes. I wondered how long the demon had been riding him.

"Jed, let's go back to the Mission. I need the yellow rope you're wearing. I'm sure we can find a different rope to hold up your pants." Dully, he nodded his head. We turned his cart around and returned to the mission.

We parked the shopping cart outside the door and went in. Caroline and Fran comforted Anna.

"Is Bob back?" I asked.

"Not yet," Fran answered.

"Fran, do you have a different rope we can give Jed?"

"No, but we have a box of belts and ties. I'll go get it."

"Jed, we need to take the yellow rope off."

He raised his arms. "Do you want me to untie and pull the rope off?"

He nodded. *Oh Boy.*

"C'mon Jed; you gotta help me with this," I said.

Jed reached down and untied the rope and slipped it out of the belt loops. He laid it on the table. Caroline picked it up, took Anna by the hand, and headed back to Bob's office.

Bob returned, breathing hard. "You found him, good."

"Caroline and Anna went to your office with the yellow rope. I'll be there in a minute."

Bob headed down the hall, and Fran returned with the belts.

Fran said, "Here ya go, Jed, you can have this belt." She handed him a worn black belt that looked a little too long.

"You go with Bob. I'll tend to Jed here," Fran said.

"Thanks, Fran. Thanks, Jed." and I followed Bob down the hall to his office.

I entered the cramped room. Bob, Caroline, and Anna had returned to their previous seats while Anna held the yellow rope. I sat down in my chair.

"Da angel said ta giv' you 'dis, Mr. Kincade," Anna said as she handed me the rope.

I gently took it from her grasp. Which piece of the armor is this? Mentally, I ran through the list. Then I announced, "The Belt of Truth," and before my eyes, the ordinary, dirty, yellow rope transformed into a belt of leather pieces held together by bronze rings.

A leather sheath hung from it, and a bronze buckle connected the two ends. It was beautiful. I put it on.

Like the other pieces of the Armor of God, it was more than something to wear. I understood the true nature of the world and God's love for us. I reached for the bag with the Sword of the Spirit. With a thought, I changed it and inserted it into the scabbard. The union of God's truth with His Word brought even greater understanding, and tears welled in my eyes. Emotion choked my voice, "Anna, t-thank you for bringing this to me. It t-truly is a gift from God," Anna's face beamed.

Caroline whispered to Bob, "It looks like a yellow rope to me."

"I know," Bob said, "But Sister, you better get used to it. You should see the Helmet of Salvation."

Anna piped up, "It's pretty."

Caroline's eyes widened, and she asked, "Sweetie, what do you see?"

"I see t'ick pieces o' dark brown stuff. It's not cloth, but like cloth. It's all hooked together with brown metal things 'n a big buckle."

Caroline shook her head and looked again. She frowned, "I only see a yellow rope."

I reached down. I pulled the Sword of the Spirit out of the sheath and the Helmet of Salvation from the bag. I slipped the hat on my head and held the sword in my right hand. I thought "Helmet of Salvation," and it transformed.

Anna stared at me, wide-eyed.

"Anna, what do you see?" asked Pastor Bob.

She replied, eyes still wide, "In Mr. Kincade's han' is a silver s'ord that glows white. On his head is a metal hat dat looks like the same as 'da belt."

"I've always thought that children were more sensitive than adults to the spiritual realm. Now, I truly believe it. Perhaps that is why

Jesus, in Matthew 11, said: "I praise you, Father, Lord of heaven and earth,

because you have hidden these things from the wise and learned and revealed them to little children."[6]

"I see a plastic tube, a yellow rope, and an old knit hat. How can Anna see something different?" Caroline demanded.

"Apparently, in the spiritual realm, these items are powerful weapons. This sword is what struck the demon of depression within our dream. And here you are now, free of depression, saved by Jesus, and have met 'the man of your dreams,' so to speak. God could have only orchestrated these events."

"You have half of the Armor of God. I wonder how we're going to find the other half," said Pastor Bob.

"Half? What's the other half?" Caroline asked.

"We still need to find the Breastplate of Righteousness, Feet fitted with the Gospel of Peace and the Shield of Faith," Bob said.

"How do we find the other half?" Caroline questioned.

Pastor Bob got on his knees and said, "We pray and wait." I also knelt, as did Anna. Caroline hesitated for a moment, unsure what to do, and she too fell to her knees. Taking turns, we all talked with God and waited.

---

[6] Matthew 11:25 NIV

Chapter 12

Caleb

Saturday Afternoon

"Mommy, I haf' ta go potty," Anna whispered. I smiled.

Bob said, "Amen," and everybody stood.

"Out the door and to the right," said Bob. Caroline and Anna left the office.

"Meet us in the dining room," Bob called out as they headed down the hall.

I took off the Armor of God, and they became everyday items again. The plastic bag bulged as I stuffed them into it and left it hidden behind Bob's desk. I noticed Caroline's untouched tray of food and picked it up.

"Bob, I'm still in shock," I said as we walked to the dining room. "Is the Dream World real or imaginary? How could we share the same dream?"

Bob replied, "For all his knowledge, man cannot fully understand how the spiritual realm works. I believe the Bible hints at it and describes it in a way we can imagine. But I suspect the reality is much more. Either you woke in a part of the spiritual world, or God just used a mutual dream to connect you. I don't know."

We stopped in the doorway of the dining area. I looked around to see if anyone was eavesdropping. "I don't completely understand this, but the angel said the Dream World is in a bubble between the spirit and physical realms. He also stated that the properties of each overlap there. That's why the Sword of the Spirit can exist and operate in both places."

"Brother Caleb, we need to put the rest of this conversation on hold," stated Bob.

We entered the dining area and found Fran had fixed us some plates of food and placed it on the staff table in the corner. I set Caroline's tray at the spot across the table. Most of the clients had left. A few milled about, reluctant to depart till the rain let up some more. Anna, with Caroline in tow, returned to the dining room. Anna let go of her mother's hand and skipped over to us. Caroline followed. At the table, I sat next to Bob and Caroline opposite me. Anna sat next to her mother. Fran swooped in and grabbed the bowl of soup from Caroline, saying something about the soup being ice cold. Bob gave thanks for the food, and we started eating. Fran returned with Caroline's steaming soup on a tray and laid it in front of her. Anna nibbled on another cookie. I took the scene surrounding me in and gave a silent prayer of thanks to God. I found all of this oddly comforting.

Caroline broke the silence and asked, "What do we do now?"

I responded, "Well, I guess I thought you'd go home and resume your life."

"I don't think I can," Caroline said as she brushed Anna's hair from her face. She lifted her head, and those green eyes gazed into mine. "I feel connected to all this and don't think I can just leave. I can't explain it, but Anna and I must be here."

I smiled, and my eyes moistened. I intentionally blinked to hide the emotion. A cheer erupted from Anna. Even though we had met only moments before, I knew I had a special connection to them.

"We need to wait until God decides to inspire us or send another piece of the armor," I concluded.

Caroline looked around to see if anyone listened. "Bob, can I ask you a question?" she asked in a low voice.

"Sure, Sister Caroline."

"According to Caleb, I had a demon clutching my mind, giving me nightmares, and he said you had one pouring despair into you. He also stated that he has seen dozens of demons walking, floating, and riding on other people out on the street. I don't know what the spirit world is truly like, but that seems like too many monsters. Is it normal for so many demons to be around?"

"I don't know," Bob replied. "Remember, this is just as new to me as it is to you. Let me think about this a moment." Bob paused, leaned back in his chair, and looked at the ceiling. He tipped forward. "It does seem the mood and temperament of the people of Stanton have steadily declined over the last three years. Or a better way to say this is, there has been increased sin in Stanton, and the effects of sin are becoming more evident. Crime statistics are up, drug use is up, and divorce rates are higher than the national norm. Last week, I read a newspaper article reporting that teens' suicide rate has increased by fifty percent this year. I have also seen it in the clients coming here. We're feeding more people than ever, and our resources are severely stretched. My despair began about three years ago. Or, more likely, I had a crack of discouragement, a chink in the armor. Whatever it's called, and it allowed the demon to keep pouring more despair in."

Caroline turned to me. "You stabbed both of the demons. Do you think you killed them? Are they dead? Is that even possible?"

"I thought I killed them, but now I don't know. It seems unlikely that flesh and blood humans could kill demon spirits. But I'm using a spiritual weapon, not a human-made weapon. What do you think, Bob?"

"Brother, Scripture says Satan and the other demons were once angels. Some say Satan wanted to become God. However, God made Satan. It seems unlikely that the thing created could ever surpass the Creator."

"What? What do you mean by that?"

Bob looked up and thought for a moment, then continued. "Humans are striving to create robots that can walk, talk, and, to a certain degree, think. It seems unlikely that humankind can make a robot better than himself. With all of our cleverness, humans may be able to give a machine the appearance of thought. However, will it ever be truly self-aware? A thinking life form? I think not. The robot will never be more than what a human makes it. The robot will not be able to surpass its creator.

"In a similar way, God created Satan. Yet, Satan thought of himself as more capable than God, and he rebelled. It's unlikely that Satan, also created by God, could surpass or replace God as the universe's creator. I don't know why Satan thinks he can do a better job than God, but he does. Scripture indicates that one-third of the angels chose to join Satan, and they became demons. Satan and his demons rule Hell. God and his angels rule Heaven. I feel like the earth is the buffer or battleground in between."

Bob took a breath and continued. "Can an angel or demon be killed? The Bible indicates that God created them, and they are immortal. By immortal, I mean they never grow old or die as we understand it. If God created them, then I assume God can unmake them. But can a mortal human yielding a spiritual sword kill a demon? It seems unlikely. Brother Caleb, I think you can make the demon ineffective for a time. It's like chopping a weed off at ground level. The plant has suffered a significant blow and cannot invade the garden as it once did. However, the roots are intact, and they will eventually grow back. It has not died."

Bob paused for a moment and leaned forward. His eyes looked directly into mine.

"I think when you strike the demons, you're hurting them severely, and you're making them unable to function for a time. However, they're likely to come back at some point and cause mischief once again.

"I once learned that death means 'separated from God.' If that is so, then the demons are already dead because they are already separated from God. Yet, they still have life, or maybe it is better to say they have existence.

"Humans have one great misfortune; they must often suffer. They need to experience trials, at least for a time, to learn, grow, be strengthened, seek God, and become what God wants. Natural events and demons may cause humans some pain in the short run, but in the long term, people become more pleasing to God."

Bob looked at Caroline and began again, "Angels are also given the freedom to choose. Satan and one-third of the angels decided to rebel against God. He must have known that would happen because God knows everything. God used Satan's rebellion to allow "choice" to enter the world."

Bob was on a roll.

"Humans have the opportunity to "choose." They are born separated from God. They grow and mature, and at some point, they make a choice. Will they follow God or not? If they don't choose God, they have decided to follow Satan, and they don't even realize it. The exception would be children who die before the age of accountability. I don't believe they would go to hell because they are not mature enough to choose. People may not think they're following the devil, but there are only two options. If you don't choose God, then, by default, you've selected Satan."

Bob looked at me again, then continued, "Humans are born with plenty of opportunities to sin. Sin is simply 'violating God's Law.' Sometimes that sin is on display for all to see, and sometimes it resides in the heart. Either way, evil is there. God allows sin on earth. He allows it in Hell, but He cannot permit it in Heaven with Him."

"Brother, I don't know why God requires blood as payment to wash away sin. All I know is the Bible says it is true. God cannot allow humans, laden with sin, into heaven. They need their sins to be washed away. In the Bible, God has always required payment for sin in blood. That was the purpose of all those animal sacrifices in the Old

Testament. Unfortunately, the sacrifices only temporarily cleansed the Jews. God sent His Son, Jesus, to the earth in human form. Jesus was God made flesh, and His blood is pure. It was God's and Jesus' plan to sacrifice Jesus as the permanent payment for all sin for all time."

Bob leaned back in his chair again and spoke to the ceiling. "God is outside of time or at least time as we understand it. Jesus' death became the payment for our sins. That payment for sin is for all time going forward and backward. That act eliminated the need for animal sacrifice."

"God then sent the Holy Spirit to be a guide for humans, but not all humans. He is a guide only for those who have repented of their sins and accepted Jesus as their Savior. The Holy Spirit can only enter those whose sin has been washed away by the blood of Jesus. God cannot abide with one who has unpaid sin in their life."

Bob leaned forward and turned to Caroline and Anna. "Sisters, today, when you accepted Jesus' blood as payment for your sin, there was a spiritual transaction. The Holy Spirit entered you and now resides in you, in your heart. The Holy Spirit may speak directly to you, but He is subtle most of the time. Subtle nudges to do what is right. Subtle nudges to reach out to another person. He whispers into your mind when praying and will act as your conscience and guide."

"God created humans with immense power. The power to think, create, and destroy. Again, it is the power of choice. Choose to help or hurt. Choose to build or destroy. Choose God or reject God."

Bob took another breath. "So, you might ask, why did God give humankind the ability to choose? The only thing that God desires is our love. That love comes in the form of worship and obedience. Does He have to have our love? No, He can exist without it. However, love without choice is not possible. Love must be freely given, or it has no meaning or value. Therefore, God permits choice. Man can choose or reject God. God is saddened when He is rejected but rejoices when someone chooses Him like you two did today."

"No, I don't think Brother Caleb can kill the demons. Kind of a long-winded answer to such a short question," Bob smiled.

"Thanks, Bob," I said. "Two days ago, being a Soldier of God never entered my mind. Yet, here I am. And with each piece of the armor that I obtain, I find my faith growing. I don't know if I am going to survive this task physically, but spiritually I will."

"Now that you're warmed up, I have another question," I said. "If God makes the angels and if they are supposed to be beautiful, then why are the demons I've seen so hideous? They're ugly, warped, and smell like death."

Bob leaned back and looked at the ceiling again.

"Again, I'm speculating. Demons were once beautiful angels. Yet those that followed Satan choose to sin. They violated God's law. Humans, when they break God's law, hide the sin in their hearts. You may never see evidence of sin on the outside. But sometimes, the sin manifests itself physically through addictions or disease. I don't mean the disease is the sin; rather, it is the consequence of participating in the sin."

Bob flipped forward, and his eyes met mine.

"However, I suspect that the angels that violate God's law cannot hide their sin in their hearts. Do they even have a heart? Initially, they were beautiful, like God's angels. Over time they've changed. They began to reflect the actual nature of their sin physically. When there is prolonged involvement in sin, it becomes ugly. So, the demons are just reflecting their sinful nature." Bob paused, thought for a moment, and continued.

"Sin affects your physical and emotional well-being. I see it at the shelter. There are lots of people that made wrong choices and could not get out from under their sin. Now, they are sometimes homeless, suffer addictions and disease. They need help, and God has sent me to help them as best I can," Bob finished.

Everybody sat quietly and reflected on Bob's words.

A couple of minutes later, Bob said, "It's getting late. I need to finish my sermon tomorrow. Especially since I have to rewrite everything."

"I would like to escort Caroline and Anna to their apartment. Then I'll go home and return tomorrow if that is okay?" I smiled at Caroline. "Is that okay with you, Caroline?" She nodded her head, yes.

Anna squealed with delight.

Chapter 13

Caleb

Saturday, Late Afternoon

Bundled against the cold, Caroline, Anna, and I said our goodbyes to Pastor Bob and left City Mission. I carried the Armor of God in the plastic bag. Caroline pointed the way down the street, and we walked in silence for a few minutes.

"In all the confusion today, I don't think I ever thanked you for getting rid of the demon in the Dream World. I've made a lot of bad choices in my life. You're the first person to come to my rescue. Thank you, Mr. Kincade, for rescuing me," Caroline smiled as I turned my head and looked at her.

"You're welcome," I replied.

We walked in silence again. Anna skipped and chatted with herself. The cold slapped our cheeks. It felt strange walking beside a woman. It had been years since I've had more than an insincere, shallow conversation with a member of the opposite sex. They often went like this:

"Hello, how are you?"

"Fine, thank you. And you?"

"I'm all right."

Then we parted ways, never to speak again.

This situation felt odd to me. Usually, the presence of a woman would tie my tongue. I wanted this walk to last forever, and I didn't want to blow it. Butterflies bumped into each other in my stomach.

"Until today, I didn't believe in demons. And even if I did, I wouldn't think it possible for them to hurt me," Caroline thought aloud. "I never imagined spirits from the next world could cause misery of this world. I always thought humans made their problems."

Anna outpaced us. "Don't go too far, Sweetie," Caroline said.

"I've got to stop thinking about this. Talk to me, Caleb," she asked. "Where're you from? What makes you tick?"

Warmth rushed to my face. Women rarely asked me anything.

"I dunno. I mean, there's not much to say. I've lived in Stanton my whole life. I didn't do well in high school and have spent my life at the bottom of society."

"C'mon Caleb, you can do better than that," Caroline good-naturedly chided me. "I'm not looking for you to reveal all your secrets, but there must be more to the story."

I kicked a stone on the sidewalk and sent it into the street. Anna, several yards ahead of us, did a little jig as she chanted in her little girl sing-song voice, "Step on a crack and break your mother's back." She glanced over her shoulder at us, "Mommy aren't you glad I'm good at missing the cracks. Oops! Sorry, Mommy," as she stepped on a crack and giggled. I smiled.

"Okay, but it's hard to talk about my life, Caroline, because most of it has been unpleasant. My father verbally and physically tormented me as a child.

"What made the torture worse was my mom's inaction. She rarely came to my rescue when my father abused me. She feared him too much. She either sat in silence or went for walks.

"She claimed to be a Christian woman, but her shallow faith, combined with a lack of self-esteem, kept her on the sidelines. I don't know if she had always been so weak or if my father beat the little strength she had out of her. There had been a few times she tried to rescue me, but my father knocked her down with his words or fists.

"Father openly flirted with other women in front of Mom. On weekends, he'd go out drinking with his buddies. He often didn't come home till morning stinking of beer, or vomit, and perfume.

"I got relief from my father by attending church with Mom on Sunday morning and Youth Group on Wednesday nights. We lived close enough to walk. I went not because I had much interest in God. Instead, I needed the break from my father, and the girls were cute.

"In school, I barely passed my courses and graduated at the bottom of my class. I'm not stupid, but I didn't see the point of doing the homework. The only real romance I had lasted about two months when I was seventeen.

"On my eighteenth birthday, I went out to avoid my father. He was in a foul mood, and I didn't want to stick around. I returned home and found my father standing over Mom. His fists bloodied, his chest heaving, and Mom lay crumpled on the floor. I thought it was Mom because of her clothes. Her face was unrecognizable. He lunged for me, but I dodged him and bolted for the door. Fortunately, I ran much faster than he did. I found someone with a phone and called the police. They caught my father dumping Mom's body in the trunk of his car.

"The trial lasted only a day. I testified against him. I hoped for the death penalty, but the judge sentenced him to twenty-five years in prison. Ironically, he was beaten to death a year later. They asked me what I wanted to do with the body. I told them I didn't care.

"I went to Stanton Community College and flunked out. I'm awkward in social situations. Once I tried to talk to these girls at a party, they claimed I 'creeped them out.' Since then, I've kept to myself."

The afternoon light faded. "I know I've been my own worst enemy. Over time, what little ambition and self-worth I had evaporated. I stopped trying. Most of my day is spent reading books from the library or working. I've been a janitor at Foe Financial Services for the last three years. That's the longest I've been at a job. Before I got this job, I was tired, tired of always failing, and tired of my bad habits. If I hadn't gone to City Mission for a meal and a message one night, I'd be more of a loser than I am. It was that sermon and a bit of conviction that helped me to turn things around. I needed to stop making excuses. I've worked hard to be on time, to do a good job. I've had two sick days in the last three years and until yesterday had never been late. And it has paid off. I feel better about myself, and I've had good job reviews. And while I see demons now, I feel I have a purpose. That I am not just a piece of human debris," I finished.

"C'mon, human debris?"

"Really."

A few moments of silence passed.

"You've heard my tale. What's your story?"

"I guess my story is similar in some ways. There's not a lot to tell; I was born and raised in Concord, New Hampshire. I was average in looks, grades, and popularity. There were a few boyfriends, but I'd get scared and sabotage the relationship when things started getting serious. I got an Associates's of Business Degree from the local community college, followed by a few low-paying jobs in Concord.

After I graduated from high school, I met Jack. He was a professor of my first class at Concord Community College. I fell head over heels in love. After a few months of intimacy, he confessed he was married, but I didn't care. It didn't feel wrong. I didn't think I could be destroying a family. All I knew was that I deeply loved Jack. He was smooth talkin', and I believed everything he told me. It had taken six years before I realized he had no intention of leaving his wife and kids."

We walked on in silence. Anna bounced ahead of us, still jabbering happily away to herself. Caroline grabbed my sleeve and stopped. She turned her head and looked directly into my eyes. "I wanted a family, with or without Jack. I stopped taking the pill and waited. Once I got pregnant, I broke things off with him. I felt hurt and used, so I did something horrible. The day before I ended the relationship, I called him, and he came over to my apartment. I bought and hid a small video camera in the bedroom and recorded our last time together. I sent the video with a long, detailed letter to Jack's wife. Then I did a cowardly thing. I didn't want to face the aftermath of my actions, so I gave away what wouldn't fit in my car. I ran away. I had no plan, no destination. I'm ashamed of what I did. I'm not as nice as I seem.

"Anna . . . slow down . . . please," Caroline's voice quivered. She wiped a tear from her eye and resumed her narrative.

"When I arrived at Stanton, I just decided to stay. But I didn't know anybody. I had little money, no job, and six weeks pregnant. I lived in my car for a few weeks while I applied for jobs everywhere. Foe Financial Services offered me an Administrative Assistant position. I'm now a Senior Administrative Clerk on the 28th floor, where I do filing, typing, and anything else the big shots ask me to do. It's weird that we both work at the same place and never met. Where do you work?"

"I'm assigned the bottom half of the building. I use to work evenings with most cleaners, but my good work and attendance got me promoted to days. Most of the time, I am on call to clean up spills, unclog a toilet, or sweep up toner."

"That explains why we never met. We're almost to the apartment. It's just a couple more blocks," Caroline said. "Shortly after Anna was born, things got tough, mentally, and financially. I had to take a lot of time off, and I hadn't accrued any benefits yet. I'm lucky I didn't get fired. I had to sell my car to make ends meet. We ate a lot of peanut butter sandwiches and macaroni and cheese. In the first couple of years, the depression was mild, but it got worse as time went on. I still functioned, but some days, barely. Anna was all that kept me going. There were times, if Anna hadn't needed me, I might've just ended it all." Caroline sighed.

"I'm glad God brought us together," I said. "It's ama. . .zing . . .," my voice trailed off. A monster strode toward us a half a block away and on our side of the street. It stood about six feet tall, and it didn't look like the imps from the Dream World. This one looked like the classic Halloween demon: slender, muscular, red with three-inch curved horns on each side of the forehead. Armed with a sword in its hand, it swaggered toward us.

"Anna, come here . . . now!" The urgency was evident in my voice. Anna stopped and turned to look at me.

"What's wrong?" Caroline asked as she looked around.

"There's a demon heading our way. It's armed with a sword and appears to be focused on us," I whispered.

I pulled the Armor of God from the bag. I pulled the cap out, put it on my head, and tied the rope around my waist.

Anna saw me putting on the Armor. "What's wrong, Mr. Kincade?" Curiosity, mixed with fear, filled her eyes.

"There's a demon walking toward us on this side of the street. Can you see it, Anna?" I asked.

"N-no," she stammered.

Thank you, God! A child doesn't need to see that.

As the demon approached, it shouted to itself. "Go round up the strays, Gorg. It's the only thing you're good at." Gorg sneered. "It's not my fault that the woman woke up. That idiot, Ort, must have run away. Now I have to find her and then wait till she falls asleep to re-insert her into the Dream Collection Center. I wasn't even on duty. Those jerks, I'll show them. I'm good at a lot of things. I know how to inflict real pain on humans." Gorg stopped about thirty feet or so from us. It stared at Caroline. "NNNOOO," Gorg wailed. "When did you become a Child of God? I'm in for it now! They'll blame me for this."

While the demon ranted, I picked up the Sword of the Spirit. Gorg lifted its sword and headed for Caroline. *The Armor of God.* As I thought the words, my Armor became shiny and lethal. Power and knowledge coursed through my veins. The sword vibrated in my hand.

But Gorg became distracted. It no longer strode toward Caroline; it focused its attention on something in an old, lidless, metal trash can between us. The container overflowed with garbage, but a white glow emanated from the top of the junk. *What is that? It can't be. It is!* A bronze metal plate with sculpted human pectoral and abdominal muscles sat on top of the trash, surrounded by a white aura. It's the Breastplate of Righteousness. It must have activated when I activated the armor.

The demon and I moved toward the container. We met at the trash can, one on each side of it. Gorg stared at the Breastplate, then looked up and saw me. Realization lit up the demon's face, and it knew I could see it.

"Stop there, demon," I growled.

Gorg stopped, surprised that I saw it. It looked at me and the pieces of the Armor of God I wore. We glared at each other.

The demon tensed; its left arm shot out, and the clawed hand grabbed the Breastplate of Righteousness. The sound of sizzling meat and steam erupted from the Gorg's fingers, where it touched the breastplate. Howling in agony, Gorg dropped it on the ground and jumped back, clutching the damaged appendage. Thinking the demon had retreated, I lunged for the breastplate, only to hear a sword whistling through the air. Reflex saved my hand from being severed.

Raising my sword with my right arm, I faced the demon. We started circling each other, waiting for the other to flinch. My brown eyes locked with the creature's red ones. The circling brought me closer to the prize, and I glanced at it. In that split second, the demon swung. Its sword sliced the air, heading for my chest. I jumped back too late. The tip of the blade ripped a trail of agony across my chest. A scream escaped my throat.

I sensed the demon readying another blow, and sparks erupted as the blades collided. We started hammering each other. Every swing of the sword hurt my chest. The battle raged intensely for minutes. The demon lunged, and its blade sliced my left side just below my ribcage. The pain sapped my strength. My blows weakened. Exhausted, I fell to my knees. Gorg's face lit up, smug with the victory. My chest heaving and in pain, I knew I would be meeting God in seconds.

The demon took a step forward and, with both clawed hands, raised the sword above its head to deliver the final blow. Closing my eyes, I waited for death. Then I heard, "Now!" streak through my mind. With strength that was not my own, I raised the sword and thrust it into Gorg's chest. The demon had a look of disbelief on its face as it dissipated.

Wounded and drained of all strength, I fell forward and hit the sidewalk with my face. I rolled over and gasped for air. I rasped, "Caroline." She rushed over, knelt beside me while Anna stood on my other side.

"What happened? Are you OK?" Caroline's voice filled with concern. She pulled something from her purse and started wiping the blood from my nose.

"My chest!" I croaked. Caroline paused, looking at my clothes. The baffled look on her face didn't register with me. She unzipped my coat, looked at my shirt a moment. Still looking confused, she unbuttoned the shirt. Looking down at my chest, I expected to see torn flesh and blood. I saw neither. A horizontal line about three-quarters of an inch wide and almost a foot long crossed my chest. The red and blistered flesh throbbed with pain. Another four-inch burn decorated my side. While the lack of blood brought relief, I knew the final blow would have been fatal.

The pain subsided a bit. "Help me up," I gasped. Anna and Caroline helped me to a sitting position, then to my feet. Leaving my shirt unbuttoned, I zipped up my jacket. I stumbled over to the trash can and grabbed the Breastplate of Righteousness.

"Anna, put this in the bag and carry it," I requested. I took the other armor pieces off and handed them to her; they joined the Breastplate of Righteousness in the bag.

"Where's the apartment?" I croaked.

"It's halfway down the block and up one flight of stairs," Caroline replied.

"Let's go. I don't think I can walk far." I lurched in the direction Caroline indicated. Walking like a drunk, I staggered down the empty sidewalk.

"Here we are." Caroline unlocked and opened the door. I dragged myself up the stairs and leaned against the wall while Caroline fumbled with her keys. She inserted the key into the lock. With a turn of the knob, the door opened.

I bumped into her as I stumbled across the threshold. Tottering through the kitchen, I collapsed on the couch as the world darkened.

Chapter 14

Caroline

Saturday, Late Afternoon

I didn't know what to think. Caleb motioned me to stay put and walked to a nearby garbage can. He said something, but I didn't hear it all.

Huh? I blinked several times. A dirty piece of clothing floated out of the trash can and dropped on the ground. Caleb grabbed the vest and jumped back like he was avoiding someone. Then he circled that rumpled cloth with the unseen opponent, swinging the plastic tube left then right. I've never seen stranger sight. I guessed he battled the demon, but I could only see one side of the fight. There was no sound other than Caleb's heavy breathing and a few grunts. Sparks flew from the tube every few seconds. Caleb's movement slowed. He tired.

Caleb, exhausted, dropped to his knees. Anna screamed and clung to my waist. Caleb knelt there, ready to receive the death blow, a picture of defeat. Then his muscles tensed, and he stabbed into the air in front of him with the plastic tube. For a split second, I saw the shocked face of a demon, and then it vanished. I blinked. *Did I see that?*

Caleb looked like a tree falling as he fell forward, hitting the pavement. He called, and we rushed over to him. Rolling him over, I asked, "What happened? Are you OK?" Blood dribbled from his nose. I grabbed a few tissues from my pursed and wiped the blood.

"My chest!" he rasped.

I examined Caleb's coat; I saw no damage to the fabric. I unzipped the jacket and inspected his shirt, looking for a gash, but found none.

Painful groans escaped his throat. Puzzled, I unbuttoned and opened his shirt. I gasped. There was a long raw, red burn seared across his chest. Another injury peeked out from his side. Mesmerized, I stared at the wounds for several moments, not sure what to do.

"Help me up," Caleb said. Anna and I helped him sit, then stand. He zipped his jacket closed and staggered over to the pile of fabric on the sidewalk. Caleb picked up a dirty fluorescent yellow safety vest as road construction crews wore. He handed it to Anna and asked her to put it in the bag. Caleb also gave Anna the plastic tube. Then he untied the rope from around his waist and pulled the hat off his head. Those also went into the plastic bag.

"Where's the apartment?" Caleb gasped.

"It's halfway down the block and up one flight of stairs."

"Let's go. I can't walk far!" Caleb said as he lurched down the street.

Anna and I ran to catch up to Caleb's staggering form. He moved like a drunkard, nearly colliding with another garbage can and a light pole. Running ahead, holding Anna's hand, I reached the street level entrance first and had it opened by the time Caleb arrived. He stumbled up the stairs before me but tripped on the top step. He managed to pick himself up but blocked the way. I gently nudged him aside. He gasped for air as he leaned against the wall by the door. I dropped my keys in my haste. I picked them up and unlocked the door. It swung inward, and Caleb fell forward as he entered the apartment. He caught himself and stumbled through the kitchen, where he collapsed on the living room couch and passed out.

Anna and I arrived at the sofa. "Anna, help me get his coat off. Pull his sleeve as I roll him on his side." I gently turned him one way then back again to slip his jacket off. Caleb's shirt fell open, and the long ugly burn looked like it pulsed with pain.

Anna's small voice asked, "Will Mr. Kincade be okay, Mommy?"

"I don't know, Sweetie." *What should I do?*

"Anna, turn the computer on for me, please? Maybe the Internet can give us some information on treating burns." Anna obeyed.

I repositioned his legs, arms, and head to make him more comfortable. *Is he passed out or in a coma?* The old computer finished booting as I sat down. Caleb didn't seem to be in immediate danger. He breathed well. Anna sat on the floor next to him.

Going to the Internet, I searched for burn treatments. Looking at the pictures and descriptions on the computer and comparing them to Caleb's injury, I decided they were not third-degree burns. According to the image, the wounds were second-degree burns. There were long blisters, but the damage didn't appear to be too deep. I placed a clean, cold, damp cloth on the two wounds.

Anna sat nearby watching. "Mommy, are we calling a doctor?"

"I don't think so, Sweetie. What would we tell them? An invisible demon attacked the man. They wouldn't believe us and think that we're crazy."

Caleb stirred. His eyes opened with a start and darted around. Once he saw Anna and me, he relaxed.

"How long was I out?" he asked.

"About ten minutes. The good news is the burns are second-degree, so if we keep them wrapped and clean, you'll heal. It will be painful for a while. Would you like some acetaminophen or aspirin?"

"Either would be great, thank you," he said. I got up, found some aspirin, filled a glass with water, and took it to him. We helped him to sit. He popped the pills in his mouth and drank the water before flopping back onto the couch.

After he took the aspirin and lay back down, I said, "The website advised a cool damp cloth followed by clean, dry gauze. Also, we need to avoid ointments and greasy compounds. I had a damp cloth on it while you were out. Sit up, and I'll wrap gauze around your chest and wounds. Then I can tape the bandage to itself and not to your skin."

With effort and some help from us, Caleb sat up again. I wrapped his wound.

"Ow . . . Ow . . . Ow!" he cried.

"I'm so sorry, but it needs to be covered."

"Keep goin'," he gasped.

I wrapped the gauze around him two more times.

"Finished"

He winced as he laid down.

Caleb moaned, "This sure hurts. Thanks for helping me."

"You're welcome," I said. "I need to fix Anna some dinner. I know we had soup for lunch, but it's the easiest and fastest thing to fix right now. There is also some ham for sandwiches. Do you want to eat anything?"

"A little soup and maybe a half a sandwich would be great, thank you," Caleb answered. He closed his eyes.

I went to the kitchen to prepare the food. I opened two cans of Chicken Noodle Soup and dumped them in a saucepan. Lighting the stove burner, I placed the pan on it. While the soup heated, I watched Anna. She sat on the floor, playing quietly with her dolls. *She'll be outgrowing those soon.* Shifting my focus, I looked at Caleb. His eyes closed, and he seemed to doze. He can't go home tonight.

I got out some bread, lettuce, mayonnaise, and ham. I made three sandwiches but cut them into quarters so they'd be easier to eat. When steam rose from the soup, I poured it into bowls. "Anna, please come and help me." I handed Anna the sandwiches on a plate, put the bowls of hot soup on a tray, and brought them over. "Food's ready," I murmured, setting the food on the coffee table. Caleb's eyes fluttered open. I helped him sit up and handed him a cup of soup. Our eyes locked. Warmth and gratitude flowed from his into mine, and we both made an awkward smile. Caleb gingerly brought a spoonful of soup up to his mouth and blew on it. Anna and I helped ourselves to sandwiches, and we all ate together in comfortable silence.

Caleb handed me the bowl. "That tasted great. Thank you."

"I've been thinking," I said. "You can't go home tonight. It's too far, and you're too weak. How 'bout you sleep on the couch?"

"Thanks, Caroline. You're right, I can't walk home, and I don't have money for a cab," he smiled.

Gathering up the dirty plates, I retreated to the kitchen. I washed a few dishes and puttered a bit.

"Mr. Kincade, do you want to play a card game?"

"Sure, Anna. I think the aspirin is kicking in. I'm feeling a little better."

Anna retrieved a deck of cards from the drawer in the coffee table. Caleb and Anna played War. I spent some time at the kitchen table clipping coupons from the newspaper and watched them play. Amazing. At noon today, I claimed Jesus as my Savior, met this man, shared my life story, he gets wounded in a battle with a demon, and played card games with Anna. "Weird Day" seemed like an inadequate description. The incredible thing is that it all feels right. I got up and joined them when they started playing "Go Fish."

Caleb never ventured far from the couch. The rest of the evening passed as we pleasantly chatted and switched to board games. For the first time in a long time, laughter filled my home. Caleb and I were talking when I noticed Anna's longer and longer blinks. "I think it's time for bed, Sweetie."

"Aw, Mommy, can't I stay up a little longer," Anna said with a yawn.

"No, it's late, and we had a big day. Go brush your teeth and get in my bed." Anna got up and headed for the bathroom. "This is a one-bedroom apartment. Anna normally sleeps on the couch," I said. "She'll sleep with me tonight. Come on, Sweetie, go brush your teeth."

A few minutes later, Anna returned clad in bright pink fuzzy jammies to say good night. She walked over and hugged me. Then she walked over and carefully hugged Caleb.

"G'nite, Mr. Kincade, I hope ya feel better."

"I hope so too. G'nite, Anna." Caleb replied and blinked several times rapidly. *Is that a tear in his eye?* Anna retreated to the bedroom.

"I'll be in there in a minute, Sweetie, and we'll read a story."

"Caleb, would you like some more aspirin?" I asked. He nodded, and I went to get it. Upon my return, I gave him the pills and a glass of water. "If you don't need anything else, I'm going to bed also," I smiled.

"Thanks for everything, Caroline. You don't know how much it means to me," Caleb said. "Good night."

"G' nite," I replied and headed to the bathroom to brush my teeth and change into my pajamas. Before going into the bedroom, I checked on Caleb one last time. While I couldn't see his eyes in the darkened room, I heard soft snores coming from the couch.

I quietly retired to the bedroom and closed the door. Anna had already fallen asleep. I pulled the covers back and curled up next to her small, warm body. She snuggled against me, and I prayed, "Jesus, thank you," and fell asleep.

Chapter 15

Caleb

Sunday Morning

MMMmmm, that smells good. The scent of bacon made its way to my nose. I tried to move, and pain flashed across my chest and down my side. I didn't think it possible for a body to hurt this much. "Did anybody get the license number of the truck that hit me?" I groaned. In pain and disoriented, my mind started filling in the blanks; Gorg, Breastplate of Righteousness, demon sword, Caroline's sofa.

Opening my eyes, I looked around. Caroline stepped into the living room with a smile spread across her lovely face. "Good morning Caleb. How ya' feelin'?" she said.

"Not bad," I lied. "Just a little tender."

"Can I look at it?"

"Sure," I opened my shirt. Sitting up was more manageable today. Caroline gingerly peeled back the tape and removed the gauze. I looked at the wound; it didn't look as bad as I expected. It looked more like a fresh, nasty scar than the burned flesh from last night.

"That doesn't look too bad," Caroline said as she carefully touched it.

"Ow! It may not look bad, but please don't do that."

"I'll re-wrap the burns to keep your shirt from rubbing against them after breakfast," Caroline said. "I hope you like pancakes and bacon."

"Anna, please set the table. We're ready to eat," Caroline called to the bedroom.

A smiling Anna bounced the room and over to the couch. "Hi, Mr. Kincade."

"Good morning, Anna," I smiled back. Caroline helped me to my feet and returned to the stove. By the time I hobbled to the table, Anna had the plates in position, and Caroline had placed the food in the center. I dropped into the chair Caroline pointed to, then she and Anna sat down.

"I suppose we should thank God for our food," Caroline said, "Except I haven't done that before."

"Me neither, but let's start," I replied. "I've heard Pastor Bob give thanks a few times. Bow your heads and close your eyes. Dear God, please bless this food to our bodies. Guide us through this day and give us wisdom as we try to do your will. Provide us with direction and help us to find the last two pieces of armor. Thank you for Your Son. In Jesus' name, we pray, Amen."

We ate our food, seasoned with small talk and laughter. It felt right, being here with Anna and Caroline. We've known each other for less than a day, yet it seemed like we've always been together. I felt complete for the first time in my life. I smiled.

"What?" Caroline asked, noticing my smile.

"Oh, nothing," I said. Caroline tilted her head and gave me a quizzical look.

Giving her head a little shake, Caroline asked, "What's the next step?"

"It's Sunday, and Bob should be preaching this morning at 10:00. Yesterday, he told me the homeless come to listen to him during the week, but on Sunday, the congregation members hear his teaching. The Deacon Board oversees City Mission and supplies some of the funding and many of the volunteers that make it work. If we leave soon, we should make it."

Caroline frowned, "Can you walk that far?"

"I think so. I'm feeling better than I did when I woke up. The only real pain comes from touching it or if I stretch too far. What do you think, Anna? Should we go visit Pastor Bob?"

"Yeah!" Anna said. We quickly cleaned up the table and put the dishes in the sink to soak.

Caroline wrapped the burns. Everything felt tender but not as debilitating as last night. I picked up the plastic bag with the Armor of God, and we headed out.

"Wow, what a great day," Caroline said. The sun bathed us in bright, warm light, and the brisk air energized us as we walked. I appreciated the dull and uneventful walk to the church. Not many people roamed the streets and even fewer demons. We arrived at the church a few minutes late. We located a half-empty pew near the back, and we sat down as the congregation finished a hymn. Next came the usual announcements and more singing, then Bob started preaching. This pastor spoke God's truth with conviction and passion. He was on fire.

I looked around at the congregation. Most people listened intently to Bob. A couple of parishioners nudged their neighbors, pointed to their pastor, and nodded their heads approvingly. I guess it has been a while since Bob preached like this. Not everybody was so enthralled with the sermon. Small children distracted some of the parents while others read the bulletin inserts. In front of me, an older man dozed. He woke himself with a snort that caused me to chuckle. It was an ethnically mixed group. Most of the people had the believer's aura, and a few shone incredibly bright.

Hearing the spoken Word and sitting with fellow believers invigorated me as I sat there and soaked it all in. Then someone shifted in their seat. Two rows ahead and to the left, I saw a shadowed person. There . . . a demon! The little imp perched on a woman's shoulder like a parrot. Its clawed hand stuck in the back of her head. I surveyed the congregation more carefully, shifting my position as much as possible and looking in all directions. I counted three demons. All were similar — the small monkey-like things sat on the shoulders of their humans. Two had their hands inside the heads, but the third had its paw reached into the man's heart. I sunk lower in my seat. Caroline gave me one of those, "What are you doing? Don't embarrass me." looks. "Demons," I mouthed and held up three fingers.

She mouthed, "Here?" My head nodded in affirmation. Panic jumped into her eyes as they darted back and forth. Then she realized she couldn't see them anyway.

I sat up higher. Whispering in the tiniest voice, "They don't seem to notice us."

The second demon was the easiest for me to see. The woman and the little monster sat on the opposite end of our pew. I tried to watch them without drawing attention to myself, but the more I watched, the more fascinated I became. Every time Bob mentioned God or Jesus, the demon winced in pain. Then the creatures' skin started to glisten, and it writhed. The Word of God caused it pain!

The sermon came to an end. Bob invited people to trust in Jesus today. Those who wanted to receive salvation should come to the front. As I watched the demon, it shifted position and had its clawed hands over the woman's ears. Standing on her shoulders, it pulled back on the woman's head like a rider pulling back on the reins of a horse. The woman stood, and it looked like she wanted to move toward the altar. The demon pulled back more, and its lips moved as it spoke into her mind. You could see the internal battle raging across her face. Then she slumped, broken, and sat. The demon won. The next thing I knew, Bob spoke the closing prayer and dismissed the congregation. Two people sported new auras of salvation at the front of the church.

We stood. One of our neighbors introduced themselves and had struck up a conversation with Caroline about the weather. I examined the congregation, looking for the demons. Two of the monsters rode past us as they exited the building. The one I observed had disappeared. It must have gone out a different way when I wasn't looking. We stood in the back and waited for Bob as he spoke with the new Christians.

In a few minutes, Bob finished. He saw us and moved in our direction. "Brother, Sister, I'm so glad you came today," he beamed. "It's been a long time since anybody responded to the altar call. I'm so pumped right now. I feel like I could save the world."

"When you're ready, we have a lot to tell you about yesterday and the service today," I said in a hushed voice.

Bob replied in a loud voice, "Brother Caleb, that is excellent news. Please wait for me in my office." And he turned to talk with the next parishioner.

We went to Bob's office. We chatted for about twenty minutes when he strode in. Once he settled into his chair, we told him about the trip home Saturday, the Breastplate of Righteousness, showed him the wounds, and reported on the demons in the Sunday service. I went into great detail when I talked about the woman who wanted to answer the call. I thought Anna might be too young, but she accepted what I said with the faith of a child.

"That explains a lot," said Bob. "During previous sermons and altar calls, I felt connected to certain people. Yet when the call came, they didn't come forward. Perhaps this is why."

Bob thought for a moment, "The next time I sense that connection, I'll pray and reach out to that person after the sermon. Perhaps that will make the difference." Another pause, then, "May I see the Breastplate of Righteousness?"

Picking up the bag, I reached in and pulled out the fluorescent yellow safety vest, the same kind I've seen road crews wear to make them more visible to drivers. With a thought, I transformed it into the Breastplate of Righteousness. "Did you do that, Mr. Kincade?" Anna asked and reached for the garment.

"You can see that, Anna?"

"Yea, it's metal held together with somethin'."

"What do you see, Caleb?" Bob asked.

"I see two roughly rectangular sheets of sculpted bronze. The front is shaped like a muscular male abdomen. At the top of each part are leather straps that rest on the shoulders and hold the front and back pieces together. The back is smooth and cupped, so it molds around the sides. The front also wraps around the sides to protect them. There are small leather straps at the bottom of each half. When they are tied together, those thongs should hold secure the breastplate," I said.

"Put it on and tell me how it feels," Bob asked.

I did as instructed. Once the breastplate settled into position, the sides tied themselves together, and similar to the other pieces of armor, the metal molded itself to my form like a warm fleece blanket on a cold winter's eve. And like the other pieces, a surge of righteous passion and power. I felt the "rightness" of God, and His protection enveloped me. "Whoa!' I exclaimed. "It tied itself at the sides and molded to my shape. I also feel the righteousness of God and our task."

"I thought it might," Bob sighed. "I wish I could see what you see. We see a regular safety vest." Caroline nodded in agreement.

"What's the purpose of the Breastplate of Righteousness?" I asked Bob.

"The original breastplate worn by the Roman soldier was to protect the vital organs. It gave them a huge advantage against their less technologically developed enemies. However, spiritually speaking, your righteousness is not effective in protecting you from demonic weapons; rather, only the righteousness of Christ can keep you safe. I don't know what kind of weapons the enemy employs, but unless you depend only on your relationship with Christ and His righteousness, you are vulnerable. While the Roman breastplate protected the vital organs, I think this one will protect your spirit," Bob explained.

I took the Breastplate of Righteousness off with awe and reverence and carefully placed it in the bag.

Bob seemed lost in thought. After giving his head a little shake, he focused on us. "Let's go out for lunch. I am not responsible on Sundays for the soup kitchen meal, nor is there any teaching. I usually eat out, so I don't get dragged into some issue or emergency. Ginny's Diner is around the corner. The food is typical American fare and very tasty. It'll be my treat," he added as an extra incentive.

Everybody liked the idea, so we grabbed our jackets, the Armor of God, and headed out the door.

Chapter 16

Caleb

Sunday Afternoon

The food at Ginny's hit the spot.

When we arrived at the restaurant, Sunday regulars filled about half the seats. Bob stopped to greet several of the patrons. We sat down in a booth in the far corner for some privacy and ordered our food. I thoroughly enjoyed the meal.

As I finished my roast beef sandwich smothered in dark gravy, Bob asked, "Brother Caleb, you said the demon called itself 'Gorg' and it was out collecting 'strays.' Is that right?"

"Yeah."

"The 'Dream World' might be more real than I believed. After all, I can't see what you see. It never occurred to me that demons had names. People must occasionally regain consciousness. They believe that they're in a nightmare. Perhaps they run around screaming, and they eventually wake up in their beds. They might even be temporarily free of the demons until the next time they sleep. Then I think the monsters will add them back to the Dream World. I wonder if everybody sleeps there or just some people? Caleb, how'd you wake up in there again?"

"I don't know. Someone called my name and startled me. I think God called. I woke up, but I couldn't open my eyes. They were glued shut. It was hard for me to move like I had been very still for a very long time. Caroline did not wake up until I struck the demon with the sword and whispered, 'In the name of Jesus, awake' in her ear."

Bob sat back and looked at the ceiling, lost in thought for a few moments. "I don't know how, but I think I'm beginning to understand the Dream World. Perhaps human spirits are transported to the Dream World when they sleep, leaving the body behind in this one. But there must be a physical component; otherwise, how could the Sword of the Spirit be in both worlds? It appears as a tube and sword in both places showing its dual nature."

"Ramiel said objects with a dual nature like the Sword of the Spirit could travel between worlds and function in both," I responded.

"Interesting. Brother Caleb, what's the next step?"

"I'm not sure. I'm afraid for Caroline and Anna's safety after the demon attacked yesterday. I don't want to leave their side in case another monster comes looking for them. Based on my wounds and the look in the demon's eyes, I don't doubt it would've hurt Caroline. Yet, at some point, we're going to need to go to work and do other things separately."

"I would feel better knowing you're around," injected Caroline. "And you're right. At some point, we'll need to separate. For tonight, though, I'd feel better if you'd stay with us. Hmm . . . what if we stop by your apartment and get your work clothes for tomorrow. Then, we'll go to our place, and you can sleep on the couch again. What do you think?"

"Yes, that sounds reasonable. It also sounds like you two will need to be careful. You could be putting yourselves into an awkward situation," Bob commented.

"Geesh, Bob . . . I get your point, but I'm not concerned about that, just their well-being. My apartment isn't far. Let's go get my stuff."

"Okay . . . okay . . . Brother Caleb, you're right. You should go home with them. Just be careful."

We all stood and headed for the diner's exit. Bob left a tip and paid the bill. We said our goodbyes. Bob returned to his apartment at the church, and the rest of us headed to my apartment. The ten-minute walk passed quickly. We chatted along the way. As I approached the entrance, it felt like a lifetime ago since I had been there last.

Then I had an unpleasant thought. My apartment's a mess. Being single, I didn't mind a bit of clutter. Okay, a lot of clutter.

"I'm sorry, Caroline, my apartment looks like a bomb went off. Until now, I had no reason to keep it tidy. Now I'm embarrassed," I unlocked the door, and we stepped inside.

Caroline surveyed the studio apartment. "This isn't so bad. Anna and I will do the dishes while you pack your things."

Caroline lifted a dishtowel off the chair's back, pulled it over to the sink, and patted the seat. "Jump up here, Sweetie, and you can play in the bubbles.

And Caleb, after you get your stuff together, then we'll straighten up your living room. Or is it your bedroom?"

"It's both."

We got to work. It felt weird. Laughter came from the kitchen area as Caroline splashed Anna. I enjoyed listening to their small talk and the clatter of dishes placed in the cupboard. I never realized how quiet and empty my life had been. How sweet the sound of a child's laughter. I discovered a hole in my soul. That hole filled as I watched them, and it felt good. It also brought fear, fear for their safety, and for losing them.

It's been a long time since I cared for someone other than myself.

Julie. I hadn't thought about her in a long time.

I never had much luck with girls. My low self-esteem and shyness proved to be significant barriers. A month after I turned seventeen, a new girl came to the youth group. I never understood why other kids didn't want to sit next to me. I showered! She sat down and told me her name was Julie. She had long, silky blond hair and pale blue eyes that melted my heart.

Opening the closet door, I grabbed a gym bag off the floor.

Surprisingly, we became good friends. She was the first real friend I ever had. We often spent time together after youth group meetings. She excitedly talked about the spiritual things we had learned and wanted to know my thoughts. She mainly wanted to know my thoughts on God.

I hemmed and hawed, weakly answering her questions. I wanted to be with her, not God. She kept after me, often asking if I died that night, did I know my destination.

One evening, I felt incredibly vulnerable. Father screamed at Mom while she cringed on the floor in fear. A bruise formed on her cheek. Angered and frustrated, I left the house and slammed the door. I wanted to hurt him badly, but I feared him more. I ran away for the evening, not returning until he passed out in a drunken stupor. I needed help. I knew it was beyond me to fix.

Julie asked about my afterlife destination again. I wanted someone to come to my rescue, but I also longed for Julie to be my girlfriend. The next thing I knew, I was saying a prayer of salvation.

I folded my work pants and shirt and stuffed them in the bag.

Julie got so excited that she gave me an impulsive hug and a kiss. As she pulled back from the kiss, her arms still wrapped around my neck, there was a long pause. We searched each other's eyes, and then we slowly came together and kissed again. It was long and wet and awkward and the most exciting thing that ever happened to me. My spirit soared.

We started "going out," holding hands and cuddling. I especially liked the long kisses goodbye. I'd never been so happy. For the first time in my life, things were going well. My self-esteem sprouted and grew. Things were great for about two months.

One day after school, I went to her house, and she met me at the door crying.

"What's wrong?"

"We're mo-moving to T-texas . . . in a m-month. My dad g-got a new job."

I placed my toothbrush, toothpaste, razor, and comb and added them to the gym bag.

The next few weeks became a blur, full of tears and brief moments together. I stood in their driveway with tears streaming down my face as they pulled away. We promised to keep in touch. We exchanged letters for a month or two, then they stopped. I felt betrayed by Julie's parents and by God. I imagined her parents moved to break us up, or God was cruel like my father.

With Julie gone, I sank back into the darkness, my fragile self-esteem withered. I never got over Julie. Instead, I replaced the pain with apathy. If I couldn't have the one person I cared about, then I wouldn't care about anything.

I looked toward the kitchen sink.

Until Caroline and Anna . . .

"That should do it for now. Is your bag packed?" Caroline's question brought me out of my reverie.

"Yeah, let's go. I didn't get much cleaning done, but it can wait."

I followed them out the door, locked it, and joined the ladies on the sidewalk.

The light faded fast as dusk approached. As we walked, talked, and laughed. I kept an eye out for demons. A few flew about in the twilight, but none ventured near us. It was an uneventful trip to their apartment, followed by a pleasant evening of sandwiches and games. A hug from Anna wrapped up the night, and they retired to the bedroom. I locked the doors and returned to the sofa. A smile danced on my lips as I fell asleep.

Chapter 17

Gloria

Sunday Afternoon

The public address speaker crackled, "Dr. Sanchez, please call the nurses' station. Dr. Sanchez, please call the nurses' station."

Aarrgh! I'll never get this article done. I had been hiding with my laptop in the conference room, trying to get it written.

I no longer resented weekend duty since my family has flown the nest. I slept at St Mary's and caught up on those tedious tasks piled up during the week. Besides, there are fewer reminders of my late husband here.

Saturday had been uneventful, and I hoped for a similar Sunday. I picked the phone and punched in the number for the nurses' station.

"This is Dr. Sanchez, is there a problem, Millie?"

"Doctor, I don't know how, but he's at it again."

Sigh. "Si, I'll be right there."

Angelo Carmichael. Mi amigo, what are you doing, and why? Angelo had been at St. Mary's Home for almost as long as I had. In the last few weeks, though, he had been more and more agitated. He ranted about needing to do something. Then yellow boots appeared in his room — brand new, bright yellow rubber boots. There'd been two pairs over the last seven days. Now a third pair had shown up. Nobody witnessed their appearance in Angelo's room, and nobody understood his obsession with them. Well-meaning aides took them from him. They thought he had removed them from the utility closet. It's typically locked because of the chemicals and sharp objects. They thought someone had been careless. The problem is the Saint Mary's had no boots like those.

Each time the aides removed the boots, Angelo had a fit and needed sedation. The odd footwear didn't bother me, but how'd they'd get there? The hall's security video showed no one entering or leaving the room with a container large enough to hold boots. The windows open two inches, plus there were screens on them. So no one passed it through the window to him.

I arrived at Angelo's door. I looked through the window and knocked as I entered the room. Angelo sat on the floor, swaying back and forth with a permanent marker in his hand. At his feet lay a bright yellow boot. He held the other boot in his hands, and he wrote, actually printed, words on it. Even though he rocked back and forth, his printing was angular and precise.

I sighed, then asked, "Angelo, my friend, what are you doing?"

He rocked back and forth as he wrote. "Writing on da boots, on da boots, on da boots," he chanted.

"Why?"

"He told me to, told me to, told me to."

"Who told you to?"

"He told me to, told me to, told me to."

Tipping my head, I read what he had written. His letters were about a half-inch high, neat like you'd see on a blueprint.

> "For our struggle is not against flesh and blood, but against the rulers, against the authorities, against the powers of this dark world and against the spiritual forces of evil in the heavenly realms."[7]

> "Blessed are those who are persecuted because of righteousness, for theirs is the kingdom of heaven."[8]

---

[7] Ephesians 6:12 NIV
[8] Matthew 5:10 NIV

"Repent, for the kingdom of heaven is at hand."[9]

Bible Scripture? I don't know much nor cared about the Bible. I did care for Angelo, and he was calm and focused. There'll be no harm in letting write on the boots. I wrote an order on Angelo's chart. "Patient is to be allowed to keep and write on the boots." I'll let him finish his little project, and then we'll see what happens.

Huh? I looked at the first lines on the boots. The words were no longer evident. As I stared at the text, they faded from sight. It seemed like the letters sank into the boot. The words at the top disappeared by the time Angelo got to the bottom. Angelo returned to the top of the boot and wrote new text over the ones that had vanished. The world started to spin, and I had to sit on the edge of Angelo's bed. Por Que?

My mind raced through the possibilities. *No. Not possible. Words cannot sink into a boot!* My mind searched for a plausible reason. It could be disappearing ink! Yes, that's it.

Angelo ignored me, so focused he was on the boots. I stood, turned, and closed the door on my way out. I wondered if Angelo knew I had left.

Returning to the conference room, I tried to focus on the biographical article requested by Saint Mary's administration. I re-read what I had written earlier.

"St. Mary's Home is a small hospital devoted to helping the mentally ill and handicapped. Most patients are non-violent, just easily confused or delusional, and require extra care the family cannot provide. They need a safe environment to live in, and St. Mary's offers that. Many of the people had been abused or neglected at some point in their lives."

That's not too bad. My fingers pecked at the keyboard again.

---

[9] Matthew 3:2 ESV

"The caretakers at St. Mary's are kind to their patients and take their job seriously. I've worked here for nearly fifteen years, and you will not find a better staff anywhere."

This article is supposed to be biographical; I better include some personal information.

"I've had lots of success treating the patients that have come under my care. Warmth and compassion go a long way towards developing a connection to the patient. Once the patients know they can trust me, then we can make real progress.

What gives me this edge? I am real with my patients.

My daughter graduated from nursing school, and my son attended the engineering program at Cornell University. I shared my joy with my patients. When my husband of twenty-five years died of a heart attack, I shared my grief with them. Ironically, they helped me more than I helped them during that time. They showed lots of compassion and love. Many of them had lost relatives and understood the pain I felt."

I'll finish this later. My thoughts drifted back to Angelo. *Angelo, what drives you to write on those boots?*

Chapter 18

Caleb

Monday Morning

I woke with a start. Loud music blared for a few moments from the next room, then stopped. Cracking one of my eyes open, I found the light on my watch. 5:45 a.m.? *Where am I?* I looked around and remembered I lay in Caroline's apartment. That's right. It's Monday. Gotta work. I sighed and rolled over.

Caroline emerged from the bedroom with a sleepy-eyed Anna.

"We'll use the restroom first, and then you can use it."

"Okay."

As they closed the door, I realized my bladder had exceeded its capacity. Suffering in silence, I waited.

An uncomfortable eternity later, the ladies exited the bathroom. I grabbed my bag and rushed in. It had been a long time since I cleaned up before going to work. Personal hygiene had not been a high priority. It seemed strange showering and shaving before work. Regularly, I got up at the last second, threw something on, and walked out the door.

Feeling refreshed, I left the bathroom and went to the kitchen. Caroline turned and greeted me with a smile that rivaled the sun.

I was smitten.

"Toast and Cheerios for breakfast. There isn't much time for anything else. Oh, there's a banana on the counter. We need to leave by 7:15. Anna goes to Grace's next door before and after school. I'm very thankful to have a neighbor like her."

Sitting down at the table, I gave silent thanks to God and helped myself to some food. Anna chatted happily, telling me about her teacher and classmates. With breakfast finished, we got ready to leave. I grabbed the bag that contained my clothes and the Armor of God. Anna and I waited in the hall as Caroline locked the door. She turned and knocked on the door opposite hers. It opened, and a distinguished older woman appeared.

"Good morning, Grace," Caroline greeted.

"Good morning, Caroline." Cracking a slight smile, Grace asked: "And who might this be?"

"I would like to introduce you to Caleb Kincade. He's a new friend, and I would like to stress the friend part."

"If you say so," Grace smirked as she gave me the once over. "Come on in, Anna."

Anna turned, gave her mom a hug and a kiss on the cheek. Then she turned and stepped toward me.

"Bye, Mr. Kincade," She hugged me and skipped into the apartment.

"Thanks, Grace, I'll see you at the usual time. Bye." Caroline hugged Grace and walked toward the stairs.

"Nice meeting you." I waved and turned to follow Caroline.

"Nice meeting you too," Grace called behind us.

We bound down the stairs and pushed the crash bar on the door, and exited the building. Once on the sidewalk, I said, "You know what she's thinking?"

"Yes," Caroline smiled, "But that's better than telling her everything."

"True," I laughed.

As we rounded the corner, we merged with the Monday morning work crowd. I stopped and looked around.

Demons.

Everywhere.

It looked like every sixth or seventh person had a rider on their shoulder. The rest flew in the air or walked, weaving their way through the crowd. None paid attention to Caroline or me.

Caroline talked and walked, not realizing I had stopped. Caroline halted, looked around, and came back to me.

"What's the matter?"

"Demons. Lots of them." Then I whispered as I surveyed the scene before us.

"Do they know you can see them?"

"I don't think so."

"Act like you can't see them. We need to take our chances and get to work," Caroline concluded as she grabbed my arm and pulled me into the main crowd.

We stopped talking and focused on getting to Foe Financial. I had walked to work thousands of times and not once had been scared. *Lord, protect us. Keep the demons blind to our presence.* We stuck close to each other as we flowed along the river of humanity. I found it hard not to stare at the demon on the shoulder next to me. I averted my eyes to be greeted by another beast hitching a ride on someone else.

Twenty stress-filled minutes later, we arrived at Foe Financial Services. Stopping outside the main entrance on Mortimer Street, I turned to Caroline. "I go in on the Pleasant Street entrance. We need to split up for the day. Can we meet here a little after 4:00?"

Caroline smiled, and her left hand rested on my right forearm, "Yes, and Caleb, have a good day. Focus on your work and try not to dwell on the demons." She gave me a brief embrace, turned, and entered the building through the main entrance.

I headed for the alley that led to the back of the building. The Foe Financial building was significant. It was the tallest building in the city, and it filled the block between Mortimer and Pleasant Streets. I arrived at my entrance and looked at my watch.

Man, I'm early. I stopped and leaned against the wall near the rear door. I closed my eyes and tipped my head back. Caroline is the best thing that has ever happened to me. How ironic that the best and worst times of my life occurred at the same time.

I opened my eyes, looking skyward. Stepping away from the wall, I continued to look up. I ran down Pleasant Street and turned around. At the top of the Foe building, a stream of demons flew in and out of the top floor. My knees buckled, and I staggered to a bench. I worked at Demon Headquarters. I sat and studied the demons. With surprising regularity, they flowed in and out of the top floor.

I sighed, got up from the bench, and walked back. Making my way to the basement, I found the time clock and punched in just in time.

Chapter 19

Gloria

Monday Morning

I had just hung my jacket up when I heard over the PA system, "Doctor Sanchez, call the nurses' station." *Arghhh, I just got here.*

My office was small but comfortable. I had a desk and chair, bookcase, filing cabinet, and a couple of plush seats for guests or clients. Photos or art, either my own or clients, covered the bright white walls. We used art to give the patients something to do, plus it often gave us insight into what troubled them.

I lifted the lab coat off the hook behind the door, slipped it on, and placed my jacket where the lab coat had been. I dared not delay, and I picked up the phone dialing the nurses' station. Millie has Mondays off, and I didn't recognize the voice.

"Doctor, it's Angelo. You need to come to his room right away."

Placing the phone in the cradle, I sighed and headed for Angelo's room. Outside his door, Lisa, one of the nurses, waited.

"Doctor, look." She pointed to the door.

Stepping up to the window, I peered inside. Angelo stood on his bed, writing. He had written on all the walls within sight with the same marker he used on the boots. He wrote numbers, the same series of numbers over and over in all different sizes and angles. The ink isn't disappearing!

The rest of the room was in shambles. Both chairs tipped and Angelo's table on its side. Every poster and picture that had adorned the walls had been strewn across the floor. In the middle of this chaos, the bright yellow boots sat in the center of the room.

"What's he writing?" I asked.

Lisa replied, "Some number. 5555856779" This isn't typical behavior for Angelo. I didn't understand it. Butterflies took wing in my stomach.

"It could be a phone number," Lisa replied. "The first three numbers match the local area code."

I kept an analytical demeanor, but on the inside, this freaked me out. "I-I'm going in; please watch from here. G-get help if something happens." I had a hard time keeping my voice steady.

Angelo faced away from me as I entered the room. He stood about five and a half feet tall and had to be on his tippy toes to reach the ceiling. His black hair and olive skin showed his Mediterranean heritage. He frantically wrote the number over and over. I examined every surface, and on all four walls and part of the ceiling, Angelo had scribed the same ten-digit number over three-quarters of the room. It does look like a phone number.

"Hola Angelo," I said with a calm voice.

Angelo spun around. He jumped off the bed and ran up to me and stopped an inch from my face. Startled, I took a step back. Angelo grabbed my shoulders with his hands and drew my face near. His wide eyes pleaded as he looked into mine.

"I . . . can't . . . get this . . . out of . . . my head," he whispered with despair.

I didn't want to agitate him further. Scared but determined, I cooed. "What is it, Angelo?"

"I don't know, but it won't go away."

"Is it a phone n-number?"

"I . . . don't . . . knooww!" Angelo sobbed as he let released me. He buried his face in his hands and collapsed on the floor. Sobs wracked Angelo's body.

I knelt and placed my hand on his shoulder. "Hang on, Angelo. I'll be back soon."

I turned and walked toward the door. Lisa opened it for me and closed it behind me.

"Has he slept at all?"

"Not to my knowledge. He's the last stop on my rounds, and I found him this way. Judging from the volume of numbers, he must've been writing all night. Do you think it's a phone number?"

"I don't know, but it seems like the place to start."

I pulled my cell phone from my lab coat pocket and looked through the window of the door. My hand shook as I punched the number into my phone. I hit send. Long seconds passed, and I heard a phone ring.

Chapter 20

Bob

Monday Morning

Monday is supposed to be my day off. One of the problems with living where you work is that you never get away from work, I thought, as I sat at my desk. At least THIS morning devotion was meaningful and fresh. Praise God.

The phone rang and brought me out of my reverie. I answered it.

"City Mission, Pastor Bob speaking."

"Hello, Pastor. My name is Doctor Gloria Sanchez. I am one of the senior physicians at St. Mary's Home. We have a situation here, and I'm hoping you can help. Do you have any connection with a man named Angelo Carmichael?"

"No . . . at least the name doesn't ring any bells. Why do you ask?"

"Angelo is a long-term patient, and we have a bit of a mystery," said Dr. Sanchez. "Angelo's behavior has been stranger than usual lately, and he has written a number all over the walls of his room. It is a ten-digit number that matches the number of your church. You're sure his name doesn't sound familiar?"

"I don't think so . . . but we get a lot of people through here. Perhaps he was here some time ago?"

"It seems unlikely, he's been a resident here a long time. I didn't think there'd be a connection, but I had to check. Thank you for speaking with me. Between this number and the yellow boots, I don't know what to think."

Chills raced down my spine. *Could it be?*

"Did you say 'yellow boots?' Please tell me more about them."

"I don't know if I should, patient privacy and all that."

"Doc, I don't want you to violate any ethics code, but I do know of a situation that may be relevant. I'm a pastor and counselor. I will keep anything you say in the strictest confidence."

I had a hard time restraining the excitement in my voice.

"Of course, you counsel people all the time. It's strange. We kept finding these yellow boots, like rescue workers, or maybe firefighters wear, in his room. We don't know the source. And he has been writing Bible verses all over the boots with disappearing ink." Dr. Sanchez explained.

"While I know nothing about Angelo, I might know something about the boots. I'd like to come for a visit this morning . . . if that's okay with you."

The line went silent for several long seconds.

"A-are you sure you want to do that, Pastor?"

"Yes, Doctor, this is important to me."

"Okay then, anytime this morning would be fine."

"I'll be there in an hour."

I hung up the phone and sat there, stunned. *God, you're incredible.* Getting up from my desk, I finished up a couple of minor things and then searched for Fran. I found her in the kitchen getting things ready for the day.

"Good Morning Fran. Do you have the church car keys?"

"Yeah, here they are. I had to do a little shopping this morning."

"I'm going to be gone for a couple of hours. Hold down the fort and answer the phone for me, please."

"No problem Bob. Can I ask where you're going?"

"I'm running over to St. Mary's Home. A doctor there called and thought I might be able to help with a patient."

"Have fun, and make sure they don't check you in." Fran laughed.

Leaving by the rear entrance, I hurried to the car. It was an ancient 1997 Honda Civic Hatchback that someone donated to the church a few years ago. While old, it had proven to be reliable. I put the key in and turned the ignition. It started without hesitation, and I headed for the exit. I turned right and merged with the morning traffic. *Dear God, could these boots be the "Feet fitted with the Gospel of Peace? This is going to be the longest 45-minute drive ever taken."* My mind raced as I drove to St. Mary's.

The closer I got to the Home, the more excited I became. *Get a grip on yourself, Bob. Don't show too much excitement. Be calm. Lord, help me choose the right actions and words.*

I pulled into the St. Mary's Home and found a vacant visitor spot. Exiting the car, I strode up the front walk to the main door. I paused and said a brief prayer, then pushed the door open.

The receptionist sat behind a desk to the right of the door. I approached her and said, "Good morning. I'm Pastor Bob Bennett to see Dr. Sanchez."

"Yes, Pastor Bennett. Dr. Sanchez is expecting you. I'll let her know you are here."

She picked up the phone and entered a number.

Stepping away from the desk, I heard her speak briefly into the phone while I looked around. The reception area felt airy, and large plants next to the big windows thrived. Several chairs and a sofa with matching navy-colored fabric formed in a cozy rectangle. Comfortable, but not too plush or opulent. Typical doctor office magazines lay in neat piles on the table.

About ten minutes later, a smart, professional-looking woman approached me. "You must be Pastor Bennett; I'm Dr. Gloria Sanchez."

"Nice to meet you, Dr. Sanchez. Please, call me Bob."

"And you may call me Gloria. Let's go to my office and chat for a minute."

"Would it be possible to go directly to Mr. Carmichael? I think if I see him and these boots, it will be obvious, really fast if I am supposed to be here."

"O-Okay," the Doctor replied as she changed direction. "Right this way," and she led me down the nearest corridor.

As we walked, she told me a bit about Angelo. He'd been at Saint Mary's for nearly fifteen years. He's not physically disabled but suffers from schizophrenia and hears voices in his head. He is usually a model patient but has been quite agitated about these boots. He wrote a number, the City Missions phone number, all over his walls. We approached his door, and I peered in the window. In the middle of the room sat a pair of yellow rubber boots. Standing on a chair behind the boots was Angelo, back to the door, writing the church's phone number on the ceiling with a black marker.

"Is Angelo prone to violence?"

"No, normally he is not aggressive, but he has been agitated for the last week. When we took the boots away, he got angry and had a fit. A few days later, a new pair appeared. I let him keep the third pair. That calmed him down for a while; he wrote Bible scripture on the boots. He started this sometime last night." She pointed to the numbers written all over the wall.

Gloria opened the door, and I followed her into the room. I stood a moment surveying the scene. As I looked at the boots, they briefly glowed. *Did I see that?* I looked at the walls with our phone number all over them. And lastly, I looked at Angelo's back. He was not a large man, approximately 150 pounds with a wild mane of black hair.

"Angelo, we have a visitor."

Angelo turned around and nearly lost his balance on the chair. He glared at the doctor and then looked at me. Recognition and joy flooded his face. He leaped from the chair and bounded straight at me like a giant puppy. He wrapped me in his arms and jumped up and down with excitement. He chanted, "You came, you came, you came!"

Just as fast as he embraced me, Angelo released me, spun around, and jumped toward the boots. Landing on the floor, he scrambled to his knees behind them and paused. With great care and reverence, Angelo picked up the boots and held them up to me.

In a quiet, solemn voice, Angelo said, "I am done. They are ready. Take them."

I approached and knelt before Angelo before accepting the boots.

"They are not for me, but another. Do you know that?"

"Yes. You are the Voice of God; the boots belong with the Soldier of God. You must give them to him," Angelo responded.

Reaching out, I accepted the boots from Angelo. As my hands touched the boots, words appeared in rapid succession on their surface. A feeling of immense power surged through my hands and up my arms. It only lasted seconds, but I felt whole, complete, and healed. With tears in my eyes, I whispered. "Thank you, Angelo."

"I must sleep now." And Angelo curled up in a ball and fell asleep on the floor. He must have gone days without sleep, and with his task done, Angelo no longer needed to remain awake.

I stood and turned to Gloria, who watched in amazement.

"W-W-What just happened? I saw words flash across the boots and a white aura around you. What's going on?"

"Could we go to your office? I'll tell you more there."

Gloria looked at Angelo. Her hands shook as she pulled the bedding off the bed. She covered him with the blanket. Gloria gently lifted his head and placed the pillow under it. He snuggled in and heaved a contented sigh.

A few moments later, we sat in Dr. Sanchez's office. I placed the boots on the floor next to my chair.

"Bob, por favor . . . tell me what happened?"

"Are you a woman of science or a woman of faith, Gloria?"

"Science. However, I'll admit science can't explain everything."

"My fear Gloria is this. If I tell you the whole story, you will want to check me into St. Mary's. What I have to say is a matter of faith, not science. There are no logical explanations. It cannot be seen, touched, or verified, but it's very real. I was meant to be called and to pick up the boots. You saw Angelo. Even though we had never met, he knew me and knew I needed to take the boots."

"No, it is not clear. Why you? I could have brought in a stranger off the street, and Angelo would've given them the boots."

"Come on, Gloria, you know it doesn't add up. You had boots appearing out of nowhere, a patient-driven to write disappearing scripture on them, a pastor's phone number scrawled all over the walls of the room, and glowing boots with words crawling all over them. Oh, and a Pastor that glowed when he touched the boots. What part of that is scientific?"

"I'm sure there's a logical explanation."

"Doctor, when you're ready to put your head aside and examine your heart, come visit me. I live and work at the City Mission. You have my number. It's all over Angelo's room."

Standing, I picked up the boots and faced the doctor.

"Thank you for the call, Dr. Sanchez. Please contact me when you're ready. I'd love to discuss faith with you. Good-bye."

I left the office with my treasure and headed for the car. I barely contained my excitement as I drove back to City Mission. I can't wait to talk with Caleb and Caroline.

*****

Gloria Sanchez sat behind her desk and watched Pastor Bob leave. On her shoulder, the Demon of Disbelief smiled.

Chapter 21

Caleb

Monday, Late Afternoon

The day dragged by, and 4:00 p.m. took its time getting here. I clocked out, grabbed the Armor of God from my locker, and headed down the alley to the main entrance on Mortimer Street. Caroline sat on a bench, waiting for me. She examined my long face.

"Caleb, what's wrong?"

Pulling her close, I whispered in her ear. "There's are demons flying in and out of the top floor. Let's go, and then I'll explain."

Hurrying, we didn't stop till we were out of breath and three blocks away. Ducking into a store doorway, I turned to Caroline.

"We work at Demon Central. When I got to the other entrance, I happened to look up. Demons floated in and out of the top floors of the building. Later on, at lunch, I went outside, and they were still there. I think we work in some kind of headquarters."

"Perhaps, this is why God has chosen you for this task."

"Maybe, but I still don't know what the task is or how to find the rest of the armor."

"Let's go see Bob," Caroline suggested. "He might have some ideas."

We marched toward City Mission.

"I called Grace earlier today. Anna's going to eat with her, so I don't need to rush home."

"Good thinking." I kept my eyes on the pavement as we walked to the City Mission. We spoke little, lost in our thoughts. When we got to the Mission's door, we walked in, and an excessively cheerful Fran greeted us.

"Hi, you two. How are you today?"

"We're good. Is Bob around?"

"He's in his office."

We found Bob sitting behind his desk. He stood as we entered the room and greeted us. We started talking at the same time. He laughed, I scowled. I didn't think it was funny.

"Alright, you go first," I snarled.

Bob either didn't notice or didn't care that I had snarled at him. He smiled and reached behind the desk and set a pair of yellow rubber boots on top. They emitted an aura like the other pieces of armor. I looked at Bob, then at Caroline, and back to Bob.

"Go ahead and put them on," Bob instructed.

I didn't even have to take off my shoes. The boots slid right over them, and I stood.

"Feet fitted with the Gospel of Peace," and they transformed. Then I transformed. They molded to my feet and calves. They became sturdy leather and brass. Bible verses visibly flowed over them. My head filled with Scripture, and I could quote entire books from the Bible. My legs felt wobbly, so I dropped into the chair behind me. The living power of the Gospel coursed through me.

Caroline and Bob just watched and waited for me to rejoin them. I forgot they couldn't see the transformation. The intoxicating sensation subsided after a couple of minutes.

I whispered, "Where did you get these?"

Bob told his story, going into great detail about Angelo and Dr. Sanchez's phone call. When he finished, I sat there, stunned, and whispered.

"God. Is. Amazing."

I reached down and slipped the boots off. After a few moments, they returned to the yellow rubber boots I first saw. I also lost the heady feeling of knowledge and power.

"Thank you, Bob. I had no idea . . . Sorry I got angry before," I said. "I too have news, and it is not as great as yours."

I told Bob about how I discovered we worked at Demon Headquarters. My thoughts whirled. The number of demons overwhelmed me. My mind raced, and I panicked.

"I've never been to the top floors of Foe Financial. I'm scared. Why are they there? So many! There's no way I can stop them! BOB, WHAT AM I GONNA DO?"

He laughed, a deep booming laugh.

I snarled again. "What . . . do . . . you . . . find . . . so . . . funny?"

Bob wiped the tears of laughter from his eyes and smiled at me.

"What makes you think you need to destroy them all? Don't you think God knows how many are there? Don't you think He picked you for a reason? Has He said you are doing this alone? You're not alone. God has given you help. Why do you think Caroline and I are here? Brother Caleb, trust God."

As he spoke, my anger faded. Bob was right. What have I done up to this point? Nothing. God had done everything when needed.

"You're right. I'm sorry, I lost it."

Feeling better but still subdued, I decided to put away the Armour of God. I tried stuffing the boots into the bag. "Bob, we need something bigger to keep the armor in."

"We have a couple of duffle bags in the back room where you slept. I'll go grab one." He left the office.

"Caroline, sorry about . . . well, what happened a moment ago. I'm scared. I don't understand. Why me? I know . . . I know . . . trust God, but knowin' it and doin' it ain't easy."

"Caleb, I can't begin to imagine what you see. It seems impossible. I grew up in the church, but everything appeared to be a bunch of stories. Maybe they had a point or a lesson, but I thought they were fiction. I never imagined demons and angels existed. But I believe you. I believe what you see is real. And even though we've known each other a few days, I am with you in this." Caroline reached over and took my hand.

Startled, I stared at her hand. Her soft skin radiated warmth and comfort into mine. No woman had held my hand since Julie. I looked up and into her eyes and saw compassion and understanding.

Bob's footsteps echoed down the hall. Caroline quickly released my hand and turned her head toward the door.

"Brother Caleb, try this one."

I took it from Bob's hand and stuffed the Armor of God into the bag. It was larger than it needed to be but usable.

Bob sat down and spoke. "Good. So, Brother, Sister, where are we at? We have five of the six pieces of the Armor of God. We know where the demons' base of operations. We don't know where the Shield of Faith is, and we don't know what we're to do with the armor once it's complete. Brother Caleb, does that sum it up?"

I nodded as did Caroline.

"It looks like we're back to waiting. Waiting for God to reveal the next step,"

"Bob, please tell me about the 'Feet Fitted with the Gospel of Peace'?"

I smiled, amused, as Bob leaned back in his chair to think. He does that regularly. A minute later, he leaned forward.

"The feet were the foundation of the Roman soldier. They needed protection so the soldier could remain standing through the battle. I think these boots are the same. The Gospel message is the foundation of Christianity. Without that foundation, Christianity would not have lasted. Scripture is your foundation! You'll need to stand on it when you face the challenge."

I thought about what Bob had said for a few moments. "I just wish I knew what I'm supposed to do?"

"I understand, Brother Caleb. I'll be prayin' for you. However, I have a more pressing matter, tho'. Are you two going to stay for dinner?"

"Do you need any help?" Caroline asked.

"Not really. We have enough volunteers tonight."

Caroline said, "Good. It's 6:30, and I need to get home to Anna. What're we going to do about tonight, Caleb? I'd feel better if you were there. But, I'm not sure that is the right thing for today."

"I'll walk you home, and then I'll go. I need to do some laundry. I also need some time to think and pray."

Caroline and I put our coats on. We thanked Bob for everything and headed out the door. On the way to Caroline's apartment, we walked in comfortable silence

Caroline's teeth chattered. "It's a lot colder than I expected."

I reached out and put my arm around her shoulder in an attempt to block the wind. Caroline leaned into me, and I enjoyed the warmth of her closeness. I also experienced an inner warmth. *Does she realize how much I care for her?*

I searched for something to say. It seemed lame to be walking without talking. I looked around my mind for a conversation starter and saw something disturbing. Several large groups of people and an equal number of demons fluttering around them approached us on the sidewalk.

"Why are so many people out tonight?" I asked.

"The Harvest Moon Festival starts tonight."

"What's that?"

Caroline explained, "It's only three years old, but the growth has been tremendous. They have the festival at night in Burns Park around the corner. It's a perversion of an ancient Celtic festival that celebrates the end of the "Light" half of the year and welcomes the "Dark" half."

"I still don't get it. Why is it starting on a Monday night? Don't these kinds of events run on weekends?" I asked.

"The festival starts on the first day after the October Full Moon and runs for six days until the Third Quarter Phase. That's why it's starting on a Monday night this year. Today is the first day after the full moon. They claim to be celebrating the autumn season and a bountiful harvest. In reality, it is a hedonist festival with lots of drinking and . . . ah . . . spontaneous foolin' around in the bushes. I made a big mistake last year. I didn't understand what the festival about and I brought Anna thinking she might like it. I deeply regretted it.

Scantily dressed, drunken women chased by equally drunken men. It was disgusting. I slapped some idiot who tried to kiss me. Anna and I didn't stay long. Several assaults were reported. Even with bad press, the festival has grown each year."

"I had no idea," I said. We arrived at Caroline's apartment. "Do you think you'll be okay tonight?" I asked.

"Yes, we'll be okay. I'd like you to stay, but I agree that it doesn't need to be tonight."

"Then I'm going to say goodbye. You need to take care of Anna, and I feel the need to get going. Can we meet after work again, same time, same place?"

"Yes, definitely," Caroline said. She reached out and gave me a long, warm hug goodbye. Excited butterflies danced in my stomach. That was the longest hug I've ever had. Reluctantly, we separated and waved to each other as I headed down the street. As much as I wanted to be with Caroline, I wanted to experience this Harvest Moon Festival. Was it as bad as Caroline said?

When I arrived at the corner, I turned and headed for Burns Park. As I approached the park, the smell of greasy food and smoke hung in the air. The noise level gradually increased, as did the number of revelers. I hadn't entered the festival yet, and I saw more demons than

I could count. Some floated above the crowd. Some walked amongst the humans, and most people had riders on their shoulders. They, too, celebrated. Ecstasy suffused their faces. I think they fed on the primal emotions unleashed by the crowd. As they moved through the mass of humanity, they reached into the revelers' heads and hearts, loosening any inhibitions the people usually had — their coarse laughter mixed with the festival-goers.

The crowd thickened as the temporary snow fences funneled us to the main entrance. I waited in line with the others. I began to regret my decision to come here, but I paid the fee and entered the park.

Once past the gate, it opened up again. Some people ran toward the lights in their excitement. I slowed. Even though there was more space around me, I felt claustrophobic. Darkness, spiritual darkness, cloaked the revelers as if they walked in shadows. Unless the person stood directly under a light, I found it difficult to see their faces.

Then I saw someone with the white aura of Christ around them. I looked for more glows, and I spied a few, but there weren't many, and the ones I saw were feeble. I suspected that those with strong faith did not seek this kind of entertainment.

Many people wore costumes that depicted something lewd, vulgar, or revealing. Neither shame nor modesty had a place here.

Barkers called out to everyone to come in and see their wares, watch a freak show or taste some sinfully good confection. One of them grabbed my arm and tried to drag me into his tent. I wrenched myself free and continued my journey. Everybody had some form of alcohol in their hands, and the scent of marijuana wafted on the light breeze. I made my way through the crowd.

Men encouraged women to reveal themselves, and many did. The men leered and chugged their beers. Lust and selfishness wove their way through the crowd like a ground-hugging fog.

I felt like a pinball spinning around and hitting bumpers that sent me in different directions. I finally cleared the revelers and found a place on the edge of the park. Throwing the duffle bag to the ground, I sat on a curb and held my head in my hands. *God, why do you allow this? Doesn't this cause you pain?* I searched for a plausible explanation but found none. Someone needs to do something, but what? My eyes fell upon the duffle bag. Is this why God had me seek the Armor? Is this my task?

I considered my actions and possible results. There are way too many demons. I couldn't vaporize all of them, but I could make a dent in them. I mentally wrestled with the options. Fear fought with conviction — someone needed to do something about this. *God, if you don't want me to take action, then you better stop me now.*

I opened the duffle bag and put on the Armor of God. With a thought, I triggered the transformation. Instantly, I was heavenly armed and felt the power of the living God surge through me. I felt invincible and scared enough to wet myself. I wish I had the shield. I decided to make one pass through the edges of the crowd. Running fast, I would surprise the demons near me and stab them with the sword. My hand rubbed my chest, and the painful scar. My resolve wavered.

What do I do, Lord? My fear grew again. I hemmed and hawed. One moment I anticipated the attack, and the next, I feared the consequences. But if God is with me, I can't fail. Right? God did not send me a clear answer, nor did the fear dissipate, but my resolve solidified. That was all the sign I needed. Before I changed my mind, I picked up the duffle bag and ran towards the nearest demon. The Sword of the Spirit whistled through the air, and the monster vaporized. My world became running and stabbing. Demon after demon wore a surprised look on their face as they disappeared.

Running like I never ran before, I stabbed another demon, spun around, and collided with a lady. She fell on her butt, and her beer splashed on me as I fell on top of her. Scrambling to my feet, her screams of anger followed me as I continued my mad dash. Every demon within my reach perished.

The crowd parted, and a seven-foot crimson monster with a massive battle-ax stood before me. It swung the weapon back and forth with ease, and its pointed, stained teeth exposed a sickening smile. It knew no fear, at least of humans.

Exhausted, my heart sank. So it wasn't God's will after all that I attacked these demons now. I stood frozen to the ground. Fear and defeat occupied all my thoughts. Then a memory wiggled and worked its way to the foreground of my mind.

"Beat your plowshares into swords, and your pruninghooks into spears."

A familiar surge of energy raced down my arm, and the Sword of the Spirit became the seven-foot-long lance again. I held it with both hands, with the lance sticking straight out from me. I ran forward like a medieval knight on horseback in a jousting match and skewered the demon through its gut. I ran through the monster's vaporous remains and kept running. I never looked back because I feared a horde of monsters followed.

I don't know how many I struck down. I could hear the cries of the demons grow louder, and I knew it was time to go. I broke through the remaining crowd and ran out of the exit. I bolted across a parking lot and street and ducked around the nearest corner. I stopped at a store entrance to catch my breath and to look for pursuit.

Nothing followed me. I took off the Armor of God but kept the sword in hand and made my way to the apartment. Fear and adrenaline energized me as I ran the rest of the way home. I arrived at my studio exhausted, and I flopped on my couch. My mind raced with this evening's episode. The fear subsided, and the adrenaline drained away, but my happiness remained as I drifted to sleep.

Chapter 22

Caroline

Monday Night

I watched Caleb walk away. Such a sweet man . . . Careful Caroline, you've only known him three days.

The old door creaked as it opened, and I trudged up the stairs. It's been a long day. I gathered Anna from Grace's apartment. I thanked her, and we returned home. Anna had eaten, but I needed something. I prepared my food and thought about the events of the last few days. God, *You are more and more real to me. Every time I see You work, my faith grows.*

I carried my plate and glass of milk to the living room. I flipped on the TV, sat down, and ate my sandwich. Anna babbled happily as she played with her dolls next to the couch. She made a dollhouse out of a cardboard box. It was almost 8:30, way past Anna's bedtime.

"Time for bed, Sweetie. Go brush your teeth and get your jammies on."

"Aww, Mommy. Can't I stay up a little longer?"

"No, it's a school night, and you're already up too late."

Anna got up and dragged herself to the bathroom as the TV droned in the background. A comedy show just ended. After the commercial, the local news anchor, Clark Myer, appeared on the screen.

Announcer: "Later on News 10 at 10 with Clark Myer."

Clark Myer: "We go to the Harvest Moon Festival at Burns Park with our very own Kimberly Vain. Kimberly, what's happening at the Festival?"

Kimberly Vain: "Hello Clark, we are broadcasting live in the News 10 lift bucket about forty feet or so above the festival. We have a great bird's eye view from here. (Camera is panning the crowd and tents below.) It's another wild year at the festival. There are lots of new food and drink vendors. Several local bands played earlier on the main stage. Police security seems lighter than I'd expect with this many people drinking. If you're going to drink, drink responsibly.

"Wait, there's some kind of commotion. A man is running through the crowd with something in his hand. (Camera zooms in on the running figure. Caroline groans. *Caleb, what are you doing?*) It's black and long; I can't tell you what it is. It looks like he is stabbing the air with it. Oh, oh, he just collided with a woman, knocked her down, and fell on top of her. The poor thing, I hope she isn't hurt. Now he is holding his weapon in front of him and is running away. Well, you get all kinds at this festival. Like I said, drink responsibly. Back to you, Clark."

Oh, Caleb, what have you done?

"Mommy, come 'n read me a book."

Caroline sighed and got off the couch. "Coming, Sweetie."

Chapter 23

Ichabod

Monday Night

The newspaper rustled as Ichabod turned the pages looking for the editorial his aide mentioned. Aahhh. Here it is.

"Ichabod Manheim Foe rules Foe Financial Services with an iron fist. The sixty-year-old CEO works hard and demands 120% from his managers. Foe is wealthy but miserly. He built up Foe Financial Services with a combination of intimidation and a keen market sense. Some people believed that Foe had help from insider knowledge. The local district attorney investigated Foe three times in the last five years. Each time, he got off on a technicality, or the witness disappeared. His ability to predict which way the markets would move made him wealthy and envied by his contemporaries. But what's most troubling is the number of politicians that look the other way when something fishy happens. Whatever Foe wants, our leaders bend over backward to make it happen. It is another example of money and power trampling the will of the people. Won't any local leader stand up against this monster?"

"HA! No, they won't," gloated Ichabod. He took a long, satisfying draw on his cigar and blew some smoke rings.

Foe sat in his opulent top-floor office suite that covered half of the building's top floor. It reflected Foe's own sense of grandeur and importance. A half-empty whiskey glass rested on the table next to him. Cigar smoke curled lazily above his head as he flipped through the balance of the newspaper. Two oversized leather chairs faced a giant TV that hung on the wall above a gas fireplace. Flames danced below while Channel 10 played on the TV above. Ichabod was not alone. His partner sat in the other chair and watched the same live broadcast that Caroline saw.

A roar erupted from the other chair. "DID YOU SEE THAT?"

"No, I wasn't paying attention."

"DON'T SIT THERE! Do something!" The partner continued, "You need to find this human. He wore the Armor of God! That means he can see and harm us. He eliminated at least three dozen of my demons. It has been 150 years since there's been a Soldier of God."

"A Soldier of God?"

"Every hundred years or so, God recruits a human, outfits him with the Armor of God, and sets them loose on us," the partner stated.

"Does he pose a danger to our plan?"

"These soldiers are an annoyance. They foul our plans and slow us down. The last Soldier of God wiped out half of my troops, but I killed him in the end. The Armor of God can take the form of various everyday human items. It changes with the times. I kept the shield and the sword from the last time and have them well hidden. I don't know what happened to the rest. Wait . . . that human had the Sword of the Spirit . . . HOW DID HE? . . . SNARK, GET IN HERE!"

A diminutive demon appeared in the doorway. Eyes down, the thing shook like a leaf in a storm.

"I JUST SAW A HUMAN RUNNING THROUGH A CROWD CUTTING DOWN MY DEMONS WITH THE SWORD OF THE SPIRIT. HOW IS THAT POSSIBLE?"

"M-Master, I just received a report from the Dream Collection Center that a break-in occurred four nights ago. A human woke up and stole a plastic tube, presumably the Sword of the Spirit."

"And why didn't I know about this sooner?" growled the master.

"Master, the DCC supervisor, notified me of the event just moments ago, and I was on my way to tell you when you called."

Foe watched the exchange. He didn't understand what the fuss was about, nor did he care. He focused on the newspaper and shut them out of his mind.

"Was the sword the only thing taken?"

"It was the only thing reported as stolen."

"Good. I'll deal with the supervisor later . . . Hmm, he will still need the shield . . . Snark, place guards around the Shield of Faith immediately," commanded the partner.

"Yes, Master," Snark responded. It turned and left the room.

"Foe, get a copy of the video and see if you can identify him," the partner demanded.

"If he is just an annoyance, is that necessary?"

A roar erupted from the shape as it launched out of the chair. Towering over Ichabod stood a twelve-foot-tall demon. The massive monster's blood-red, leathery skin smelled like rotten flesh to Ichabod. Smoke escaped from its mouth and ears. It oozed evil and hatred as it glared at Icabod with its crimson eyes.

"I AM ANTIVERITAS, the Corrupter of Truth. Slave, remember, who the Master is here. If you ever question me again, I will end your puny life and send your spirit straight to hell. Is that clear?"

Ichabod glared at the demon and pulled out his phone. He dialed the TV station. A few moments later, he mumbled a few words into the phone. "It's done. They'll email a link later tonight. I'll have someone analyzing it first thing in the morning. Are you satisfied?" Ichabod sneered.

"I still don't like the tone of your voice, human, but it will do for now. Don't forget who's in charge."

Chapter 24

Demons

Monday Night

Snark left the office and returned to its station. The spirit realm is similar in some ways to the physical world. Everyone has a purpose, a job, and they need the proper tools to carry out their work.

Being an Administrative Demon, Snark sat behind a mundane desk with IN and OUT baskets on each front corner stacked high with what looked like documents. A quill lay next to a blood-red bottle of ink. However, these reports were not written on paper, rather parchment made from some kind of skin. There were many desks and Administrative Demons on the top floor of the Foe Building.

Dane, Snark's administrative neighbor, leaned over and whispered, "What did the master want?"

Fuming, Snark replied, "What that puffed-up jerk always wants, something done now. The Master wants guards placed 'Immediately' around some old piece of junk. I'll assign some guards alright . . . when I'm good and ready."

Chapter 25

Caleb

Monday Night

I got off the couch and headed to the bathroom. I had a hard time brushing my teeth since I couldn't stop smiling. Satisfaction permeated my entire being as I prepared for sleep. Happy does not come close to describing how I felt. I've never been so alive as I ran through the festival and slashed and stabbed demons. Sleep came slowly as I relived the festival. Soon a warm fog enveloped me, and I sensed motion like moving through fluffy dream clouds. A few moments passed, and a shape drew closer and flew next to me. The fog thinned, and I saw Ramiel, the angel, who spoke to me a few days ago.

"Where are we . . .," my voice trailed off as Ramiel put his finger to his lips. He gestured to keep silent. The fog cleared, and we floated high above the Dream World. A sea of beds stretched out below me. I moaned, "Oh no!" and turned toward my companion.

The Angel glared. He raised his finger to his lips again and to watch the scene below. My stomach knotted.

Below us, stretched rows upon rows of sleepers laying on beds, and demons moved among them. As I watched, I noticed a pattern. The demon's movements were not random.

My vision zoomed in like binoculars. The magnification effect startled me, but I soon got used to it. I focused on a man's peaceful face. A small demon landed on the man's chest and reached into his head. As the imp withdrew its arm, I saw a wispy golden strand clutched in its claw. The wisp twisted, attempting to escape the demon's grasp. As the strand cleared the man's head, his face contorted with fear and anger. He tossed and turned on the bed but settled down in a few moments. He remained asleep, however his once peaceful expression was replaced with a frown.

The demon opened the container that sat next to the man's head and shook the wisp into it. The cylindrical bucket was about the size of a gallon paint can. When it lifted the cover, I saw more golden strands writhing like snakes on the inside. My vision zoomed out, so I looked from a distance again.

Below us, I noticed something new. A circular bodied demon, three feet across, floated towards the imp we had been watching. It had eight arms and no legs. I wanted to vomit. From the top, it looked like a giant blood-red spider hovering in the air. A covered container dangled from each appendage. It approached my demon, dropped off an empty can, and picked up the one lying there. The spider demon cruised to the next row and the next set of victims. The spider performed the same service for seven more demons in seven more rows of sleepers. *What are they doing?* I looked at my companion quizzically. He motioned to keep watching.

We followed the spider demon. When it reached the central aisle, it turned left and increased its speed. We watched from high above, unsure of its destination.

It flew toward the far end of the cavernous room where an elongated semi-circular wall stood inside the gigantic chamber's outer wall. It reminded me of a stage. In the center of the stage, an immense cauldron rested upon a dais three steps high. The demon set all the buckets down and emptied each into the massive container. Golden filaments flowed like water into the larger vessel. They writhed within the enormous kettle, looking for an escape. The spider demon picked up all eight containers, turned, and floated back to the sleepers. As it left, another took its place, emptying eight more buckets. A regular parade of red spiders moved down the center aisle to the cauldron.

I stared at the massive vessel. *What could those filaments be?* The wisps looked like golden smoke but moved like something alive inside the large container. The cauldron was black like cast iron. Its eight-foot diameter and thick walls meant it weighed tons. I pondered what we witnessed. We hovered against the ceiling, and I looked at Ramiel. His raised eyebrows gave me a "C'mon, connect the dots" look.

And they did connect.

Dreams. The demons stole the dreams of the people of Stanton. That explained a lot. Dreams gave you two things: Hope and love.

Hope gives you goals, something to look forward to, to anticipate. It allows you to reach for something beyond yourself. The impossible becomes possible with hope.

Love gives you the capacity to put the welfare of another before yourself. You genuinely wish the best for other people. Love gives you the ability to commit to people as a friend or a spouse. Love gives you spiritual strength. With love and hope, you can endure almost any hardship.

Hope and love together make God a possibility. If you accept that God is real, then there is a purpose for your life, and something better awaits us when this life ends.

Without our dreams, people become selfish. It's all about me and what I want and when I want it. Crime, divorce, suicide, and drug addiction had soared in Stanton. Without love, you don't care about yourself or others. Self-pity, despair, and depression had become the norm—something I understood.

Without a dream, there was nothing to work toward or anticipate. There's no striving or struggling toward a goal. Without hope, you cannot truly love. Now I understood why hedonist festivals like the Harvest Moon had become famous. And that's why the festival crawled with demons.

All of this came as a flash to me. This epiphany must have come from God because until recently, I lived without hope. And I realized

God wanted me to destroy the cauldron and return the dreams to the people. It looked indestructible. *How am I supposed to destroy it?*

I was about to turn towards Ramiel when I noticed a unique decoration hanging in the center of the stage wall. It was round and about twenty inches in diameter. It looked like a battered galvanized garbage can cover. It briefly glowed. *The Shield of Faith!* I glanced at the angel. He gave a brief nod. So it was more than destroying the massive container. To complete the Armor of God, I needed to re-enter the Dream World.

Ramiel indicated with his hand that I should follow him. As we approached the wall, the fog returned, and my companion faded from sight. I woke with a start on my couch.

This time, I knew it wasn't a dream. Anger boiled to the surface. *How can God expect me to go against an army of demons? I am one man!*

Fear followed the anger. "If you want me to die, just kill me now," I yelled at the ceiling. "There's no way for me to win this battle. Do you treat everybody like this? Giving them impossible tasks?"

Fearful and angry, I got out of bed. The clock read 6:57 a.m. *What's today? . . . it's only Tuesday. This is going to be a long week.*

But I had to go to work. With a groan, I stripped off my clothes, tossed them in the corner, and headed for the bathroom. I cranked up the hot water. Steam filled the room, and I stepped into the shower. A few minutes later, I toweled off and got dressed. My mood had lightened some. I knew I needed to talk with the others. Maybe they had some ideas. Breakfast consisted of a couple of generic strawberry toaster pastries stuffed into my mouth.

Grabbing the duffle that held the Armor of God, I headed for work. The demons mixed with the morning crowd. I felt exposed and pulled my hood up while I kept my head down.

I jumped as loud ringing erupted from my pocket. Grabbing the phone, I answered it.

"Hello," and I yanked it away from my ear.

"YOUR LITTLE RUN THROUGH THE PARK WAS ON TV LAST NIGHT!"

I stepped into the mouth of an alley. "Caroline? Is that you? What're you talkin' about?"

A little calmer but still louder than necessary, Caroline explained. "Last night, Channel 10 News broadcasted LIVE from a lift bucket above the festival. They recorded your run through the park. It showed you pushing through the crowd, tripping over people, and stabbing the air. The good news is they just said you were one of the many drunk people there. Someone will know you weren't drunk. They will know you killed demons last night. They will come after you."

Initially alarmed, then I thought about what she said. I smiled. "Are you telling me demons watch TV?" I laughed and started walking towards work again.

"Don't you laugh at me," snapped Caroline. "You don't know what demons do in their off time."

My amusement faded. Caroline might be right. Maybe it was a dumb move.

"But Caroline, you should've seen it. Almost every person there had a demonic escort. I saw the demons releasing inhibitions and whispering foul ideas into their ears. The creatures laughed as the people numbed their senses with alcohol and drugs. I had to do something. I knew I couldn't take them all on, but maybe I could take a few out. So I acted."

"I understand, Caleb - but I wish you hadn't done that."

"Okay, maybe you're right, but I have news. I was visited by Ramiel last night. I know the next step and . . . I'm afraid."

"What happened?"

"He took me to the Dream World. Ramiel showed why the Dream World exists and why the sleepers are there. He also showed me the Shield of Faith."

"No! In the Dream World?"

"Yeah, 'n I gotta go in and get it."

"Oh, Caleb." Caroline's voice wavered.

"There's more, but I gotta go. Meet me out front at 4:00." I hung up. That conversation almost made me late. I punched in, gathered my equipment, and got to work. The day dragged on and on. Fear latched onto my soul, and my innards roiled. *How can I release the dreams, grab the shield, and live?*

Chapter 26

Gloria

Tuesday Morning

"I DIDN'T' KNOW! YOU DIDN'T TELL ME! YOU CAN'T CONDEMN ME IF I DIDN'T' KNOW!" I yelled.

Images of a courtroom mixed with scenes from my past surrounded me. A deep voice resonated with authority filled the chamber.

"You did know, and you CHOSE not to hear. You CHOSE not to believe. I've sent many of my people to you, dozens of opportunities to accept my grace. You've cast each aside like a piece of trash. You will be judged. You will get what you deserve."

"It's just a bad dream, that's all. You'll wake up soon, and all of this will fade," whispered another voice through my mind.

I ignored the whisper and sobbed.

"I didn't understand. Si, you're right. I didn't believe it. My head said it couldn't be true, and my heart said it was. I listened to my head. Please, I beg of you, one more chance."

"Your head is right; hearts are full of irrational emotions. Listen to your mind," cooed the whisper.

Softer, but with authority, the deep voice declared, "Child, you have one more opportunity in this life. If you do not take it, you'll suffer eternal punishment. In this matter, you need to trust your heart."

"This is a dream, full of lies and deceit. Truly there will be no consequences. You've nothing to fear," the whisper insisted.

"I don't believe you." I woke with a gasp. My heart raced, my breath ragged and drenched in sweat. I rolled out of bed and stumbled to the bathroom. The clock on the counter read 6:00 a.m. I turned the water faucets on and splashed my face. The double sink vanity was too big for one person. I glanced at the other basin and imagined my dead husband, Mateo, standing there, dragging an electric shaver over his stubbly beard. He wore that irrepressible grin that made him look younger than his years. He had a touch of gray in his hair.

However, a year ago, he died of a heart attack. We spent the evening at home, and he fell asleep on the couch. I went to bed, thinking he would eventually wake up and come upstairs. The following day, I found Mateo still sleeping on the sofa. I laughed and said, "C'mon, sleepyhead, wake up! You'll be late for work." I shook his shoulder and felt his forehead. Cold! Mateo died in his sleep. I called 911, but there was nothing they could do. That had been the worse day of my entire life.

I looked in the mirror at my reflection. My sullen visage stared back at me from the mirror. Dark bags hung under my eyes, and wet strands of hair clung to my face. My olive skin had more wrinkles than I remembered, and a few gray hairs stood out against my charcoal-colored hair.

It's a dream, just a dream. Reassured the whispers in my mind.

"Gloria, it was only a dream, now get over it and get ready for work," I reprimanded myself.

I took a hot shower and got dressed. I missed Mateo's love and laughter.

For breakfast, I wolfed down a bowl of granola, after which I brushed my teeth and left for St. Mary's Home. I felt a little better and mentally mapped out the day while en route. Arriving at my usual time, I greeted Jean at the reception desk as she handed me a couple of messages. Flipping through them, I walked to my office. None were significant, so I tossed them into my inbox. Lifting the lab coat off the hook behind the door, I put it on and started my rounds.

I enjoyed the rounds. Speaking with each patient for a few minutes helped me get the pulse of the place. Afternoons typically held counseling sessions.

The hall clock said ten o'clock—time to see Angelo. I'll also need maintenance to paint his room. I arrived at Angelo's door and looked in. He's been much calmer with the boots gone. Unlocking the door, I entered the room. "Good morning, Angelo. How are you today?"

Angelo sat in his chair and closed the book in his lap. The book title was printed in large gold letters. *I didn't know Angelo read the Bible.*

"Hey, Doc, I feel much better today."

He seems more lucid than usual. I jotted a note in my notepad. "Angelo, can we paint your room and get rid of that phone number?"

"Sure Doc, the Feet fitted with the Gospel of Peace is where it needs to be."

I mentally rolled my eyes and then smiled at him. "You seem calmer now than you've been in a long time. I'm so happy that you're doing better."

"Me too. Say Doc, can I ask you a question?" He said.

"Sure, Angelo, go ahead."

Angelo stood and faced me. He gazed directly into my eyes with unusual intensity and said, "Your last opportunity is today. Are you going to follow your head or your heart?"

What! I staggered backward, fell against the door, and slid to the floor. His question felt like a gunshot to my chest.

"Are you going to follow your head or your heart?" insisted Angelo.

"H-H-How'd you know that?"

"I don't know how, but I know it's true," Angelo replied.

Scrambling to my feet, I wrenched the door open and slammed it shut as I left the room. My legs felt rubbery, and I staggered to my office. The door banged shut behind me, and I collapsed in my chair. I covered my face and sobbed. Tears squeezed between my fingers. Last night's dream returned with renewed intensity. Fear like I never felt before assaulted my being. My head and heart battled each other. *I've got to get out of here!*

Picking up the phone, I called Jean at the front desk. "J-Jean p-please cancel all my appointments t-today. C-call Dr. Franklin and see if he can cover this afternoon. I'm not w-well and need a personal day. I'm leaving now and will n-not be available."

Confused, Jean sputtered, "Y-yes, Doctor."

I took my lab coat off, threw it on the chair, and slipped on my jacket. I practically ran out of the building, got into my car, and spun the tires as I left the parking lot. I drove and drove. I aimlessly drove around for an hour. My mind grasped for some logical explanation. *What am I doing? Where am I going? I know, I'll call Claire.*

Claire has been my psychic counselor since Mateo died. When I was in mourning and troubled, she seemed to say what I needed to hear. I dug my phone out of my purse. I entered her number and pushed the call button. I drifted towards the oncoming traffic and jerked the wheel back as the oncoming car horn blared at me. The phone at the other end rang and rang. *C'mon . . . c'mom answer!*

A click. "This is Claire, your Psychic connection to the unseen world. How can I help you today?"

"Claire, this is Gloria Sanchez."

"Hi Gloria, how are you?" asked Claire.

"I-I'm not doing so well. I must see you today!"

"I don't know, Gloria. I am pretty booked, but let me look." Pages rustled in the background. "That's right. I had a cancellation this afternoon. Can you come at 2:30?"

"Not till 2:30 . . . Is there a time sooner?"

"Sorry, Gloria, that is the soonest I can fit you in."

"Okay, I'll be there. T-thank you, Claire." I hung up the phone and slumped back into the driver's seat. *What do I do now? I've got hours to kill.*

I ran my second stop sign today. And I realized I had been driving recklessly. *I must stop somewhere before I hurt myself.* I passed a Harvest Moon Festival sign on the corner. I decided to go there to waste time and get some lunch. At the entrance, I paid an admission fee and stopped by the first sandwich truck. I ordered a small, assorted submarine sandwich and soda. A short distance away stood an empty park bench, so I walked over to it and sat down. I ate mechanically. The sandwich had no flavor, and my stomach churned. I dumped half of it plus my drink into the closest trash can and strolled around the park. Festival Barkers tried to get my attention, but I brushed them off. I thought a walk would settle me, but it didn't. 2:30 seemed to be an eternity away.

As I walked, I felt the battle waged between my heart and my head. Whispers kept reassuring me that science has proven there is no God. The whispers felt like a mosquito buzzing in my ear. I stayed as long as I could stand it. I got back in my car and drove.

I arrived at Claire's at 2:10 p.m., sat in my car, and waited. The radio played music I didn't hear. I tried to make sense of it all. There must be a logical, rational answer for all that had happened today. I looked at the dashboard clock about every minute, waiting for the appointed time.

A man walked out the front door at 2:28. His feet hadn't even stepped onto the small parking lot when my door slammed, and I marched up the sidewalk to the entrance. I burst through the front door and found Claire sitting behind a small writing desk.

Claire stood, concern covered her face. "What's so urgent that you needed an immediate session?" Claire asked as she motioned me toward the next room. Her large desk filled half the office, and a round table big enough to seat four around it occupied the other half.

In the middle of the table sat a crystal ball. The stand the crystal rested on looked like a clawed metal hand; the palm faced the ceiling, and the ball rested on the splayed fingers. Claire mirrored my movements as I sat down on one side of the table.

Even though I tried to remain calm and analytical, tears welled up in my eyes. I shared my nightmare and the encounter with Angelo. "How could he know about my dream?"

Claire reached across the table and held each of my hands. The crystal ball rested between them. "Dear Gloria, Angelo knows nothing about your dream. He's unstable. You know that. He just made a random statement that seemed to relate to your nightmare. What he said was nothing. It was the timing that made the difference. If you didn't have the dream, would his words have affected you?"

I slowly shook my head, no.

"Then don't let it affect you now."

"You're right, Claire," I said as the panic subsided. "It's ridiculous to believe Angelo could have known about the dream. I mean, I didn't tell a soul except you."

"That's right, Gloria, in this matter; you need to trust your head."

I stared at Claire. "W-would you repeat that, Claire?"

"In this matter, you need to trust your head."

"I-I'm sorry. C-Could you say that one more time?"

Claire's smiling face full of patience slowly said. "In-this-matter, you-need-to-trust-your-head."

"I-I-I've g-g-got to g-g-go." I stood, turned, and ran out the door.

I bolted for my car and jumped into the driver's seat. The engine roared, and gravel flew as I raced out of the parking lot.

Tears obscured my sight, and I pulled over to the roadside. I sobbed uncontrollably. It isn't possible. *Am I hallucinating? What is happening?* The phrase Claire used mirrored my dream, except "heart" replaced "head." I heard "head" and "heart" in my mind at the same time. But what happened to Claire? All three times, when she

159

uttered the word "head," for a split second, she turned into a monster. It was like a camera flash showing her true nature for just a moment.

"Not true, you can't believe your eyes. Claire never changed. That makes no scientific sense," uttered the whisper.

With unexpected resolve, I said to myself, "I saw what I saw. Claire is a monster."

I still didn't know what to do. I turned the car off and rested my head on the steering wheel. *Think Gloria!* So much had happened in the last twenty-four hours that challenged everything I believed to be true. I ran the events of the previous day over in my mind. What did Pastor Bob say? "Doctor, when you're ready to put your head aside and examine your heart, come visit me . . . I would love to discuss faith with you."

I straightened up and started the car. I knew what to do. As I wove my way through the busy Stanton streets, I honk my horn the moment traffic slowed. A trash can clanged as it hit the sidewalk when I clipped it with my bumper. I swerved into a parking space on the street. The clock on the dashboard said 4:00 p.m., and I exited the vehicle.

I marched to and yanked the main doors of the City Mission open. A kind-looking woman sat behind a desk near the door. "Hi, I'm Fran. Can I help you?"

I took a deep breath and tried to compose myself. "I'm looking for Pastor Bob Bennett. Is he available?"

"I don't know if he's available," Fran smiled. "But you can go down that hall. You'll see him in his office."

I nodded my thanks and walked where she pointed. I went past a couple of open doors, and then I saw Pastor Bennett behind his desk. I stopped and stepped back from the opening so he couldn't see me. *You don't want to do this. Weak people turn to God. You're strong, and you don't need God.* The whispers raced through my mind.

Chapter 27

Caleb

Tuesday Afternoon

The Shield of Faith is in the Dream World. That thought hung in my mind all day long. My watch read 4:15. I'd been waiting in front of the Foe Building for 15 minutes and no Caroline.

Where is she? My impatience grew.

"Hi, Caleb."

I jumped.

Caroline chuckled. "Nervous?"

"Yes! We need to talk . . . in private." Her face went from amused to concern.

Taking her hand, I headed for the City Mission. I wanted to get away from Foe's.

Two blocks later, Caroline protested. "Caleb, slow down. You're crushing my hand; I can't keep up."

Slowing down, I spied a bench in front of a shoe store. Dozens of women's shoes and large sale signs decorated the other side of the glass.

"I'm sorry, let's sit here." Releasing her hand, I motioned toward the bench. "Wait, watch the bird poop." Caroline sat, and the droppings forced me to sit close to her.

Looking around for eavesdroppers and keeping my voice low, I told Caroline everything about my trip to the Dream World with Ramiel the night before. "It's impossible for me to defeat all those demons. There's n-no way . . . n-no way to do this."

Caroline smiled and took my hand. "Caleb, you're doing it again. You're not trusting God. Hasn't He given you what you needed when you needed it? What makes you think you're alone? Bob and I will help. You know that, right? Have you prayed about this yet?"

"Well . . . no." I'd been too wrapped up in myself to even think about asking God for help.

"Caroline, you are my anchor."

She stood and pulled me to my feet. "I'm not sure I like being compared to an anchor, but I understand what you mean," she said, her eyes sparkled with mischief. "Let's go see Bob." Hand in hand, we headed for City Mission.

Chapter 28

Gloria

Tuesday Afternoon

I stood by the coat rack outside and out of sight of Pastor Bob's office for several minutes, fighting my doubts and the whispers. Scenario after scenario played out in my mind; what I'd say, how to act. I wanted to be professional, clinical. The whispers of doubt buzzed in my ears like flies buzzing around my head.

Why am I so nervous? I plunged into the pastor's office with new resolve and plunked into the chair in front of the desk. Words gushed out of my mouth.

"HolaPastorBob.CouldWeHaveThatDiscussionAboutPuttingTheH eadAsideAndExaminingTheHeart?"

My brave front lasted seconds, and I broke down, burying my face with my hands. Tears squeezed between my fingers. Soon I felt the weight of an arm around my shoulders and tissue pushed into my hands. Dabbing my eyes, I turned and found Bob sitting in a chair next to mine. His head bowed, eyes closed, and he spoke.

"Lord, please extend your love and protection over Gloria. Help her know you love her. Keep the demons at bay. Give her peace. Touch her, so she knows you are real."

Relief seeped in, my body relaxed. I blew my nose.

"I'm glad you're here, Gloria. Tell me, what's going on," he cooed.

I told him the entire story, the doubt he planted, the horrible courtroom dream, Angelo's question about following my heart or head, and Claire's transformation. And like a mosquito, whispers buzzed in my mind. *He can't help you. He lies. Being here is stupid. Go home.* But I ignored the buzzing.

"I think I can help you, Gloria, but this is a matter of the heart and faith. You won't find any scientific verification. I know there's a strong demonic presence in this city. There is also an active presence of God."

The tears stopped. A scuffling noise behind us caused Bob to turn his head. I saw him nod. I wiped my eyes and turned to look at whoever was behind us. A plastic tube thrust past my head. I quickly stood and faced my assailant—a middle-aged man towered over me. A woman was behind him. He had a black plastic tube in his hand.

Bob took my hand. "Don't be afraid. Sit. Please."

The two strangers entered the office. The woman sat in the desk chair, and the man stood next to her. He still held the plastic tube. I slowly sat down, suspicious of these newcomers.

"Doctor, you probably won't believe this, but you had a demon attached to you. These are my friends. The woman is Caroline, and the man is Caleb. He can see and kill demons with weapons God has given him. He stabbed a small demon that sat on your shoulder. It's gone."

A small demon? That is crazy talk! Who are these people? My mind spun with disbelief. Wait . . . Hold on. The mental spinning stopped. There was a dark part of my mind. Cracks grew across the darkness, and they widened, letting beams of light enter. I felt chunks of night crumble, allowing my mind to be awash in the light. I felt light as a feather and the whispers. The whispers . . . were . . . gone!

"Bob, I think I believe you."

Warmth flowed from my head to my toes. A different kind of tear ran down my cheek.

"In your dream, the voice said you have one more opportunity to avoid the punishment you deserved. Is that correct?"

I nodded my head.

"The opportunity is to accept Jesus Christ as your Savior and Lord. If you don't accept Jesus, then you will suffer eternal punishment when you die. Are you ready to accept Jesus as your Savior?"

My throat was tight with emotion, and I couldn't speak. I nodded my head again. Tears threatened to spill from eyes again. Caleb and Caroline came out from behind the desk and stood behind us. Their hands rested on our shoulders.

"We are going to pray now. Repeat after me, and as long as you mean it, you will be a child of God, your sins forgiven, and Heaven will be your reward, not Hell. Bow your head, close your eyes. Repeat after me."

"Lord God, I am a sinner. I repent of those sins and unbelief and seek your forgiveness . . ."

"Lord God, I am a sinner. I repent of those sins and unbelief and seek your forgiveness . . ."

"You are the creator of all things . . ."

"I believe Jesus died on the cross . . ."

"His blood as payment for my sins . . ."

"So I may be forgiven . . ."

"Jesus, I ask you to be my Savior . . ."

"I repent of my sins . . ."

"Help me to live a life pleasing and obedient to You for all eternity . . ."

"Amen," we concluded.

I wiped my eyes. I felt new and clean.

Chapter 29

Caleb

Tuesday, Afternoon and Night

Caroline and I arrived at the City Mission. Fran sat at the reception desk and warmly greeted us. She also indicated Bob had a visitor. We headed toward his office to let him know we were there.

Looking through the doorway, I could tell the woman was distraught. Bob sat next to her, hand on her shoulder. She shook as she cried. Then the demon's face appeared above the collar as it crawled from her chest to her back. It looked frantic. It scrambled all over her head, neck, and back. The imp's hands repeatedly entered her skull and through her back to pull at the strings of her mind and heart. With feverish intensity, I heard it whisper disbelief into her ears to distract her from Bob.

I set the duffel bag down and pulled out the tube. With a thought, it transformed into the Sword of the Spirit. Bob glanced at me, and I mouthed the word "demon" while making a stabbing motion. Bob subtly nodded his head. The little monster jumped on Bob's hand, trying to get him to release the woman. Every time it touched Bob's skin, it wailed in pain, and puffs of smoke rose from its feet. It paused as frustration and fear covered its face. I stepped forward and stabbed the demon. I heard the familiar pop as it vaporized.

Caroline followed me into the office. Bob told the woman who we were and what had just happened. The next thing I knew, they prayed the salvation prayer, and the woman cried, this time for joy.

Bob introduced us properly. "Caroline and Caleb, this is Dr. Gloria Sanchez from St. Mary's Home. She's Angelo's doctor. Angelo provided us with the boots, which are the Feet Fitted with the Gospel of Peace. Gloria, this is Caleb Kincade, Soldier of God, and Caroline Sullivan, a friend."

Gloria wiped her eyes. "Pleased to meet you, but I must confess, I feel embarrassed."

"Doc, I don't mean to be rude, but I need to talk with the Pastor." I turned to Bob. "I know where the last piece is, and I know what we're supposed to do."

"Caleb, that's great."

"Oh, okay, I . . . guess I'll go," a subdued Gloria said.

"Brother Caleb, you are rude! Sister Gloria, you stay put. I'm going to speak with Caleb down the hall."

Bob turned me around and headed out of the room. "Brother, I think we need to include her. Let her be a part of whatever happens. She's fragile. Sending her away like this is going to feel like rejection. Her new faith will crumble."

"But Bob, you don't know what's coming. This next part is treacherous, and I expect to die."

Bob's eyes filled with concern. "Brother, it's that dangerous?"

I nodded. Bob closed his eyes for a moment.

"That doesn't change anything. We still need to bring Gloria into our little group."

"This is stupid . . . but okay."

We returned to the office. Bob sat in his desk chair, and I stood next to Bob. Caroline sat in the chair next to Gloria.

"Sister Gloria, Brother Caleb has a story you need to hear. It's going to sound impossible, but it's true."

Gloria shifted her attention to me.

"Gloria, we've decided to include you in our group here. It's strange to say 'group' because we didn't know each other five days ago. But God brought us together, and Bob thinks you have a part to

167

play in all this. A lot of what I am going to say may confuse you, but please hold your questions for now."

"Caroline and I woke up in this Dream World. It's a place that seems to be part spirit realm and part physical reality. In this place, people sleep in rows upon rows of beds, and demons do things to them in their sleep. Last night an angel returned me to this world. We did not talk. We had to be silent to keep the demons ignorant of our presence. Somehow the demons have plugged into people's minds while they sleep. While we're sleeping, they come by and harvest our hopes and dreams. They look like golden wisps of fog, but they flow like water when poured from the collection pot. The demons took the collected dreams and dumped them into a large black cauldron at the end of the great room where the sleepers lay. There is a wall behind the cauldron. In the center of the wall hangs a decoration, the Shield of Faith. The Shield is the last piece of the Armor of God. It looks like a metal garbage can lid, battered and discolored. I need to enter the Dream World, destroy the cauldron, grab the Shield of Faith, and escape again. Simple right? There is only one real problem."

"What's that, Brother?" Bob asked.

"THERE'S NO WAY I CAN PULL THIS OFF! There're thousands and thousands of sleeping people, maybe thousands of demons. And there is the little matter of getting into the Dream World. The first time I was there, God woke me. The only reason I escaped was that God pulled me out before the demon attack. The second time, an angel brought me. I know God wants me to do this, and I am willing, but I see no hope of surviving. I'm not sure it will even do any good. The demons will still be around. How do I get past them?" I ranted.

"Jesus faced a similar situation."

"C'mon, Bob. I don't think so."

Pulling out a Bible, Bob continued, "Jesus knew his time on earth was short. He knew he'd be betrayed. In Matthew 26:36-46, it says:

"Then Jesus went with his disciples to a place called Gethsemane, and he said to them, "Sit here while I go over there and pray." He took Peter and the two sons of Zebedee along with him, and he began to be sorrowful and troubled. Then he said to them, "My soul is overwhelmed with sorrow to the point of death. Stay here and keep watch with me.

"Going a little farther, he fell with his face to the ground and prayed, 'My Father, if it is possible, may this cup be taken from me. Yet not as I will, but as you will.'

"Then he returned to his disciples and found them sleeping. 'Could you men not keep watch with me for one hour?' he asked Peter. 'Watch and pray so that you will not fall into temptation. The spirit is willing, but the body is weak.'

"He went away a second time and prayed, 'My Father, if it is not possible for this cup to be taken away unless I drink it, may your will be done.'

When he came back, he again found them sleeping, because their eyes were heavy. So he left them and went away once more and prayed the third time, saying the same thing.

Then he returned to the disciples and said to them, 'Are you still sleeping and resting? Look, the hour is near, and the Son of Man is betrayed into the hands of sinners. Rise, let us go! Here comes my betrayer!'"[10]

Bob continued, "You see Brother Caleb, Jesus, even though He is God, He is also a man, subject to the feelings and sometimes the limitations of the human body. He wanted to do the Father's will but didn't want to bear all the world's sin. Jesus knew humanity would be better for it in the long run, but His human body still feared the process. In the end, He trusted God and hung from the Cross.

"Brother Caleb, you are faced with a similar situation. You know what to do, but the fear of it is stopping you. But you are not alone.

---

[10] Matthew 26:36-46 NIV

God has already helped you. You also have three of us. We will do whatever is necessary," Bob concluded as his eyes met mine.

"You're right. God had provided when the time was right. And He has provided all of you. Bob, your knowledge of the Bible is key to helping us determine God's will."

"The Scriptures promise that God answers all prayer. Have you prayed yet?" Bob asked.

"No, I haven't. Can we pray now?"

"Of course."

Everybody bowed their heads and closed their eyes. Bob prayed aloud. Caroline chimed in occasionally while Gloria remained silent. Soon their voices faded into the background. *Lord, I need help and a plan. I surrender to you.* Several moments passed, then a new urge grew within me.

I opened my eyes and looked around. The others had their heads bowed and eyes closed. Bob's voice sure and confident. Reaching down, I opened the duffle bag and pulled out the Armor of God. I set each piece on the floor before me, trying to be quiet. I reverently put each piece on. The rustle of the Armor caught Bob's attention. His voice trailed off when he opened his eyes to watch me. The women also opened their eyes and again turned toward me—the *Armor of God.* In the spirit world, I knew I was a weapon, but my friends could not see. Their eyes were blind, and they needed to see. I needed them to see.

With the Sword of the Spirit in my right hand, I raised both arms to heaven. I closed my eyes. *Ask.* Crying out, I declared, "Lord God, please give them eyes to see and ears to hear. I ask this in the name of Jesus Christ,". . . and . . . and . . . nothing. I expected the clap of thunder. A rush of wind. Something, but instead, nothing. Disappointed, I opened my eyes. Feeling pretty foolish, I started to apologize, but the words caught in my throat.

I scanned their faces expecting to see pity or disbelief. Instead, I saw awe, amazement, and puzzlement.

Gloria broke the silence. "Caleb, I'm confused. What're you wearing? And what's that white glow?"

Relieved, I raised my eyes to heaven and said, "Thank you, Lord."

Looking at Caroline, then Bob, "I didn't think anything had happened. Can you see the armor?"

"Yes, Brother Caleb, we can. I believed you before, but seeing just makes me want to praise God further."

Caroline got up and stepped around the desk. She placed her hand on my chest, feeling the Breastplate of Righteousness. Then she reached her hand up and touched the Helmet of Salvation. "I knew, but I didn't know. I gotta sit down." Caroline returned to her chair.

Responding to Gloria's questions, I said, "The glow you see is the aura that surrounds those that have trusted Jesus Christ as their Savior. What just happened is that God granted you the same ability that I have; to see the spirit world. What I'm wearing is five of the six pieces of the Armor of God. They are the Breastplate of Righteousness, the Belt of Truth, the Helmet of Salvation, the Sword of the Spirit, and the Feet Fitted with the Gospel of Peace. The only piece missing is the Shield of Faith. I know where it is, but how do we get it?

Bob, shaking his head, said, "Brother Caleb, I had no idea. All we saw you wearing were common, everyday items. Yet, in the spiritual world, you're anything but common. I didn't fully believe you were equipped to do battle for the Lord or capable of taking on demons." Bob leaned back in his chair, reflecting on what happened. Speaking toward the ceiling, he said, "I wonder what God sees when He looks at us. Is it the junk of our lives or the spiritual warrior?"

Tipping forward, he continued, "God has answered our prayers. I think we're ready to enter the Dream World."

Timidly, Gloria asked, "Does that include me?"

"Do you see the Armor of God?" I asked.

Gloria nodded.

"Then He has given you this gift for a purpose. Whether the purpose is for today or tomorrow, it is not for me to say."

I removed the Armor of God and returned it to the duffle bag. Turning to the others, I said, "Entering the Dream World will be as easy as falling asleep. The real question is, what happens once we get there?"

Bob and Caroline shrugged their shoulders.

"Maybe I can help," Gloria said. "I develop strategies for clients facing unknown situations. Tell me what you know, and we should be able to develop a rough plan when we arrive."

"N-Not me. I-I can't go," Caroline stood, knocking the chair backward and grabbed her things. Tears glistened in her eyes. "I've been there, and I'm NOT going back! Anna, I need to pick up Anna. I can't get hurt or, worse, killed in there. What would happen to my little Sweetie? Make your plans without me." She gave me a brief hug and fled.

Flabbergasted, I stared at the space where she just stood. The thought of Caroline not being a part of this was unthinkable to me.

Bob put his hand on my shoulder. "Come, my brother. We need to make some plans."

For the next several hours, I described the dream realm as best I could. Gloria filled page after page with notes and ideas. We looked at possible entry points. How could we move without detection? Do we battle demons immediately or sneak around? We ran every angle we thought possible. We prayed and then prayed some more.

"Do the demons know the shield hanging on the wall is part of the Armor of God?" Bob asked. I shrugged.

"Earlier, you said Gorg's hand sizzled when it touched the Breast Plate of Righteousness, and the demon's feet smoked when it jumped on my hand," said Bob.

I nodded.

"Then it seems like the demons don't know it is the Shield of Faith. If it was activated and they handle it, they'd be burned and know it was the Shield. If it wasn't active and they did not get burned when handling it, they may not know what it is. Perhaps they hung it for decoration. Or they know what it represents, and it is the bait for a trap. Our only real hope is they are ignorant of its purpose," Bob concluded.

Gloria surveyed at all the paper that surrounded them, said, "We've talked plenty about getting in and what to do when we are there. But how do we get out of this place? My understanding is we need to go to sleep to enter this realm. But this causes a contradiction. The sword came from this Dream World and physically appeared in our world once you woke up. But you haven't carried something from the physical world into the Dream World because you start asleep. So how do you know you can bring something into the Dream World? The Dream World is a spiritual place with real connections to the physical world. In theory, physical/spiritual materials should pass through in both directions, but if it doesn't, then what do we do? It seems we'd be in big trouble," stated Gloria.

"Caroline gave a clue for leaving the Dream World. I woke Caroline, and she left to find an exit. When the demon approached, she cried out to Jesus, and she woke in her bed. The same happened to me. I faced the big demon and cried out to Jesus to save me. Then I, too, returned to my apartment. I'm pretty sure we say that, and we can exit the Dream World and return to our world."

Bob injected, "I've been thinking about the nature and differences between the spiritual and physical realms and where does the Dream World fit. The Armor of God has two natures. The physical nature causes the Armor of God to look like junk. Then there is the spiritual side that can't be seen in the physical world. The Dream World lies between the physical and the spiritual worlds. It's like a bubble where the laws of both realms apply. Not only can our spirits travel there while we sleep, but so can objects with both physical and spiritual natures. I have to believe the Armor of God will accompany us to this Dream World."

"It will," I said. "Ramiel told me dual-purpose objects could travel between worlds. I wonder if any other such items can exist in both realms?"

"But you don't know for sure, do you?" Gloria accused.

"No, I don't know for sure, but this is where faith comes in."

"I'm still very new to this whole "faith" concept," replied Gloria with a tired smile. "When do we do this?"

"Bob, can I sleep here tonight? It's 10:00 p.m., and I'm exhausted. I also think the closer we are physically, the better we might connect to the Dream World."

"Then I would like to stay also," Gloria stated.

"Okay, Caleb, you're with me in my apartment. Gloria, you can sleep in the back room where Caleb slept last week. Keep your door locked. I don't typically expect problems with the homeless men that stay here. We try to keep things buttoned up just in case," Bob cautioned.

We escorted Gloria to the storeroom with a cot. Bob picked up some linen on the way and helped her get as comfortable as possible. He gave her a Bible, one of the New Testaments he regularly gave to new Christians.

Bob and I returned to his small, three rooms, if you count the bathroom, apartment. It was reasonably clean, cleaner than my own.

"I'm sorry I don't have a couch," said Bob. "The recliner, or the floor, it's your choice. I'll be back in a few minutes." He went to the bedroom.

I unzipped the duffle bag and carefully put on the Armor of God. A thought, and it transformed. The aura might be a problem. The demons might see us sooner than we want. I put the boots on last.

When I did, Scripture and insight rushed into my mind. Man, I wish I had this all the time.

Bob came out of the bedroom with a Bible in his hand. "We are going to a spiritual realm, and this is a holy book. I thought it might make the transition between worlds."

"I am not sure how we are going to connect in the spirit realm. All I can think of is as you go to sleep, pray to be taken there. Keep it in the forefront of your mind as much as possible. Let's go to bed now. Hopefully, Gloria has drifted off already," I said.

I had a hard time believing I could sleep. My nerves tingled away. *God, I know I can trust you, but I'm scared and need you to help us with this task.* I drifted off to sleep while praying.

Chapter 30

Caleb

Tuesday Night

A familiar white fog surrounded me—the place between worlds. Only one direction felt right. Hands out in front of me, I kept walking, and soon they met a white wall. The fog thinned, and the wall ran straight in both directions. There it stood, smooth without blemish, wrinkle, or doors. This was unexpected. A distant "Caaaaleb" floated to my ears.

"OVER HERE."

Footfalls grew louder.

"Brother Caleb, keep talkin'."

"Over here, keep comin'."

A human silhouette appeared in the fog. As Bob got closer, I saw more and more detail.

"You've got the Armor of God on."

"You've got your Bible, excellent. Any sign of Gloria?"

"Caaaaleb . . . Booobb, where are you?" Gloria called.

"I'll get her," Bob said and went in the direction of her cry.

I heard Gloria and Bob exchanging calls trying to locate each other. I examined the wall again. I poked and rapped it with my knuckles. *How are we to get through?* Foolishly, I kicked it out of frustration. I was still hopping around on one foot with my back to Bob when he returned with Gloria.

"Brother Caleb, what happened?"

"Nuthin', never mind," I responded and turned around to face them.

"Look who else we found," Bob beamed.

Delight danced across my face. "Caroline . . . Why are . . . I didn't think you'd be here."

"Nor I, but God has other plans, I guess," she smiled.

Gloria ran her hand over the wall. "It's hard, warm, and silky smooth."

Caroline approached the wall and ran her hands over it. "When I stood on the other side, trying to leave the Dream World, I faced a blank wall. When I looked away and turned back, an outline of a door appeared. I didn't have to seek it out. Do ya' think there's a door along here?" she asked.

"Bob, how about you and Gloria walk 200 paces to the right. Caroline and I will go 200 paces to the left. If and when you find a doorway, return, and we'll meet here."

We separated—the fog filled in behind us as we moved apart and obscured our vision. I ran my hand along the wall as we walked because there was no contrast between the wall and the fog. With my other hand, I held Caroline's.

We walked and counted our paces; 10 . . . 50 . . . 100 . . . 200.

"There's nothin', but the smooth wall," I said, "Let's go 100 more before we turn around." We walked 100 more paces—still nothing.

"C'mon on Caleb; we need to get back."

"Okay," We turned, and 300 paces later, we found Bob and Gloria.

"I thought the hardest part would be getting out. I'm wrong. Gettin' in is harder," I said.

Bob turned to Caroline. "Exactly what did the door look like again?"

Caroline closed her eyes so she could mentally picture the door. "It was about eight feet high and outlined in blue. Along the outside of the arch was written. 'Come to me, all you who are weary and burdened, and I will give you rest.' I pushed against the door. It swung outward. I stepped through the doorway, and I woke up in bed."

"I think Scripture reveals the door to us, but will any verse or a specific one form a door?" Bob speculated. He flipped through his Bible. "Let's try the one Caroline read, Matthew 11:28."

Bob stepped up to the wall, lay his hand on it, and with a firm voice commanded, "Come to me, all you who are weary and burdened, and I will give you rest."[11] We watched. We waited, and nothing happened.

"Caroline, did you do or say anything else before you saw the door?" Gloria asked.

"That's right. I shouted something. Caleb told me something right before I left him in that room. The demons pursued me, one saw me, and I yelled: "Jesus save and protect me." I pushed against the door, it opened, and I woke in bed. All I know is I was scared and desperate to get out of there," Caroline said with tears of frustration building in her eyes.

Bob lay his hand on the wall and repeated Caroline's words. Nothing happened. He tried different combinations. Still, nothing happened. Caroline took a turn saying the same things. Nothing changed.

"Are we barking up the wrong wall?" I asked.

"God brought us all here for a reason. I doubt He would bring us this far and expect us to turn around and go home," Bob said. "There appears to be more than one way in and out. Caleb woke up from a dream. Caroline exited via a door before waking up. Caleb also flew above with the angel and observed the activity below and then flew back and woke up."

"Do you think the urgency of the need determines it?" Gloria asked.

"What do you mean?" Caroline queried.

"Caleb, faced with a demon, urgently needed to wake up, and he did," she explained. "Caroline recognized her urgent need for Christ to

---

[11] Matthew 11:28 NIV

protect her and needed an exit. The angel needed Caleb to witness the dream collection and the shield. If Caleb hadn't revisited the Dream World, then the shield would've been lost, the Armor of God incomplete. If the Armor is not complete, then Caleb's task might fail. Perhaps our need or the urgency to get in is not great enough? I'm scared. I don't want to enter. Maybe I'm holding us back?"

"That's an . . . inter . . . resting . . . observation," mused Bob. The proverbial wheels turned in his mind.

"Form a circle and hold hands," Bob instructed. Looking at each of us, Bob said, "I am going to pray aloud. Close your eyes and shut everything else out. Each of you must stress your need and desire to accomplish God's will in this place, at this time, silently. Act as if God is standing before you and beseech Him."

"Lord God, Creator of Heaven and Earth, we desire only to do your bidding. We are your slaves. My brother and sisters and I need to enter the Dream World to accomplish the task You've set before us. We are stuck and confess our need for You. If it is Your will for us to continue, then allow us entry into the Dream World. If we misunderstood the task, then please instruct us. Make your will clear. We urgently desire to do this for you. Please help us. In Jesus's name, we pray, Amen."

I slowly opened my eyes. Past Bob's elbow was a bed.

"We're in," I whispered. "Be extra quiet now. We want to avoid detection as long as possible."

Motioning them closer, I squatted down. The others followed suit.

"Try not to be shocked by what you see. We can't assist anyone now, but if we succeed, all the sleepers will be helped. Keep looking up as well as around. Remember, demons can fly. We need to move toward the center and get oriented. I don't know which direction to go. I'm hoping something will look familiar once we go further. Ready?"

Caroline, Bob, and Gloria nodded. Determination and fear covered their faces.

Crouching, I moved toward the aisle next to the first bed. Caroline followed, then Gloria and Bob brought up the rear. We passed at least two dozen beds before I popped my head up to get oriented. *Make the demons blind, Lord.*

A sharp intake of breath behind me spun me around, and I glared at them, putting my finger to my lips. Gloria pointed to our right. A demon squatted on the chest of a woman sleeper, claws buried in her forehead. Drool dripped from its toothy maw, and an evil grin twitched at the corners of its mouth. The sleeper thrashed, cried out, and then settled down. The demon laughed. It pulled its hand from the sleeper's head, and a golden filament followed. It dropped the dream wisp into the bucket held by its other hand, kicked off the sleeper, and floated away from us. We breathed a collective sigh of relief and continued down the row. As we neared the central aisle, I stopped and motioned to the others to stay low. I slowly raised my head to see what dangers lay around us. I could see distant shapes moving about in the gloom. Screams and mocking laughter punctuated the atmosphere. I ducked back down and motioned them forward.

We continued our creep and neared an intersection, and I crouched next to the last bed. From my left, I heard heavy footfalls. I quickly motioned to my companions, and we each rolled under a bed. A massive pair of mottled, red-brown feet with a five-foot stride walked by. Each toe, tipped with an inch-long claw, clicked on the floor as it passed. The sounds faded as the creature got further away. We crawled out from under the bed.

Profanity filled the air, and we rolled back under the beds. Carefully sticking my head out, I saw one of the spider-shaped demons. From each limb hung a collection bucket. It faced the way the giant monster had gone.

It snarled, "You big oaf, you almost dumped my load. Bad enough that I gotta travel da whole length of this stinking place." Profanities filled the air again as the spider demon turned toward us. I ducked back under the bed. It went past us to the left down the central aisle.

Now we knew which direction to go, but we still did not know how far. Checking once again, I rolled out from under the bed. My colleagues did the same. I motioned them to turn around, and we headed back to the wall. Once we cleared the beds, we squatted down. "The spider demon went that way," I whispered and pointed in the direction the imp traveled. "I thought it would be safer following the wall now that we know the direction. It helps that the cauldron is at the very end instead of in the middle of all these beds. Are there any questions?" Everybody shook their heads.

Standing straighter but still bent over, we walked along the wall. We made better time. We saw shapes in the distance, but nothing near us. We walked for almost an hour. The wall gradually curved inward, and the rows of beds got shorter. We had reached the end and crouched behind the last bed in the final row.

"We're almost there," I whispered.

I stood. Halfway up, someone grabbed my belt from behind and jerked me back down. I turned to glare at Caroline. She put her finger to her lips for silence and pointed. The floor vibrated with footfalls, a demon's head towered over us. If it looked down, we'd be done. I curled like a five-year-old child hiding from an angry parent. It had teeth like a saber tooth tiger with four-inch fangs hanging out of its hideous mouth. The creature's skin had the typical mottled tones of red and blood red. It turned and strode out of sight. I slowly got up and looked over the bed. This eight-foot-tall monster carried a 5-foot sword in its hand as it marched away from us. I ducked back down.

"Guards!" I whispered. "There weren't any guards the other night." I peered over the bed and saw three of them. The closest guard walked away from us toward the central aisle. A second one walked down the center aisle toward the shield and cauldron. I saw a third demon walk in our direction from the dais's far side. All three monsters met at the intersection near the cauldron and the Sheild of Faith. Then they turned and slowly marched away from each other.

I dropped down and waved everyone closer. I whispered, "The cauldron is a couple of hundred feet away. It's on a dais about three steps above the floor, and the Shield is behind it on the wall. The demon is heading back this way. We'll hide under the beds a couple of rows back and wait until the guard turns."

We retreated a half dozen rows and hid. Looking under the beds, we watched the demon's feet approach. They slapped the floor and got louder. I winced, like fingernails on a chalkboard. The demon's claws scraped the floor on the turn and gouged the surface there. We waited for the footfalls to become fainter. We crawled out and returned to the last row of beds.

I pointed ahead of us. "See the gap between the two walls over there?" The Shield of Faith wasn't hung on the white cavern wall but on an inner wall that ran parallel to the outer. They nodded their heads.

"When I tell you to move, that's where you're going. We'll hide there and make plans. The Shield of Faith is hanging on the wall behind the cauldron. When the demon turns, we'll crouch and move along the outer wall and hide behind the edge of the inner wall. Hopefully, the dim light will mask us from the distant demon."

We hid again as the creature approached. When the large feet disappeared from view, we silently left our hiding spots. In a single file, we moved along the outer wall and hid behind the curved inner wall. We waited. My heart pounded in my ears.

"The next time the demon turns, I'll run up behind it and stab it with the sword. Once it's down, we'll run for the Shield of Faith. You three dump the cauldron. I'll grab the Shield of Faith and take out the other two demons. Then we'll get out of here."

"I don't know, Brother Caleb," Bob stated, his face filled with concern. "It seems like a lot could go wrong with that plan."

"I'm open to suggestions," I said. "Anybody got any better ideas?" Caroline and Gloria shook their heads.

"Look, I know you're scared. I am too. All we can do is trust God to see us through this," I paused. "We do this together. You ready?" All three nodded.

We could hear the demon's approach. Its feet made a scuffing sound as it turned. I stole a peek around the corner and saw its back. Springing to my feet, I ran up behind it and prepared for a mighty thrust. One of the metal rings jingled on the armor jingled. The monster turned with a roar and stepped sideways. Missed! Off-balance, my momentum carried me past the demon. I turned and ducked as the beast's mighty sword sailed over my head. On the next swing, our blades struck, and white-hot sparks flew in all directions. Fear filled my soul. *Jesus, save me and give me strength.* I swung again, and my sword dug deep into its arm. The flesh smoked and bubbled. The beast howled and yanked its arm away. The Sword of the Spirit leaped out of my grasp when it twisted its arm away from me.

I expected the demon to vaporize, but it didn't. I hesitated. Then the massive sword whistled toward my head. I faked right, jumped left, and rolled beyond the creature's reach. I jumped to my feet and looked for an escape route.

The massive monster clawed at the Sword of the Spirit, and wherever he touched it, the skin burned, and it roared in pain. The creature grabbed it one more time and pulled it free. The sword flew down the aisle toward the dais. I raced past the demon and heard the thunderous footfalls of the beast chasing me.

I dove for the Sword of the Spirit, snatched off the floor, and rolled over, and held it straight out. The demon bounded toward me, its arm raised, sword poised, ready to stab me. Instead, it impaled itself on the Sword of the Spirit. A final roar escaped its throat as it dematerialized, and its sword fell to the ground.

Breathing hard, I stood and looked for the others. They had made it to the center of the dais. The women struggled to dump the cauldron.

I charged down the aisle to help Bob. The floor thundered as the massive demon ran toward Bob. He stood several feet from the dais and faced the beast lumbering down the central aisle. He held the Bible open, pages outward; an incandescent glow surrounded the book. "In the name of the Lord, STOP DEMONS!" he yelled. The demons paused. The one in the center aisle raised its sword and shield, and like a mad rhino, charged Bob. "And these signs will accompany those who believe: In my name, they will drive out demons. . ."[12] Bob declared with authority and power. A fireball rocketed from the Bible and burned through the creature's shield and chest. It toppled and vaporized as it fell. The shield clattered on the floor. The recoil from the fireball launched Bob backward, hitting his head on the dais. He lay there, groaning.

I faced the remaining demon, and it charged. These demons were faster and nimbler than they looked. At the last second, it dodged left and swung its sword. The tip clipped my shoulder. Flesh blistered and boiled. I screamed. It turned and swung again. Pain erupted in my thigh as the sword tip of that foul weapon raked my flesh. I looked up and saw the sword race toward my heart. I dodged sideways. The demon's momentum carried him past me, and I stabbed it deep in its side. It turned to vapor before it hit the floor.

Caroline ran to me. "Are you okay?" she panted. I nodded, yes. "The cauldron is too heavy for us to tip."

I glanced toward Bob and saw Gloria helping him up. He staggered like a drunken sailor, but he was on his feet.

I ran past them and up to the Shield of Faith on the wall. I tried pulling it down, but it stuck fast. I dug the sword under the edge to pry it off. It didn't work. It wouldn't budge. Desperate, I tried again to pull it down. It stuck like it was part of the wall. I sobbed. We're so

[12] Mark 16:17 ESV

184

close. Muffled cries of alarm drifted toward us from the depths of the Dream World.

I cried out, "Jesus, help us." Then I had the oddest sensation. The boots warmed and vibrated. A surge of energy raced through my head; Scripture coursed through my mind. It permeated my being. I knew what to do.

With authority, I called out. "Is not my word like fire," declares the LORD, "and like a hammer that breaks a rock in pieces?"

The Sword of the Spirit transformed into a mighty, glowing, silver sledgehammer that pulsed with power. Surprised, I stared at it for precious seconds. Then an idea skittered across my mind. With a mighty heave, I lifted the hammer and swung at the wall. The entire wall exploded into a million pieces, and they became smoke before they hit the ground. For a moment, the Shield of Faith hung in the air before it fell. I left it on the floor, turned, and ran to the cauldron.

With another mighty swing, I struck the giant container. The metal shattered like glass. All those hopes and dreams hung suspended for a second before they fell to the floor. They flowed and transformed the dais steps into a golden waterfall and spread out across the floor. Then like leaves on a windy autumn day, they began to swirl and became airborne. They rose higher into the air and blew towards the sleepers.

Caroline picked up the shield and handed it to me. It didn't look like much; two feet in diameter, banged up, it appeared to be an old garbage can cover rather than a mighty shield. I held it in my left hand and whispered, "Shield of Faith." The thing expanded and transformed unexpectedly. I expected it to be round and bronze. Instead, it became rectangular, curved, and I could kneel behind it and be completely hidden. The shield weighed a couple of pounds, and it looked like wood and leather. I held onto a wooden rod that ran its length.

Caroline pointed down the central aisle. "We've got to go." In the distance, reinforcements flew or ran hard down the aisle.

"Caleb, those flying demons . . ." Gloria yelled.

A pack of demons flew toward us, straight down the center aisle. They carried something in their hands. Crossbows! The lead monster reached behind its back and pulled an arrow from a quiver. The arrow tip ignited as the demon laid the shaft on the neck of a crossbow. The scene repeated itself all down the line of airborne monsters.

"Quick, get behind me!" I shouted. Bob, Caroline, and Gloria got behind me. The first volley of arrows soared in our direction.

Gloria screamed, "Caleb . . . the shield won't protect all of us." Almost on cue, the Shield of Faith expanded in all directions, and we all hid behind it.

The first arrow hit and rebounded off the shield. However, the rest of the shafts were going to hit us nearly simultaneously. Thud . . . Thud . . . Thud. The burning arrows clattered all around us. More arrows flew, and the Shield of Faith repelled them all.

"Let's move," I yelled. Clustered together, we moved as a unit. I kept the shield between our attackers and us; we turned right and shuffled for the cavern wall. The demonic shafts continued to rain down on us. Then the rain of fire stopped.

We peeked around the shield at the demons. "What're they doing? Why have they stopped?" asked Gloria. "Wait, look at the beds!"

Everywhere we looked, the people stirred. Their hopes and dreams returned to the sleepers. They woke up rubbing their eyes. As they looked around, they screamed or yelled when they saw the demons. They jumped up and started running in all directions.

"They're going to stampede and kill themselves," Caroline declared.

With a booming bellow, I shouted, "Over here. The way out is over here." The Sword of the Spirit, still a mighty sledgehammer, throbbed with power. I handed Bob the shield. "Guard our backs," I ordered. I ran to the wall, and with an incredible swing, I struck the wall. It sounded like a giant gong. The wall boomed and drowned out the people's cries. The crowd paused. The demons stopped. They watched as I swung again—another boom. I swung a third time, and nothing happened. Not even a tiny scratch appeared on the wall.

Lord, help us. What are we to do? I prayed.

A voice spoke into my mind: *Grow!*

Confused, I tried to decipher the thought, and then it occurred to me. We stood in the spirit world, and the laws of physics don't work the same here. I closed my eyes, prayed, and focused on growing in size. As I did, I found my faith grew also. With God, I could do anything.

Caroline yelled, "Caleb, what's happening to you." I opened my eyes and looked down. I was nine or ten feet tall, and the hammer grew proportionally to my size. I didn't waste any time, and with a mighty swing, I brought the hammer to bear on the wall.

BOOM! The sound deafened us. I swung again.

BOOM! Demons and sleepers covered their ears while fractures appeared at the point of contact.

BOOM! Fractures rapidly spread across the wall in all directions as far as I could see.

I swung one last time. With the impact of the hammer, the entire wall surrounding the Dream World shattered and fell. I watched it collapse in both directions. Fractures raced up the ceiling, and like the demons, the chunks of the chamber vaporized as they fell. Few hit the floor, and white fog billowed in from the other side of the wall. Chaos reigned. People ran everywhere.

"Run into the fog," my amplified voice bellowed. People heard and reacted. I watched streams of people running into the mist. A horde of demons flew toward us—time to go. With one thought, I returned to my standard size and grabbed Caroline's hand. Bob grabbed Gloria's arm, and we ran into the fog.

Chapter 31

Demons

Wednesday, Early Morning

"AAARRRGGGHHH," roared Antiveritas.

The demon messenger had curled into a ball on the ground. Antiveritas picked the imp up by the scruff of the neck. It uncurled itself and tried to avoid eye contact with the massive demon.

"Tell me again what happened." Antiveritas snarled.

"Four humans entered the Dream Collection Center. They . . . they vaporized the . . . the guards . . . smashed . . . dream . . . cauldron. Th . . . they released the dreams . . . woke the sleepers . . . shattered the wall . . . all the dreamers escaped," whimpered the little demon.

Antiveritas ripped the messenger in half, and it became a wisp. Turning, he focused all his rage on Ichabod Foe. Antiveritas grabbed him by the shoulders and picked Foe up until they were eye to eye.

"I . . . HOLD . . . YOU . . . RESPONSIBLE. You were supposed to find the Soldier of God, and you didn't. If he isn't in front of me in twenty-four hours, you will suffer," growled Antiveritas.

The blood drained from Ichabod's face. With a gulp, he nodded. Antiveritas dropped him, and he landed in a heap on the floor. He scrambled to his feet and limped to the door exiting the office. On the other side of the door, Foe paused and took a deep breath. *I am damned.*

Foe looked at his watch, 8 a.m. "Nogah, come here," Foe commanded.

A four-foot demon materialized in front of Foe.

"How may I serve Master-r-r," Nogah growled.

"I'll be in the conference room," snarled Foe. "You summon every demon on duty last night in the Dream Collection Center. I want to speak to each one. You get them here, and you get them here NOW!"

"Of course, Master-r-r. It will be as you have commanded."

Chapter 32

Caroline

Wednesday Morning

That was incredible! Anna! I jumped out of bed and bolted to Anna's room. She slept soundly. From my bedroom, the alarm rang.

I showered, woke Anna, got us both dressed, fixed breakfast, plus made two lunches. During all that time, I kept reliving the events of last night. Caleb was amazing. Bob used the Word of God to take out that colossal demon.

At 7:30, I left Anna with Grace and headed for work. I felt exhilarated, electrically charged.

I exited my building and merged with the heavy pedestrian traffic. I just about skipped down the street. Wait a minute . . . something's different.

Bob

Wednesday Morning

I woke, sat up, and looked at the clock, 6:30 a.m. We're back, and we're alive. "Thank you, Jesus!" I shouted.

Someone pounded on my bedroom door. "Bob, are you in there?" Caleb yelled through the door.

Getting up, I opened the door. Caleb stood there with a wide grin. "Did all of that happen?" he beamed. "You were amazing. I doubted about the Bible . . . I'm so glad I was wrong."

"I forgive your doubt, Brother Caleb," I said, all serious. He paused, unsure of my meaning. I laughed and gave him a friendly tap on the shoulder.

"Hey . . . Take it easy. The demon sliced me a few times last night." Caleb lifted his shirt and exposed a long, nasty burn across the ribs. I also saw the previous burn scars from a few days ago. "It's tender. I'll be sore for the next coupla' days."

Seconds later, someone pounded on the apartment door. "Hola, you guys awake?" Gloria called.

I swung the door open. Arms encircled my neck, and Gloria smothered me in her embrace. Released, she bounded past me and did the same to Caleb.

"I've never been so scared!" exclaimed Gloria.

For thirty minutes, we talked, relived the night, and praised God for a successful mission. I was excited, pumped up. I had never felt so good, so alive. Purpose and hope had returned to me.

"What time is it?" a panicked Caleb cried.

"7:10."

"Dang, I gotta go to work. Can I jump in your shower? I'll have to wear my clothes from yesterday," Caleb said as he moved to the bathroom.

That left me alone with Gloria. Her face beamed, and her smile wide with dazzling teeth. Her eyes sparkled and danced. Things felt awkward; I never had a woman in my apartment before.

"Sister Gloria, are you hungry? I don't have much, just some bananas and apples, plus bread and peanut butter."

"I'm famished. The banana and apple would be great. When Caleb leaves, I'll leave. A hot shower and clean clothes are calling me. I had better let St. Mary's know I'll be late." Gloria took the apple from my hand, rinsed it under some running water, and wiped it dry with a towel. She bit into the apple as she pulled her phone from her purse.

I excused myself to the bedroom, quickly put on some clean clothes, and rejoined Gloria.

Caleb emerged from the bathroom in his work clothes. He picked up the duffle bag, and he stored the Armor of God inside it.

"Man, I'm gonna be late," Caleb said.

"I can drop you off," Gloria volunteered.

"Thanks, that'd be great," he replied.

Caleb's cell phone range. He dug for it in his pants pocket and flipped it open. "Hello . . . Hi, Caroline. Uh-huh . . . What? . . . We will . . . Meet you after work. The same place? . . . OK . . . bye," Caleb hung up. "Caroline's all excited and says we need to go outside."

I opened the apartment door and led the way to the Missions' main entrance. Unlocking the door, I exited first. The others followed, and we stood on the sidewalk in front of the mission. The weather was fantastic. The warm air felt good, and the sun shone brightly. Lots of people crowded the streets heading for jobs or errands.

"Brother Caleb, what are we looking for?" I asked.

"I dunno," Caleb replied. "Caroline just said to go outside."

Then we heard it. Laughter. People smiled and greeted each other. Someone skipped, another leaped for joy. So different than yesterday. A man in a business suit approached, his face aglow and his large front teeth exposed in a huge smile. Reaching for my hand, he said, "Good morning. Isn't this a beautiful day?" He also shook Gloria's and Caleb's hands. He continued down the sidewalk and waved to all he met.

"There're no demons . . . on the street or the people. Yesterday, there were dozens of them," observed Caleb.

A spontaneous display of whooping, high fives, and praises exploded from the three of us. We danced around the sidewalk, bumping into people trying to get past us. Caleb stopped and looked at his watch. "I gotta go. Gloria, can you still take me?" he asked. Gloria nodded and headed down the block to her parked car.

"Bob, we'll meet you here after work," Caleb called from down the block. Gloria hit her clicker, and I saw her taillights flash as the doors unlocked. They got in the car and drove off.

I just stood on the sidewalk and smiled at all who passed. I stood there. My body felt like a sponge soaking up the joy and excitement of the passing crowd. Strangers shook my hand, wishing me a great day. I looked to the heavens to praise God. *What's that?* Up in the sky, above the building across the street, hovered two shapes.

Demons! So they weren't gone. They had only retreated. I returned to my office, subdued. We won a battle, but the war continues. Picking up my Bible, I went to the sanctuary where the riot of colors greeted me. The bright sun streamed through the stained glass. I sat in a sunbeam and opened my Bible. Bowing my head, I prayed.

Chapter 34

Ichabod

Wednesday Morning

Fear and anger smoldered behind Ichabod's eyes. He had interviewed demons for hours, and all he had were inconsistent descriptions of the assailants. The only monsters that had gotten a good look at them were no more. Once the people woke up, mayhem broke loose.

"Send in the next one," Ichabod shouted.

A six-foot-tall demon entered the room. "What's your name and rank?" snapped Ichabod.

"Slov, DCC Supervisor, t'ird class," it snarled.

"What do you know about the DCC disaster last night?"

"Nah, I saw people runnin' around, the wall crashin' down. You should've seen 'dat. Then all da humans ran into da fog."

"Anything else? Anything at all?" The demon shook his head. "Get outta here, you useless piece of . . ." Ichabod waved his hand dismissively.

Slov reached the door when he turned and said, "Dere might be sometin' else. A couple o' days ago, a couple o' sleepers woke up in da DCC. I couldn't find da name of da first one, but I did for da second. I sent Gorg to fetch her and make sure she got re-inserted into da DCC da next time she slept, but he never came back. Gorg was an idiot, but he never disobeyed. I reported it to my supervisor. I don't think he cared."

The wrinkles on Ichabod's forehead deepened. If this Soldier of God was with her when Gorg found her, he might have . . . hmm.

"What's this woman's name?"

"Caroline Sullivan . . . lives on Grand," stated the demon as he turned and exited.

Ichabod picked up the phone and entered a phone number.

"There's a woman on Grand Avenue . . . name Caroline Sullivan. Find out everything you can, then locate and follow her. If you lose this woman, you're dead. Report back this afternoon." Ichabod hung up and smiled for the first time that day.

Chapter 35

Caroline

Wednesday Morning

I thoroughly enjoyed the walk to work. It seemed like everybody greeted or smiled at me. My good mood vanished when I reached the Foe Financial Services building. Looking up, I saw demons, lots of them swarming around the top of the building. It looked like someone poked a stick into a hornets' nest. And I was one of the pokers.

I arrived at my desk without incident. My mood soon improved as I realized the happiness on the streets spilled into the buildings too. The good cheer and smiles were contagious. All day long, I heard snippets of conversations.

"I feel alive for the first time in a long time."

"I don't remember much about the nightmare, but now I feel great."

"A huge load has been lifted off my shoulders."

If only I could tell them what happened. The workday passed pleasantly and quickly. I can't wait to see Caleb and the others tonight.

Chapter 36

Gloria

Wednesday Morning

The shower felt great. My happy mood escorted me to St. Mary's. Only an hour late, not bad. Striding through the front door, I greeted Jean with a hearty "Good Morning."

"And a great morning to you, Doc," replied the happiest Jean I'd ever seen. "Isn't it a beautiful day? I feel so good. Best night's sleep ever."

"Yes, it's amazing how a good night's sleep brightens your outlook." I returned the smile.

The rest of the day went just like my morning. Everybody, employees, visitors, and the patients were all in high spirits.

One patient I met said that the sun rose in her mind for the first time in years. Another said the whispering had stopped.

I wanted to tell everybody why they felt so good but knew I couldn't. I'd be the one admitted into Saint Mary's.

Time flew by, and I realized I hadn't visited Angelo yet. The mid-afternoon sun streamed through the hall windows as I made my way towards his room. When I opened the door, Angelo looked up. He stared at me a moment. A serene smile decorated his face. He stood up and walked over to me. He threw his arms around me, gave me a long, warm hug, and whispered in my ear, "Welcome to the family, Sister. I'm proud of you. I know what you did."

I broke his embrace and stepped back. *Does he know? How does he know?*

"What did I do?"

"You accepted Jesus as your Savior and helped release the hopes and dreams of the people. You were there when Caleb popped the bubble, and the sleepers woke. You also show them the way out." He calmly said. "For the first time in a long time, my mind is at peace."

"What happened to you?" I asked as we sat down in the chairs at his little table.

"I've always felt connected to God and Jesus. However, my mental stability had always been fragile. I've been seeing counselors most of my life. Fifteen years ago, images and voices from the spirit world flooded my mind. Angels, demons, plots, deception, agony filled my head. I couldn't understand it all, and what I did understand terrified me. It was too much. My mind overloaded, you might say, "short-circuited." During it all, God periodically whispered to my soul and told me I had a role to play in the future. I needed to be patient, and when the time was right, my sanity would be restored. So I waited, trapped inside my head while my mind short-circuited."

Tears streamed down my cheeks. Angelo grabbed a tissue and wiped them for me.

"Oh, Angelo. I didn't know. I couldn't understand then, but I can now." I reached across the table and placed his hand between both of mine. "I'm so sorry. I was blind to what was truly happening to you."

We continued to chat. I told Angelo details of the adventure that I wouldn't have told anyone else. After a while, I asked, "So should I be filling out some discharge papers for you?"

His response startled me. "Not yet. You've won a battle, but the war still rages. There will be consequences for your actions."

His words chilled my heart.

Chapter 37

Caleb

Wednesday Morning

Gloria dropped me off, and I punched in two minutes late. Dang, the second time this week. Time flew. The good moods of the other employees lasted all day. Even more surprising, they saw me. Usually, I'm invisible to the office workers and managers, but not today. Today they smiled and said hello. I thoroughly enjoyed the day, well, most of the day. At lunch, I stepped outside and looked up—what a mess. Countless demons swirled around the top of the building. *This isn't over, is it, Lord?*

I punched out at the end of the day and just about ran to the front of the building where Caroline waited. She smiled as she ran to me. Her arms opened to hug me. She drew me close and brought her mouth to my ear. With the slightest whisper, she said, "Have you looked up?"

"Yea," I whispered back. "Let's go."

Caroline released me. I grabbed her hand, turned, and pulled her down the street, heading toward the City Mission. A block later, I realized I still held her hand. Embarrassed, I mumbled an apology and let go. We walked another half a block. Then I felt her fingers seeking mine. I looked at her. She gave me a shy smile and squeezed my hand. With our fingers interlaced, we went to find Bob and Gloria. I slowed our pace. Suddenly, I wasn't in a hurry to find them.

Chapter 38

Ichabod

Wednesday Afternoon

At 2:00 p.m., Foe's phone rang.

"What've ya got? She works for me . . . Here? . . . uh-huh . . . Administrative Assistant . . . 25th floor . . . Got it. Any husband or boyfriend? You don't know; well, find out . . . Anything else? Okay, you listen. Call Alec in personnel. ONLY Alec. Get her photo and address. Then you follow her. Do you hear me? Whatever you do, don't lose her. I want to know where she goes and who she's with. Then find out who those people are. You call every couple of hours. Got it?"

Foe disconnected, took a deep breath, and smirked like the proverbial cat that ate the canary.

Chapter 39

Wednesday Afternoon

Foe's henchman sat on a bench near the Foe Financial Building's main doors and waited for Caroline to leave for the day. Alec had emailed a photo to him. He had it up on his phone when he spotted Caroline walking through the main door with several of her co-workers.

Instead of leaving, she walked over and stood near him. He thought she spotted him, but he kept his cool. After all, he was a professional. She began to pace along the front of the building like a caged lioness. *She's waiting for someone.*

Foe's henchman didn't look too remarkable. He stood five foot ten inches with a well-muscled body hidden by loose non-descript clothing. A two-day-old beard adorned his pockmarked face. His stained jacket kept him warm while a filthy baseball cap hid his tight military haircut. The frayed brim obscured much of his face. He pulled it down as far as possible over his face and still covertly watched Caroline pace.

She fumbled through her purse and pulled out her cell phone. She dialed a number and spoke into the device. Ball Cap heard and mentally filed away much of what she said. Caroline hung up and continued to walk up and down the sidewalk.

About fifteen minutes had passed when a man arrived carrying a duffle bag. The two embraced, and they departed rapidly down the walkway. Ball Cap nonchalantly stood, hustled a bit, and fell into step behind them. He tried to listen to their conversation. Their subdued voices, combined with the usual street noise, made it hard to understand most of what they said. That didn't matter. He was a patient hunter. He only had to be observant and stay in the background for now. Ball Cap wasn't too concerned about being detected. The targets only had eyes for each other.

Chapter 40

Caroline

Wednesday Afternoon

I'm giddy as a schoolgirl. Caleb's face was in my mind's eye all day long. I recognized the symptoms of infatuation, and I hoped it turned into something more. God brought us together, but is that all?

I dialed Grace's phone number. "Hi, it's me."

"Hi, Caroline," she replied. "Let me guess. You're calling to ask if I can watch Anna longer."

"You're right. I know this is the third day I've called. I'm sorry for the short notice. Is it okay?"

"Of course, dear," said Grace. "Anna is such a delight. I love having her here."

"Can you put her on?" I asked.

"Hi, Mommy."

"Hi, Sweetie. Mommy's gonna be late again. You be a good girl for Miss Grace, OK?"

"OK, Mommy. Wait! Mommy, David ate some paste today in art. The teacher got real angry at him."

I laughed then replied, "I'll see you later, Sweetie. I love you. Please put Grace back on."

"I love you too, Mommy."

I could hear some noises as the phone exchanged hands. "Thanks again for watching Anna," I said.

"You're welcome, Dear," and with that, I hung up and dropped the phone in my purse.

Where's Caleb? I wish he'd hurry up. As I paced backed and forth, I kept thinking about what'll be like when Caleb arrived. *Would we hug? Would we kiss? You've got to relax, Caroline.* If only those demons would go away. Of course, the demons that brought us together.

Caleb came around the corner of the building and marched straight toward me. My stomach started to twist, and my heartbeat harder. A broad smile parted my lips. I hugged him as an excuse to put my mouth near his ear.

"Have you looked up?" I whispered in his ear.

"Yeah," Caleb breathed his reply. "Let's go." He grabbed my hand. My heart beat faster, and I couldn't stop smiling. About a block later, he dropped my hand and mumbled something. He looked embarrassed. What should I do? I argued with myself. *Go for it.* I reached out with my shaking hand and took his hand in mine. It felt warm and calloused. I squeezed it as our fingers intertwined, and I peeked at him. His eyes registered surprise, and then they twinkled. I could've stayed in this moment forever.

We relaxed and acted like any new couple out for a walk making small talk and laughing. We reached City Mission way too soon, and reality reasserted itself. We did have pressing business with Pastor Bob. The demons suffered a setback, but they weren't gone.

We walked through the Mission's door, exchange pleasantries with Fran, and headed to Bob's office. Bob's door stood open, and he saw us coming. He grinned, got up, and walked around the desk. He gave each of us a quick embrace and returned to his chair.

"Gloria called. She's on her way," Bob said. His smile faded. "You know we're still in trouble?"

"Yeah," Caleb replied. "You should see the top of the Foe building. It looks like angry wasps are swarming around their nest. What'll they do next?"

"I don't know, Brother. I don't know what the demons will do, but whatever it is, it's going to be nasty," a somber Bob replied. "I've got another, less important issue, though. We're short volunteers. I need to help with this evening's meal and preach a short message."

"We can help with the meal," I volunteered and looked at Caleb. He nodded in agreement.

"That'd be great. Thanks."

Just then, Gloria arrived. Another round of greetings and embraces occurred. I felt like we were old friends, yet only a few days ago we didn't know each other.

Gloria sat down. She told us about Angelo and what he said. Gloria explained his mental illness and how God used him to help us. She also explained to us his warning; there will be consequences for our actions. My heart skipped a beat, and a shiver ran up my spine, and I felt fear. Fear for me, my friends, but especially for Anna. If anything happened to me . . . I couldn't face that possibility.

"Brother and Sisters, I sense a lot of anxiety in the room. We need to pray," Bob said. "We need to rely on God, trust Him. He's helped us every step of the way. There's no reason to doubt Him now."

We took turns praying, beseeching God, and asking for guidance, peace, and patience. I felt better by the time we finished.

"Go get your assignments from the cook. I'll start the service. Fran will play a little intro music on the piano. I'll lead us in a few hymns. Caroline and Caleb, do you think you could help me lead the singing? Then I'll deliver my message and give thanks for the food. Then you'll be on to serve the meal," Bob said. "But right now, I need you guys to leave so I can finish my message."

With that, Bob gently kicked us out of his office. We headed for the kitchen to see how we could help.

Chapter 41

Wednesday, Late Afternoon

Ball Cap stood outside the City Mission Soup Kitchen and wondered how he'd get inside without drawing attention to himself. Dinner wasn't for a couple of hours. *I'll try the direct and act stupid approach.*

He yanked the door open. Fran, a bit startled by the sudden motion, greeted him. "How can I help you this glorious day?"

With a faked smile, accent, and urgency, Ball Cap said, "I haf'ta go to da bathroom RREEAALL bad. Is dere one I can use?"

"Oh, of course. Go down that hall, past the pastor's office, and it's on the right at the end."

"Bless you," lied Ball Cap.

He strolled past the Pastor's office. There were four people in there. The target and her boyfriend, a man he assumed, were the Pastor and an unknown woman. He entered the bathroom and peed into the urinal. He left the bathroom without washing his hands and returned to the front desk.

He smiled and said to Fran, "T'anks, I feel much better. Say, I saw someone I might know in da pastor's office. Who is 'dey? If it's who I tink it is, I'll wait for t'em.'

The always helpful Fran replied. "There's Caroline Sullivan, Caleb Kincade, Gloria Sanchez, and Bob Bennett, the pastor. Does that help?"

"Too bad, it's not who I t'ot it was. T'ank you for da help and lettin' me use da bat'room. G'bye." Ball Cap smiled. Once he hit the sidewalk, he looked for a place to inconspicuously camp until the targets exited. He pulled his phone from his pocket and called in their names.

Chapter 42

Ichabod

Wednesday, Late Afternoon

"That's great news. Give me those names again," Ichabod instructed. He scribbled them on a piece of paper. "Were they carrying anything?"

"Kincade's been carrying a duffle around."

He's the Soldier of God. "We're going to need some leverage," said Foe.

"Ya know, Sullivan's got a daughter. I heard her talkin' on the phone," Ball Cap said.

A delicious thought occurred to Foe. "I want you to snatch the girl."

"OK. I heard the target say the sitter's name is Grace, but I don't know where she lives," said Ball Cap.

Foe brought up Caroline's personnel file on the computer. "There's a woman listed in the emergency contacts named Grace, who resides in the same building. She's at 592 Euclid Street, Apartment 2a. Sullivan lives in 2b. Find the girl and take her to the old industrial park. You know where I mean?"

"Yeah, at the end on the right, got it."

"NO mistakes, hear me? Let me know the instant you have her." Ichabod hung up. He leaned back in his chair, face somber. Then the corners of his mouth curled up in an evil grin. This is going to be fun.

Chapter 43

Grace

Wednesday Evening

A knock on the door startled Grace. Walking over to it, she peered into the peephole. A man stood there with a package in his hands. A dirty baseball hat partially covered his face.

"Yes, who is it?" Grace called through the door.

"It's Quick Delivery Ma'am. I know it's late, but I can't go home until this last package is delivered. It's for Anna Sullivan, but nobody's home across the hall. Can you sign for it and give it to her later?"

"Anna's here," Grace volunteered. As she turned the deadbolt, she called out, "Anna, Dear, come here. Somebody sent you a package."

Anna scampered over, and delight suffused her face as Grace turned the knob. The door flew inward and knocked Grace to the floor as the man barged into the apartment. She struggled to get up. The mystery man punched Grace in the face, and she crumpled. The man slammed the door closed, stripped a piece of duct tape from the roll in his hands, and taped Grace's mouth. He flipped her over and bound her hands. He pulled a dirty cloth sack out of his coat pocket and slipped it over her head.

Anna stood, frozen with fear. The intruder stepped over Grace; his arms reached for Anna. She came to her senses and blood-curdling wail. He caught her by the wrist, reeled her in, and put his hand over her mouth. Anna bit his finger, and they both screamed when he pulled his hand away from her face. His right hand balled into a fist, and he jabbed Anna on the cheekbone below her left eye. She fell and lay there whimpering while he ripped another piece of duct tape off the roll. Then the man taped Anna's mouth and hands.

The whole process took less than a minute. The intruder paused with his ear up to the door, then he opened it and stuck his head outside into the hall. He picked up the large canvas bag he had dropped beside the apartment door. Bringing it inside, he laid it parallel to Anna.

The man returned to Grace. She moaned beneath the sack over her head and struggled to free her arms. He checked to make sure her hands were still secured and then taped her ankles together. The Ball Cap clobbered Grace again. She didn't move after that.

Anna laid on her side and watched him. When he turned toward her, she fought the bindings, her screams muffled by the tape. Baseball Cap picked up the squirming girl by her biceps and lifted her till they were eye to eye. "Don't make me mad, girl," he snarled. She kicked her legs to escape and nailed him below the belt. The man dropped her as he doubled over in pain. Anna scrambled to her feet as Ball Cap recovered, reached down, and grabbed her ankle. Baseball Cap pulled Anna off her feet and onto her back. He towered over her and slapped her in the face.

"Stop, or I'll hit ya harder," he threatened and drew his hand back.

Anna whimpered, but fire blazed in her young eyes. Ball Cap picked her up, placed her in the canvas bag, and zipped it closed. Surveying the room, he paused to made sure he left nothing behind. The canvas bag squirmed, and he kicked it until it lay still. Picking up the duffle, he locked the doorknob as he closed the door to the apartment.

A short time later, Grace stirred and struggled against the duct tape. Tears stained the cloth bag as she lay on the floor.

Chapter 44

Caroline

Wednesday Evening

What an incredible night we had serving the homeless and worshiping God with my new friends. Caleb and I shared a hymnal. It was just the excuse I needed to stand close to him. When I looked into his eyes, my heart melted. *Oh, Lord, please let these feelings be real.*

After Bob's message, we helped serve the meal. Caleb and I fixed our plates of food also and ate dinner together. Everything was finished by 7:30. There were plenty of people to help clean up, and Bob thanked us for our assistance. Gloria offered us a ride home that Caleb and I enthusiastically accepted. On the way to my apartment, I sat in the front, and Caleb sat behind me. Before we got into the car, I searched for an excuse to sit in the back with him, but none came to mind. So I climbed into the front seat when Gloria suggested it.

As we approached my apartment, I asked, "Gloria, would you like to come in and meet my daughter, Anna?"

"Si, I'd love to."

A pool of light from the street lamp showed an empty parking spot near my building. Gloria pulled into it, and we clambered out of the vehicle. It seemed unnaturally quiet. Closing the car doors shattered the silence, and the sound echoed off the buildings. The main entrance was just a bit further down the street.

I felt uneasy because I had been gone too long. To break the quiet, I said, "Anna stays with my neighbor Grace. I don't know what I'd do without her."

The front doors creaked as Caleb opened them, and I led the way up the stairs. "I live over there," I said, pointing towards the right. Our footsteps sounded loud in the hall. "Here we are," I said and rapped my knuckles on the door. No response. I knocked again, nothing. A little fear worked its way up my throat. "I-I don't know where they could be."

"Ssshhh," Caleb said. Then I heard it. A muffled cry came from the other side of the door.

Caleb grabbed the doorknob and twisted it. Locked! He took a step back, charged the door, and bounced off it. The door, clad in steel, could not be forced open.

"Do you have a key?" Caleb asked.

Fear constricted my throat. "In my apartment . . . I'll get it," I gasped as I turned and crossed the hall to go to my apartment. I dug into my purse, looking for my keys. *Where are they?* I held the bag open under the light by my door and found them. With the key in hand, I tried unlocking my door. My hands shook so bad I kept missing the keyhole.

"Let me," Gloria offered and took the keys from my hand.

Behind me, I heard Caleb say through the door, "Grace, hold on. Caroline is getting the key."

Gloria got my door open. I ran inside and pawed through the kitchen junk drawer, where I kept Grace's key. Things scraped and rattled as I sifted through the contents. *Where is it?* A sob escaped my lips. I pulled the drawer right out of the cabinet and dumped it upside down on the counter. Screws, scissors, and rolls of tape scattered across the counter. *There!* I snatched up the key, ran back, and handed it to Caleb.

He unlocked the door. As he twisted the knob, I shoved him aside and raced into the apartment. I glanced at Grace, bound and lying on her stomach, and ran past her, calling, "ANNA, WHERE ARE YOU? ANNA." I tore through each room, opening closets, looking under the bed and behind the sofa. She was gone. "Where's my baby?" I called and returned to the entrance.

Caleb and Gloria had freed Grace and helped her into a chair. Dropping to my knees at her feet, I grabbed both of her hands. I shrieked, "WHERE'S ANNA, GRACE? WHERE IS SHE?"

Grace's head slumped forward, and her shoulders shook with sobs. I nearly crushed her delicate hands in mine, and I struggled to get my voice under control. "Where's Anna? What happened?"

"Anna's gone," Grace cried. "Delivery m-man . . . sob . . . package for Anna . . . unlocked the door . . . barged in . . . moan . . . moved fast . . . hit me . . . tied me up." Spasms wracked her body.

Frantic, I asked, "But where's Anna?"

Grace regained some composure and said, "Anna screamed . . . I heard him hit her . . . couldn't see anything. I think he gagged and tied her up. I heard rustling and the sound of a zipper closing . . . some kind of duffle bag, maybe? Then I heard the click of the lock, and the door closed. I tried to get loose, but I don't have the strength. I'm so sorry."

Gloria asked, "Shouldn't we call an ambulance?"

Sniff. "That's okay, I'm bruised, but nothin's broken. We gotta get Anna back!" Grace declared.

I had only heard, "Anna's gone," and I froze. I didn't move or cry or yell, nothing. Emotion and thoughts filled my mind as I processed what I learned. Fear joined the panic: fear for my daughter, myself, and my friends. Questions plagued me. How did they find us? What're they going to do to my baby?

Caleb knelt beside me. He forced me to release Grace's hands. His hand caressed my cheek as Caleb turned my head so I could look directly into his eyes. He took my hands into his. "Caleb, what are we going to do?" I pleaded in a small voice.

Before he could answer, a phone rang somewhere. My purse lay on the floor behind Caleb. I stared at it. Everything seemed so unreal.

Caleb turned around, grabbed the bag, and handed it to me. I opened it and pulled out the phone. The Caller ID showed "Private." I answered.

"H-hello," I sputtered. Caleb put his ear next to mine and listened.

A deep voice spoke, "If you ever want to see your daughter again, you'll do what I say. Understand?"

"Yes-s-s," I said in a hoarse whisper.

"You, your boyfriend, the pastor from City Mission, and the lady doctor need to be at the old industrial park at 10:00 p.m. sharp. Look for a light in a window and go through the door next to it. We'll be listening to the police radio, and I'll have watchers all around. If I get even a tiny hint, the police are involved, your daughter dies, and we disappear. If you're missing one member of your party, then she dies, and we disappear. Got it?" the voice threatened. "Just to let you know, we're serious . . ." BANG! I jumped. A gunshot blasted my ear, followed by Anna's scream. "Don't be late." The phone went dead.

"What do we do?" I wept. "He's got, my baby."

Caleb explained to Gloria and Grace, "Someone's got Anna at the old abandoned industrial complex. It's a couple of miles from St. Mary's. He said all four of us: Caroline, myself, Bob, and you (pointing to Gloria) are to be there at 10:00 tonight. They'll kill Anna if they see a cop or if any of us are missing."

"Call the cops anyway. Let them handle it," Gloria snapped.

"NO, he'll kill her," I cried.

"He wants to KILL US!" Gloria countered. "We destroyed the Dream World, and he wants revenge. Does it make sense for all of us, plus Anna, to die?"

"You bitch." I lashed back. "Wouldn't you die for your kids?"

"Yeah, but Anna is NOT my kid," came the cold reply. "And I'm not ready to die."

"We gotta get Anna back. I'd d-die if anything happens to her." Caleb took me into his arms, and I sobbed into his shoulder. My cries filled the room. Several anxious moments passed.

With my face buried in his shoulder, I heard Caleb say, "Gloria, Christ is our Lord and Savior. Now we follow wherever He leads. Whether we die today or 50 years from now, it doesn't matter. Our destination is Heaven. Guilt would consume me if they killed Anna, and I didn't try to save her. I don't think you could either. For good or bad, we're in this together. You need to go with us tonight.

Caleb had finished speaking, and I turned to look at Gloria. She stared at the ground. A tear hit the tiled floor. She looked up, and another tear ran down her cheek, "You better call Bob and let him know we're on the way."

Chapter 45

Angelo

Wednesday Evening

"NNNOOOO!!!" Angelo howled. His hands tore at his face in anguish.

"GONNA DIE, GONNA DIE, GONNA DIE," he chanted as he rocked back and forth on the floor with his knees drawn up under his chin.

"NO, NO, NO, GONNA DIE, GONNA DIE." Images flooded Angelo's mind, images of death and evil. His brief time of sanity slipped away.

An orderly opened the door. "Angelo, cut it out, or I'll restrain you," he bellowed. Angelo cowered on the floor. The door banged closed as the orderly left in a huff to continue his rounds.

Whimpering, Angelo just rocked back and forth. He stopped rocking. Alert, he answered an inaudible question, "Yes, I will." He reached for the shoes that laid askew on the floor next to him. Once the shoes adorned his feet, he stood. "It is? It's unlocked??"

Angelo walked to his door and saw it had not latched when the orderly banged it closed. He cautiously pulled it opened and poked his head into the hall. With new-found purpose, he slipped into the corridor and moved along the wall until he reached the security door. That door was also not fully closed. He dropped to his knees and pushed it open just enough for him to squeeze through. The orderly faced the reception desk and flirted with the nurse stationed there. Angelo crawled on the floor, putting the furniture between him and the front desk. The coat closet lay along his route, and a winter jacket hung on a hook. He stood, quietly lifted it, and rolled it up into a ball so he could carry it under his arm. He silently dropped to the floor and continued to creep to the front entrance. He probably could have just walked out since the orderly and nurse only had eyes for each other. Angelo opened the front door. Its well-oiled hinges gave no sound, and he disappeared into the night.

Chapter 46

Caleb

Wednesday Night

Gloria drove. I sat in the back seat with my arm around Caroline as she cried into my shoulder. The passing street lamps created an oscillating pattern of light and dark. In front of the City Mission, Bob paced within an island of light. Gloria tapped the horn, and Bob lifted his head. He held a plastic bag in his hand. Gloria stopped in the middle of our lane. Bob needed to cross the road to get to us. A horn blared as an oncoming car slammed on its brakes. He mouthed an apology as he passed in front of Gloria's car and got in the passenger side. She punched the gas pedal, and the tires squealed. Bob asked no questions since I told him everything on the phone earlier.

Bob began to quote Scripture; his deep voice never wavered.

"The LORD is my light and my salvation;
whom shall I fear?
The LORD is the stronghold of my life;
of whom shall I be afraid?"[13]

"He gives power to the faint,
and to him who has no might, he increases strength.
Even youths shall faint and be weary,
and young men shall fall exhausted;
but they who wait for the LORD shall renew their strength;

---

[13] Psalm 27:1 NIV

they shall mount up with wings like eagles;"[14]

"Fear not, for I am with you;
be not dismayed, for I am your God;
I will strengthen you, I will help you,
I will uphold you with my righteous right hand."[15]

There was more scripture, a lot more. But as he spoke and prayed, our fears lessened, and our faith strengthened. Caroline lifted her head to listen; her tears dried up. Gloria sat higher, straighter. The knots in my gut loosened, and I knew that whether we lived or died, God would prevail.

Gloria pulled up to the main gate of the abandoned complex and slowed to a stop. "This should be the place. I drive by here often, and the gate is usually closed."

"Wait, I need to put on the Armor of God before we go in. Bob, did you bring the clothesline?" Nodding, Bob handed me the plastic bag. It contained a piece of white rope.

I stepped out of the car, and I put on the Armor of God. I slipped the yellow rubber boots over my shoes. I threaded the yellow rope through my belt loops. I tied it tight to help my pants stay up. On went the yellow safety vest, and I saved the knit cap for last. I needed a way to wear the Shield of Faith and the Sword of the Spirit so my hands could remain free. I took the white rope, threaded it through the garbage cover handle, and made a makeshift sling for the shield. I tied the two ends together and slung it over my back. I stuck the plastic tube behind the yellow rope at my waist. If I weren't so fearful for Anna, I would have laughed at how ridiculous I must've looked.

---

[14] Isaiah 40:29-31 ESV
[15] Isaiah 41:10 ESV

I opened the rear door and got into the car. The garbage can cover and the plastic tube jabbed me in the back. I stepped out, took the cover and tube off then sat down again.

"How come it doesn't look like the armor we saw last night?" questioned Gloria.

"I haven't activated it. Until I give the command, it is dormant. At this point, it looks like junk to me too, and that's what I'm bettin' on."

Gloria drove down the central driveway. We looked all around for a light, and we found it near the end of the road. "There . . . to the right," said Caroline.

Gloria turned and parked in front of the door next to the light. I looked at my watch, 9:58 p.m. We were on time. We got out of the car and moved toward the entrance. I tried the handle; it turned, and I pulled the door open. I entered first, followed by the women, and last came Bob. A faint electric glow came from the end of the hall.

"Hello," I called out.

"M-mister Kincade?" came the muffled reply. Caroline shoved me aside and ran past me. We ran to catch up. The light brightened as we approached. We entered a large room that had a single bulb hanging from the ceiling. Debris lay strewn about; papers, boards, damaged chairs, an upside-down table with broken wooden legs sticking into the air, and more. Under the circle of light sat Anna on an old wooden office chair. Her hands were tied in front of her, and she had several bruises on her face and arms. Her gag and blindfold hung loosely around her neck. Caroline had her arms around her, crying and reassuring Anna.

"All of you step into the light, NOW," a harsh voice came from the shadows. I waded into the pool of light and stood next to Caroline. Bob and Gloria followed and stood behind the chair.

Two figures appeared at the edge of the circle. Both were human; there didn't seem to be any demons. The older man stepped further into the light and kicked a piece of debris across the floor. Caroline lifted her head at the sound. He had a gun in his hand. So did the other man on the edge of the shadows. Caroline's sharp intake of breath signaled she recognized the man.

Caroline gasped, "Mr. Foe! I . . . What is . . . I don't understand. Why are you doing this?"

"Why?" he responded. "My Dear, everybody answers to a higher authority. By your aura, I see you belong to Jesus. I answer to . . . a . . . different power. A long time ago, God abandoned me when I needed help. And I was helped, but not by Him. A power greater than your God offered me a deal, and I took it. Weren't you among the many that wondered how I rose to power so quickly? How I built my financial empire? I had help, supernatural help. It was the perfect arrangement until you messed it all up. I find it hard to believe that the four of you destroyed the DCC."

"The DCC?" Bob asked.

"The Dream Collection Center. It's the facility you destroyed last night. Did you believe there wouldn't be consequences for those actions? Didn't God tell you it would be the last thing you'd do on this earth?" ranted Foe. "Where is your mighty armor, Caleb?" I feigned a surprised look. "Yes, I know all your names and quite a bit of your histories. And what is that junk you're wearing?"

"This is the armor I wore last night," I replied.

Foe snorted, "There's no way that's the Armor of God. Well, it doesn't matter. You're coming with me. There is someone who'd like to meet you. Step toward me, then turn around."

I complied but did not like the direction this took. Baseball Cap pointed his gun at the others. "Put your hands behind your back," Foe ordered. He crossed my wrists and tied my hands together. The ropes had a little slack in them. *Foe must not know how to bind a man's hands*. He turned me to face him.

With a smile on his face, Foe spoke to the henchman. "Wait 15 minutes, and then kill them. I don't care how."

"What do you want done with the bodies?"

"I don't care. Just make sure there's no way to trace it back to me."

"No, you can't," Caroline cried. "You told us that if we did what you said, you'd let Anna live."

"No, I said you wouldn't see her alive again unless you did what I said. She's alive, and you saw her. I kept my promise. Now you'll both die," Foe chuckled.

Foe stepped behind me and poked me hard in the back with the gun. "Get moving," he growled. I hesitated and turned to Caroline. This was worse than I ever imagined. It never occurred to me that we might get separated. It dawned on me that I might never see them again this side of heaven. It was easy to talk tough and spiritual, with no guns around. Now I feared for Caroline and my friends. I projected my terror and love for her through my eyes.

Foe pushed me forward. I tripped and sprawled on the floor. "Get up." He commanded and grabbed my arm and hauled me to my feet. He gave me another push toward the doorway in the back of the room. A line of dim lights lit the way down the hall. We left via the building's rear entrance, where his black sedan waited. He opened the trunk. "Get in." Foe snarled. As I tried to step into the trunk, he shoved me from behind, and I fell in.

"I don't want you getting any ideas about escaping," Foe said. The trunk slammed, and all was inky black. I heard the driver's door open and felt the car sag when Foe sat down. A few moments later, the engine roared to life, and the car started moving.

Chapter 47

Bob

Wednesday Night

As soon as the sound of Foe's footsteps faded, I addressed the assassin. "Listen, you don't have to do this. It's not too late to walk away," I pleaded.

He lifted his gun. "First, you assume that I find this distasteful. Well, I will enjoy this," he sneered. "This is how it's going to play out. I'm going to shoot the doctor first and then you, Pastor. Then I am going to finish the kid slowly while mama watches. Lastly, I am going to have some . . . fun . . . with mama." He leered at Caroline, "and when I am done playing around, I'll kill her. Lastly, I have a great place to dump your bodies. They'll never find you. I'm not sure whether I'll dump your car in the river or torch it here. After all that, I'll go home to a nice warm bed for a great night's sleep after a job well done. Might as well get started," he said, his voice stone cold as he lifted the gun.

"Wait, it hasn't been 15 minutes," Gloria screamed, holding her hands before her face.

"Lady, do you think I care?" He raised, steadied the gun, and fired.

"N-N-N-O-O-O," Angelo cried as he sailed out of the darkness between Doctor Sanchez and the assassin. The bullet hit him in the chest, and he fell to the ground. Surprised, the gunman hesitated, and I made my move. I scooped up a two-by-four lying on the floor. I swung the board hitting his arm and sending the gun across the room. I readied another blow, and then my skull rang like a gong from the impact of his fist. He hammered me with expert blows. I didn't have a chance. I collapsed to my knees, and blood streamed from my forehead and nose. My right eye swelled shut. *Dear Jesus, give me strength.*

He walked over to the gun and bent to pick it up. I wobbled to my feet. He turned, aimed, and Caroline came flying in. She pushed his arm up, and the gun fired into the ceiling. Caroline held on tight as he pummeled her with his left hand. They danced around the room, and the gun went off three more times. Agony exploded in my arm as a bullet passed through my left bicep. He shook Caroline loose, and she fell to the floor by my feet.

"You're gonna pay, lady," he growled. He aimed the gun, and I charged him like a linebacker. My shoulder hit him in the gut. He sailed up and backward, followed by a sickening crunch. The assassin lay on his back with one of the broken, sharp, wooden table legs protruding through his torso. He lifted his head and looked at the wooden spike protruding from his abdomen. He wore a surprised look on his face; then, his head flopped back as he died.

I breathed a sigh of relief and went to check on Caroline. Loose debris and bits of paper started to fly about the room. I saw the spirit of the dead assassin rise from his body. He looked around as his death registered. He looked down at his torso.

"This isn't the way it's supposed to be." He took a couple of steps toward me. "I'm supposed to get a reward," said the specter. I caught movement out of the corner of my eye. I saw dark wispy shapes with embers for eyes in the shadows at the edge of the light. They leisurely circled us; their red eyes focused on the fresh soul. A hole opened beneath his feet. An unholy smell wafted up from the opening, as well as shrieks of agony. A plume of flames erupted from the rift in the floor.

"NO . . . NO! You can't do this to me. It's not supposed to be like this," the apparition cried, and like water going down a drain, the assassin's spirit twisted and sank into the floor. His elbows caught the edge of the hole where he hung there, engulfed in flames and wailing in pain. The opening widened slightly, and he disappeared into the abyss. The dark spirits followed him, and then it closed.

Screams assailed my ears, and I turned. Gloria sat on the floor, crying. Angelo's head lay in her lap. She applied pressure to his wound, but blood oozed between her fingers. He gurgled with every breath.

I turned to Caroline. Anna lay on the floor with her abdomen soaked in blood. She barely breathed. Caroline pressed on the wound with the palm of her hand, trying to stop the bleeding.

I pulled out my cell phone and dialed 911. I put it up to my ear and nothing, no reception. A cry escaped my lips, and I ran outside to find a signal. Once out, I found a weak one and redialed 911. They answered the phone. "There have been shots fired and people wounded and killed at the old industrial park. We need at least three ambulances and police. The main entrance is open, and we're in the warehouse at the end on the right. Please hurry."

The operator asked a few more questions, and I am not even sure I answered them. "I gotta go," and I hung up. Running back inside, I found both women still sobbing and trying to stop the bleeding. Anna looked terrible, but the flow of blood had slowed.

Angelo was a different story. The bullet must have hit a major artery.

This can't be happening. Fearful and frantic, I looked around for anything that might help Angelo: an old first aid kit, something to use as a bandage, anything. Someone stood in the shadows, and I heard faint sirens in the distance. "Quick, you need to help him; he's going to die," I cried.

Angelo opened pain-filled eyes. "Doc, you're alive . . . I'm so happy," he smiled.

"Oh, Angelo, why'd you do that?" Gloria wept.

"God asked . . . me to . . . save . . . y . . ." his body relaxed as he released his last breath.

Tears poured from Gloria's eyes as she rocked back and forth, hugging Angelo.

The figure stepped into the light and, with a gentle voice, said, "No, he's not going to die. He's going to live truly. You've done well, Angelo. It's time for your reward. Are you ready?" The newcomer held out his hand.

"Are you crazy?" Gloria screamed. "He's de. . . " Her voice trailed off as Angelo's arm lifted and grabbed the hand. The stranger pulled and took a step back, and as he did so, Angelo stood. But Angelo also lay on the ground in a pool of blood. I looked at the one then the other, and it dawned on me. The stranger was an angel.

"Thank you, Doctor, for all the care you gave to my earthly body. I am well and whole for the first time. Goodbye, for now, Doc. We'll meet again." Angelo turned to the angel and spoke one last time, "I'm ready." They stepped towards the shadows and faded from sight.

Gloria laughed and cried, joy and sorrow intermixed. I turned my attention to Caroline. Anna still lived, but barely. The sound of sirens and tires sliding on gravel stopped just outside the building. I ran out and signaled them. I led the police into the room, followed by the paramedics.

We hurried down the hall; I said over my shoulder, "There are two men dead and a little girl shot in the abdomen. She needs your attention first." They came into the room. Two paramedics immediately started working on Anna; a third checked the dead bodies, and the police surveyed the scene.

Exhaustion gripped me. I turned over a chair and flopped down. The third paramedic made a call on his radio. The police searched the area. *Oh, Lord, what do we say? We should have some common reasons for being here.*

Somebody set up some lights. More and more people arrived. Additional police and medical personnel entered the room. A couple of people with "Medical Examiner" on their backs took care of the bodies. Flashes lit up the room as someone else took photographs. Little red numbers sprouted like mushrooms at various points on the floor.

A paramedic came over to me. "All right, let's check you out."

"Why? I'm fine," I said in a daze.

"No, you're not. I see at least one bullet wound on your arm, and your face looks like it's been used as a punching bag," the paramedic replied.

A man in a suit with a badge on the lapel entered the room. He spoke briefly to a uniformed officer who pointed towards me. The paramedic worked on my injuries as the suit walked over. He scowled like he swallowed something distasteful.

The officer spoke, "My name is Detective Wright. What's your name, and what happened here?"

"I'm Pastor Bob Bennett, Senior Pastor of Stanton Community Church." The paramedic probed my wound, " HEY!"

I turned my attention back to the detective, and my mouth vomited most of the story. I talked so fast; I wasn't even sure what I was saying. "Slow down, Pastor. Please start at the beginning. Go slow and think about what you are saying," Detective Wright insisted.

"Earlier tonight, myself, Dr. Gloria Sanchez, Caroline Sullivan, and Caleb Kincade, served dinner to the homeless at the City Mission. Anna, Caroline's daughter, stays with a neighbor when Caroline works or is at the Mission. An assailant, I assume it was the dead guy over there . . ." I recapped the whole evening for Officer Wright. I even mentioned the Dream Collection Center, but I made it sound like I didn't know what that was. I gave him the details about the fight with the assassin. I told him about Angelo and his death, minus the angel. I just hoped no one told a conflicting story.

"We didn't know what he planned, and I know we should've called the police, but he said he'd kill the child if we did."

The paramedic had to cut my shirt sleeve off to get to the bullet wound. I raised my arm gingerly so the medic could wrap it with bandages. I winced, and with my good eye, I peered around the room. Anna lay on a stretcher going toward the exit, and Caroline followed. I couldn't see Gloria.

I turned back to the detective. "None of us are rich or famous, and we didn't understand what he wanted. We arrived, hoping to quietly and quickly resolve whatever the issue was.

"Officer, we need to get him to the hospital. You can question them there," said the paramedic. "Pastor Bennett, please lie down." He supported me as I sat, then laid back on the gurney.

As the paramedic strapped me down, I said, "One more thing, Detective, I don't know who the dead guy was, but Caroline identified the other man as Ichabod Foe, CEO of Foe Financial Services."

The Detective grunted and shook his head. They wheeled me out, loaded me into the ambulance, and whisked me away.

Chapter 48

Caleb

Wednesday Night

Pain assaulted my senses. I kept trying to loosen the rope. It was looser, but I still couldn't free my hands. Junk and sharp objects filled Foe's trunk. Every time he hit a bump, something stabbed me. I felt the wet stickiness of blood between my skin and clothing. Time became a long series of jolts and jabs. I had no idea where Foe intended to go or how long I would have to endure this torture.

I focused on removing my bonds. They loosen but not loose enough to free my hands. I couldn't believe Foe didn't recognize the Armor of God. As much pain as I was in, I feared more for the others than myself, especially Caroline and Anna. *Damn you, Foe! Lord, please keep them safe.*

Chapter 49

Caroline

Wednesday Night

The world around me disappeared, and Anna was the only thing that existed. *I SHOT MY DAUGHTER!* My soul tore—every molecule of my body cried out in anguish. *Lord, let her live . . . please!* Consumed with fear for Anna, I barely functioned.

I didn't know what to do. Anna lay unconscious before me as I knelt next to her. I slipped my sweater off and rested her head on it. My tears cascaded down my face while the blood staining her t-shirt grew. *Must stop the blood.* I pressed my palms against the bullet hole. The external bleeding stopped, but I knew the blood pooled inside my baby.

I didn't know the paramedics had arrived until one of them gently moved me aside. "Let us take care of her," he murmured. I stood to make room for them, which broke my fixation on her. I surveyed the space around me, looking for the others. The dust hung in the beams of the work-lights as if time had stopped. Two men lifted the assassin off the broken table leg. More responders poured into the room. I looked down and didn't miss the grim look that passed between the paramedics. A third one tried to attend to my injuries. I couldn't understand what he wanted and pushed him away. He tried again: I punched him. He marked something on a clipboard and departed.

Where are the others? Gloria sat on the floor and cradled Angelo's body. Bob perched on a stool, surrounded by medics and police. *Where's Caleb? I need him!* Then I remembered. Foe took him.

229

Some detective tried asking me questions. I gave him our names and where we lived, but I couldn't focus on what he said. He gave up when they put Anna on a stretcher, and I trailed behind them outside. They threw open the ambulance doors and loaded Anna's gurney. I tried to climb into the ambulance, and the paramedic held up his hand to stop me.

"Sorry, Ma'am. Normally you could ride back here, but your daughter is too badly injured. I need room to work. I'm sorry," said the paramedic. He was gentle but firm.

The mama bear in me rose on its hind legs. "I WON'T LEAVE MY BABY!"

Exasperated, he said, "Jump in the front seat, hurry," he said as the door closed.

I ran to the passenger door and found it locked. The driver fumbled with the buttons on his armrest. I heard a click, yanked the door open, and jumped in.

The engine roared, and the tires spun on the gravel. The siren wailed.

"Thank you," I whispered. The driver grunted a reply.

We sped through intersections and weaved around the few cars on the road.

I prayed for Anna the entire trip to the hospital. Outside the passenger window, a staccato of light and dark kept pace with the ambulance. I moaned and didn't even know what I was praying, but I trusted God would understand them.

Upon arrival, the hospital doors burst open, doctors, nurses, and orderlies spewed out. Everyone carried some kind of instrument or device. Each seemed to be yelling something into the organized chaos. I opened the door, thanked the driver again, jumped out, and raced to the back of the ambulance. They offloaded Anna and wheeled her into the emergency room. I followed and stood on the edge of the triage room. Doctors and nurses swarmed around Anna, hooking her up to the equipment calling out orders and questions.

Suddenly, like a swarm of locusts, they flew out of the room, pushing Anna in front of them. A couple of nurses jogged ahead to open doors. I ran to keep up. A middle-aged nurse intercepted me, grabbed my bicep, and pulled me aside.

"I'm sorry, but you can't go past this point. Come with me, please. I'll show you where to wait." I fought her and pulled my arm free. Her hand shot out like a striking cobra; her nails bit into my forearm. She spun me around to face her. "Ms. Sullivan, please, you can't go in there. There is nothing you can do right now. Come with me."

She took me to a private waiting room. The nurse sat me down and asked questions about our names, address, insurance, and more. She slipped mysterious papers in front of me, and I signed without reading them. She turned on the TV and left.

A few minutes later, she and another nurse returned with various medical supplies.

"What's that for?"

"Why, for you, Dear," she purred. "You're banged up pretty bad. You have a black eye, several lacerations. The cut on your cheek needs stitches, and there's dried blood everywhere. Let's do what we can here instead of moving you to the emergency room."

Sitting there in a daze, I let her work. *My baby!* Soon, another nurse joined her. They rubbed, scrubbed, and bandaged me. The nurses finished and a Doctor entered the room. "Ms. Sullivan?" he asked.

Nodding my head, he sat beside me on the sofa and continued, his soft voice filled with compassion.

"The bullet did a lot of damage to her abdomen. We believe it nicked a small artery, which explains all the blood. Fortunately, we think it is small nick; otherwise, she wouldn't have made it to us alive. Her small intestines are perforated and digestive fluid leaked into the abdominal cavity. Not only do we need to fix the damage to the artery and the small intestine, but we need to clean the spaces between her organs. If we miss anything, she'll get a massive infection. She's going to be in surgery for hours. If I can, I will send word, but I can't make any promises." He got up and left.

Tears welled up in my eyes as I bowed my head. My shoulders shook with sobs. My body felt like a gaping, open wound. I hurt so badly; I didn't know if I could ever heal. *Lord . . .*

Chapter 50

Gloria

Wednesday Night

I wasn't injured. Angelo's body stretched before me, his head rested in my lap, but his spirit had left with the angel. I ran my blood-stained fingers through his hair. I had known him for ten years, yet I never really knew him until this moment. I didn't know what to feel, grief at his death, relief that I lived, or joy that he was with Jesus. I did not doubt that his spirit was whole, and he celebrated with the angels.

The paramedics and the police arrived. The medical personnel gave me the once over and discovered I was uninjured. Then the cop started in with the questions. I told him almost everything, but I didn't mention that we did destroy the Dream Collection Center nor about the Armor of God. I did identify Foe and then relived the events of the night. The ambulances with Bob, Anna, and Caroline, were probably at the hospital by now. *When is this cop gonna let me leave?*

"You're free to go for now, but we'll have more questions for you later, and don't leave town. I'm not making you go down to the station because I believe you. Do you promise to stick around?" Detective Wright asked.

I opened my purse and handed him my business card. "Please call anytime." My voice sounded hollow, and I walked down the hall toward the exit. My mind, spirit, and body felt numb. The car door creaked open. It took three tries before I stuck the key into the ignition, and the engine roared.

I didn't know what to do. Bob, Caroline, and Anna had gone to the hospital, and Caleb was missing. I guess I'll go to the hospital.

It took about fifteen minutes to get to the hospital. Generally, I split my time between visiting patients at the hospital and St. Mary's. I'm friends with many of the hospital's staff.

The quiet Emergency Room made me uncomfortable. It was too quiet. Shouldn't I hear something going on in the triage rooms? Shouldn't doctors and nurses be scurrying about helping my friends? Then a familiar voice came from the reception desk. "Hey, Doctor Sanchez. What's brings you here this time of night?"

"Hi, Jenny. I see you pulled the graveyard shift this week." I tried to put some levity in my voice.

"Yup, this week and next . . . Doctor Sanchez, is that blood? Are you okay?

"I've been involved with something terrible tonight. Three friends of mine are injured and here. Their names are Bob Bennett, Caroline, and little Anna Sullivan. Anna was shot. Can you tell me where they are?" A few tears dropped on my blouse. I reached for the tissue box on the counter and wiped my eyes.

Jenny turned to the computer and started typing. She read the screen and looked up at me.

"The young girl is in surgery. Her latest status is not optimistic. The mom has been tended to and is waiting in the private family waiting room."

She typed a few more things into the computer.

"Mr. Bennett is in Alcove 20 at the far end."

"Thanks, Jenny," I said. I turned and strode past the bays. The curtain hid any activity in Alcove 20, and I heard muffled voices behind it.

"Excuse me. This is Dr. Gloria Sanchez. May I come in?"

I heard Bob's weak and weary voice, "It's 'tokay wi' me. C'mon on in G'oria."

I moved the curtain to one side and entered the room. I checked the alcove number on the wall next to me because I didn't recognize Bob.

Eyes, black and blue, were nearly swelled shut. His forehead, cheek covered with a bandage, and his lips swollen. He sat on the gurney bare-chested, so I saw every bruise and cut on his chest and arms. The doctor snipped the last stitch to close the bicep wound where the bullet passed through. I wanted to throw my arms around him but didn't dare.

" 'Twite da sight, eh?" Bob half smiled, then winced.

"Yes, you are quite the sight to s-see." My voice and smile cracked as my professional demeanor waivered.

I recognized the doctor. "Thanks for taking care of my friend Doctor Anderson."

He smiled, "You're welcome, Doctor Sanchez."

He finished with Bob. Doctor Anderson opened the curtain, peeled off the latex gloves, and tossed them into a medical waste bin as he walked to the desk across the aisle. The attending nurse took away the used instruments on a metal cart. Doctor Anderson returned and handed Bob a slip of paper.

"We sent a prescription to the hospital pharmacy for pain management. You can pick it up on the way out. Sign here and here, and you're free to go. Also, you need to go see your Primary Care Physician in a week to take out the stitches."

T'anks Doc," Bob said as he put his torn shirt on. "Doc, our fewrend's daugh'er is in sur'ery with a gu'shot wound. D' you know 'ere her mot'er is waitin'?" Bob said through his damaged lips.

"I know where she is. I'll take you," I interjected. "I think we'll also stop by the laundry and see if we can't find some kind of shirt for you to wear home. You can return it later."

Bob stood, staggered, and fell back against the examination table.

"I'm a bi' uns'eady."

"Sit down, and I'll get a wheelchair," I ordered. I found one in the next cubicle and returned. "Get in. I'll give you a ride."

We wound our way through the maze of hallways. Fortunately, I knew where to go.

Upon arrival, I hit the button to open the door. Caroline lifted her head. It took her a few moments to recognize us.

"Is that you, Bob?" she cried as she got up and hugged him.

"Ow . . . care'ul . . . everyt'ing hurts."

Caroline came over, put her arms around me, buried her head in my shoulder, and sobbed. I engulfed her with my arms.

"I'm not sure Anna's going to make it," she wailed into my shoulder. She pulled back a little.

"I've tried to release her and give her to God, but it's so hard."

I helped her back to the couch, and she sat down then wheeled Bob closer. I sat next to Caroline.

Bob reached for our hands. "Let's pway," he said.

I don't know how long we prayed; time became meaningless. Then a tiny voice near me spoke. "Mommy, why can I walk through walls?"

Chapter 51

Caroline

Wednesday Night

"Mommy, why can I walk through walls?" Anna asked.

My head shot up, and there stood Anna. I saw the door through her. She looked angelic, innocence personified. My heart, already torn, shredded, and I couldn't respond. *My baby's dead!* Grief closed my throat, and tears splattered on my blouse. I fought to regain my voice. I didn't want to frighten her. I didn't know if she could understand what death meant. "Oh, Baby . . . your body's hurt . . . the doctors tried to fix it. How do you feel?"

"I hurt real bad b'fore, but I feel good now. What's over there?"

I looked where she pointed. "I see a wall, Sweetie."

"No, Mommy, on the other side of the wall. I see kids playin'. Someone's comin'."

We all looked at the wall. Then someone else passed through it.

The newcomer towered over us. He had a long coat on which hid his bodily form. His face radiant and decorated with a broad smile. Power, spiritual power washed over us. He came over and knelt before Anna.

"Hello, Anna. Are you ready to go?" he asked. Anna's head bobbed up and down.

"A-are you an angel?" I whispered.

He nodded. "I'm Ramiel. Caleb has mentioned me."

I struggled to get the words out, "A-are you g-gonna take my baby away?"

"Didn't you give her to God?" Ramiel questioned.

"Yes-s." Fresh tears streamed down my face.

"Mommmeee, can I go play?" Innocence asked.

I nodded my head. She stepped toward the wall, stopped, and turned.

"Mommy, why are you cryin'?"

"I-I'm s-sad S-sweetie. I-if you go play, I-I c-can't come with you. B-but don't w-worry, Jesus will t-take c-care of y-you."

I buried my face in my hands as I wept and, indeed, released Anna. *I give her to you, Jesus.*

I raised my head. I wanted to watch her as long as possible. Anna reached up and took the angel's hand. He looked down at Anna as she looked up at him. Their faces beamed with happiness as they strode towards the wall.

Anna stopped, as did the angel. She turned and looked over her shoulder at me. Her little eyebrows furrowed. I could tell her mind struggled as she thought about my words. She looked up into the Ramiel's face again.

"Mr. Angel, do I haf' ta go?"

Chapter 52

Caleb

Wednesday Night

The vehicle stopped. The car lifted as Foe stepped out of the vehicle. I heard him walk around to the trunk, and it popped open. The bright ceiling lights hurt my eyes and caused them to water.

"Get out."

Sore and stiff, I wasn't moving too fast. I got about halfway out of the trunk when Foe grabbed my shirt, pulled, and I fell to the ground.

"I see you're still wearing that junk. It's very fashionable."

I slowly stood and looked around. We were in the parking garage below the FFS building. Only Foe and his management team parked there. An express elevator sped the managers to the upper floors bypassing three-quarters of the building. I always thought they did this so they wouldn't have to mingle with us commoners.

"Get moving," he growled, digging the gun in my back. "There's someone who wants to meet you." He kept jabbing me as we walked toward the elevators. Trying to keep one eye on me and the other on the keypad, Foe punched in his code—a hum and clatter of cables emanated from the other side of the sliding door. I continued my attempts to loosen the ropes tying my hands behind my back whenever Foe turned his head.

He laughed. "You're in for a real treat." The door slid open; Foe pushed me forward with the gun barrel. I tripped and fell against the back wall of the elevator. He stabbed the button for the top floor. My stomach sank as we rocketed upward. The elevator door slid opened, and the barrel of the gun prodded me forward again.

We stepped into Foe's cavernous reception area. To the average human eye, it appeared as a colossal, open, empty waste of space. Most people saw a single desk in the middle where an aide usually sat, but I saw something else. The place hummed with activity. Demons of every shape and size sat hunched over desks or carried strange objects. Many flew about on mysterious missions. They zoomed through the glass, in and out of the tower at various speeds. Some turned and looked at me, but most of the monsters ignored me. After all, I'm just a human.

We crossed the expanse of the reception area and entered his equally large office. We approached the center of the room, and Foe shoved me so hard I fell to the ground. I worked my way to my knees and stood. As I loosened the ropes, my eyes followed Foe to the liquor bar next to the fireplace. He pulled a bottle of imported beer from the refrigerator and popped the cap off. I scanned the office. Islands of furniture surrounded by an ocean of floor dotted the room. Like little suns, each island had lights suspended above. A giant plasma TV, leather chairs, and fireplace formed one island against the back wall. A large conference table with twenty chairs created another. Lastly, an immense desk and technology center sat in the center of the last island.

"Is this him?"

I jumped and turned around. An immense shape stood in the shadows by the window. Foe strode over with his bottle in hand.

"Yes. You asked for the Soldier of God, and I delivered him." He took a long drink from the bottle and stuck the most arrogant pose I'd ever seen.

The demons back faced us. In the gloom, I hadn't seen it looking out over the city. The gigantic monster stood at least twelve feet high and four to five feet wide. The massive creature only wore a loincloth. His crimson skin smoked in some places and oozed corruption in others.

It turned.

"I am Antiveritas, Corrupter of Truth. You are the Soldier of God. You have caused me trouble, and now you're going to die a horrible death." Flames danced in his eyes; fangs filled his mouth below its snout. Two ram-like horns curled in a spiral around each side of his head—immense power like waves of heat radiated from it. Pure evil washed over me. My spirit quivered like a tower of jello, and I wanted to puke. *Oh, Lord, help me.*

"FOE, YOU IDIOT," Antiveritas roared, followed by a long string of profanity. "You let a fully armed Soldier of God in my presence."

More profanity followed. While Antiveritas raved, I dropped the ropes I had loosened. I reached around, grabbed the Shield of Faith, the Sword of the Spirit, and thought, *Armor of God.* The armor transformed into its true nature.

"Look at him, Foe. Look what you've done!" Antiveritas bellowed.

Foe turned, and his jaw dropped as he stammered, "I-It was junk."

Antiveritas reached out, stuck a clawed finger into Foe's skull, and stirred. Foe collapsed like he'd lost all his bones.

A moment later, Foe's spirit emerged and stood above his former body.

"N-N-N-O-O-O," came an unearthly howl. Foe's spirit dropped to his knees, lifted his arms, and yelled skyward. "Jesus, save me. Be my Savior. Forgive my sins. Don't let them take me," Foe pleaded. He looked at me expectantly. "Am I saved? How do I get to heaven?"

"That's not how it works," I replied.

A couple of dark spirits with ember eyes emerged from the floor and lazily swirled around Ichabod Mannheim Foe. A hole opened below him, and he darted sideways to keep from falling in. Screams and smells of decay emanated from below. Even more of the ember-eyed shadows erupted from the opening and swirled around the room. Foes spirit turned as he followed the elusive apparitions. They flew faster and faster, closing in on him.

Antiveritas laughed, "See you in Hell, Foe."

The hole quickly widened, and Foe screamed a long sorrowful wail as he dropped into the darkness. His screams mingled with the rest of the damned.

The mirth left Antiveritas's face. I sensed many presences near me. Turning to my left, I saw six giant demons, like the guards at the Dream Center. To my right stood six more. All carried swords or lances.

"Kill him."

The demons lifted their swords and strode toward me. Coarse chuckles escaped their throats as they anticipated my demise. They expected an easy kill because they thought I was alone.

But I wasn't alone. The Holy Spirit filled me with strength, knowledge, and speed. The Shield of Faith protected me and blocked the demon's swords. The Sword of the Spirit parried the demon's weapons and sliced through them, turning them into wisps. Their swords couldn't pierce the Breastplate of Righteousness. A steady stream of Scripture flowed from my throat.

"The LORD is my strength and my song; he has become my salvation. He is my God, and I will praise him, my father's God, and I will exalt him."[16]

"I can do all things through him who strengthens me."[17]

"Fear not, for I am with you; be not dismayed, for I am your God; I will strengthen you, I will help you, I will uphold you with my righteous right hand."[18]

---

[16] Exodus 15:2 (NIV)
[17] Philippians 4:13 (ESV(
[18] Isaiah 41:10 (ESV)

The living words flew from my throat like darts. Each time one of them landed, it caused the demons pain; you could see it in their eyes. I jumped and spun, slashed, and stabbed with skill, not of my own. I turned to look for the next attacker, and there were none.

Laughter erupted from Antiveritas.

"Well done, Soldier of God. Well done," Antiveritas mocked with a demeaning tone. "You are much better than the previous one. He was weak, and I easily defeated him. Yes, you're a more exciting challenge than the last."

"It would be unfortunate to let talent like yours go to waste. Do you know I have the authority to grant you anything you could wish for?" Antiveritas bragged. "Look out the window. Anything you see, any riches or women you can claim for yourself. You don't have to return to that loser life you had before God tapped you to do his dirty work. All you have to do is bend your knee and worship me."

Puzzled, I asked, "How do you know what kind of life I have?"

"Once I learned your identity, I learned quite a bit about you. You might say I asked around. Ha!" A puff of smoke escaped from his mouth as Antiveritas laughed. "Well, do you want to rule the world?"

"My sheep listen to my voice; I know them, and they follow me. I give them eternal life, and they shall never perish; no one can snatch them out of my hand," I quoted from John 10.[19]

Antiveritas winced at the Word of God. "Hmm, perhaps that was a little too grand of an offer," the demon contemplated.

"I could name you heir to Foe's empire and fortune. I'd even let you spend the money any way you wanted. Just think how much you could help that poor soup kitchen. You could start and fund dozens, even hundreds of organizations to help the poor and other Christians. I'd even let you evangelize and bring thousands to a saving knowledge of Christ. Just think of all the good you could do. Just bend your knee and worship me. No one needs to know."

---

[19] John 10:27-28

I replied, "You're just a pawn of Satan, and while your words sound sweet, they drip with deceit. As scripture tells us, 'You belong to your father, the devil, and you want to carry out your father's desires. He was a murderer from the beginning, not holding to the truth, for there is no truth in him. When he lies, he speaks his native language, for he is a liar and the father of lies.'"[20]

Antiveritas eyed me, "Your daddy aptly named you. You are nothing but a dog before me. He told me how you cowered before him." Antiveritas roared with laughter. "Your father even told me that you'd wet yourself as he tormented you."

Realization illuminated my face; dread filled my soul.

"Yes, I've spoken with your daddy today. Would you like to see him again?" Antiveritas asked, and with a wave of his hand, Father rose through the floor and stood next to Antiveritas.

Emotions washed over me; fear, loathing, hatred, anger like waves, they crashed against the shores of my spirit. I felt like a ten-year-old again standing before my drunken father, waiting for him to beat me with the switch I had cut.

"Kneel before me, you worthless excuse of a man and take off that junk," my father commanded.

I dropped to my knees and fell forward. Antiveritas roared with laughter. Prostrate, I lay before my father shaking.

"You still haven't taken off that junk. DO IT NOW!" father yelled.

I felt like that little boy again, terrified of my father. Waves of memories and fear pummeled my spirit as I recalled the torment and punishment he doled out upon me. *Help me, Jesus!*

As one of the waves receded, a rock appeared in my mind. I leaped onto the rock and clung to it as the tide washed over me. God's love flowed through me while the waves of fear and loathing subsided.

My quivering stopped, and I spoke words to the floor.

"WHA'D YA SAY, BOY?" Father screamed.

---

[20] John 8:44 (NIV)

I slowly stood and looked into my father's ghostly eyes.

"See what great love the Father has lavished on us, that we should be called children of God! And that is what we are!"[21] I said. "YOU are not my father. God is my Father, and Jesus is my Lord. You're a sad soul condemned to Hell forever. I pity you, and I'll never be like you. Return to that pit. You got what you deserved."

Father turned to Antiveritas, "M'Lord, I tried. Please don't send me back. Let me serve you here!"

"Take him away." Arms reached up from the floor and pulled my father down. Fathers' cries sounded much like Foe's. He knew he faced an eternity of never-ending torture.

Antiveritas frowned. Then it looked off into the distance like it saw something far away. A cruel smile split its face.

"Little Anna was shot in the struggle after you abandoned them. She died on the operating table a few moments ago. Jesus is not going to save her, but I can. Renounce Jesus, bend your knee to me, and I will restore her life."

Fear slammed into the pit of my stomach. I bent over as one punched, and tears blurred my sight.

"Oh, sweet Anna, what have we done?"

My legs gave way, and I knelt before Antiveritas.

---

[21] 1 John 3:1

Chapter 53

Caleb

Thursday, Early Morning

I knelt on the floor, slumped forward with my chin on my chest. Antiveritas towered above me.

Anna's dead! I felt like all meaning and joy in the world drained out of me. *How did this happen? How could God allow a sweet child like that to die in such a horrible way?*

I considered Antiveritas's offer because I'd give anything for Anna to live. Then a tiny tendril of hope sprouted.

I lifted my head, and with little confidence, I demanded, "You're a liar. Why should I believe you?"

"While I do love to lie, the truth often serves me better. Foe's agent failed. Your friends live; however, during the battle, Caroline shot Anna. Oh, it was an accident, but she died on the operating table." Antiveritas savored each word as he circled me. "It's not too late. I sense you love her and her mother. You thought you had found the family you've always desired. Will Caroline understand when she discovers you could have saved Anna? I can restore her life if you bend your knee to me," boasted Antiveritas.

A battle raged within. Anna deserves to live more than I. Caroline shouldn't forgive me. Our relationship would crumble. *What do I do, Lord?* I can save Anna. I just need to . . . No, I can't! Then a soft voice spoke words of love, comfort, and truth into my mind and heart. I knew God loved Anna more than I ever could.

I slowly stood and responded to Antiveritas through gritted teeth. "And we know that in all things God works for the good of those who love him, who have been called according to his purpose."[22]

Antiveritas no longer looked smug. His stony face showed no emotion, and I sensed he was a volcano about to blow.

"Very well," Antiveritas responded.

A massive battle-ax materialized in his left hand and a giant broadsword in his right. He swung the ax over his head and down. I jumped aside. The ax head buried itself in the floor where I had stood. The impact almost knocked me down.

With resolve and inspiration, which could only have come from my Lord, I knew what to do. I learned a lot from the Dream World. With a thought, my spirit grew to the same height as Antiveritas. I looked him in the eye.

Antiveritas roared again and swung his blade. Our blades collided, and sparks flew. We danced around the large office. Blow and counterblow, our swords rang with every clash. The Shield of Faith protected me from most blows. He stabbed, I jumped aside, but his sword managed to slip between the Belt and the Breastplate and seared my waist. No blood, only burns, from the spiritual wounds. Pain radiated from the seared flesh. I parried, and the Sword of the Spirit bit deep into his ax arm. Antiveritas yelled in pain, and smoke rose from the wound. He dropped the ax. Another swipe of his sword and the tip sliced deep into my left shoulder cutting the breastplates strap. Another flick of his sword tip cut the strap holding the breastplates side closed and another trail of burnt flesh. I couldn't hold up the Shield of Faith any longer and the breastplate flapped back and forth.

I barely dodged two more swings. One scored a long burn below my throat and across my open chest setting it on fire with pain. Another raked my right cheek from ear to chin. More bruises and

---

[22] Romans 8:28 (NIV)

abrasions appeared all over my body as Antiveritas hammered me. I cut deep into his right thigh. The demon's flesh smoked and sizzled with the sword buried in his leg. I yanked the blade out and stepped back.

Antiveritas withdrew. We both still stood and both wounded, but I was worse. Exhaustion and pain were all I felt and desperation set in.

"It is not too late, Soldier for God. Bend your knee and worship me, and I will spare your life."

Anna's dead. I loved Caroline and I'd never be able to tell her. The regrets in my life began to pile up. I was about to die. "Not today Caleb," spoke a voice, and a plan formed in my mind.

Antiveritas attacked. With a thought, I shrunk to my normal size as his sword passed where my head had been. I dropped the Shield and ran forward. With all of my remaining strength, I swung the Sword of the Spirit and severed Antiveritas' right leg below the knee. He teetered there for a moment and in the time I stabbed the other leg in the calf. For a second, he stood with a startled look on his face.

Antiveritas fell like a tree on his right side and hit the floor with a crash. I stepped in and drove the Sword of the Spirit through his eye into his skull.

An explosive release of power knocked me across the room, where I hit the far wall. The Sword of the Spirit and I clanged as it hit the floor. I sat there, head ringing with pain. I watched Antiveritas dissolve as he became smoke and dissipated. Agony attacked my body. I wanted to sit there forever, but I had to get up. I struggled to my feet and picked up the Sword of the Spirit.

Chest heaving, sword tip dragging on the floor, I turned and considered my next step. *Oh no!* I faced a host of lesser demons that came to watch the battle. I teetered for a moment and raised the Sword of the Spirit. Pandemonium reigned as demons took off in all directions. They flew through the roof, floor, or window.

In seconds, I stood alone. Well, not entirely alone. Ichabod Foe's body laid there in a crumpled heap.

I called 911, identified myself and my location. I asked for an ambulance and said I was hurt, and my assailant had died. Exhaustion threatened to knock me out. I realized police and medical people were on the way, and I wore the Armor of God. Burns scored my skin, yet the Armor of God was mostly undamaged. The Breastplate of Righteousness and the Helmet of Salvation had a few dents and a couple of straps were cut, otherwise it didn't look damaged. Gingerly, I stripped the Armor of God from my bruised and burned body. After I removed each piece, it returned to its earthly appearance.

Unfortunately, the duffle bag sat in Gloria's car. I stumbled around, looking for any container to hold the Armor. Foe's office was frustratingly sparse. I felt light-headed and knew I wasn't going to last much longer. I opted to put the Armor of God in a pile next to one of the oversized leather chairs.

Then I figured out I had another problem. My shirt remained undamaged since the spiritual weapon did not tear clothing. I ripped it off my body. I looked around for a lighter or matches, anything that could start a fire. I noticed several metal fire pokers in a rack next to the fireplace. I turned on the gas and lit the fire. The last thing I needed to do was I set two of the pokers into the flames.

I don't know how I remained conscious. When the metal glowed red, I took one of the pokers and wrapped Foe's fingers around the handle. Next, I positioned it like Foe had dropped it when he collapsed. The floor beneath the poker smoked. I returned to and sank into the overstuffed chairs. I struggled to remain conscious as I waited for my rescuers, but that battle did not last long.

Thursday, Early Morning

Two policemen entered Foe's office with guns drawn, followed by paramedics pushing gurneys loaded with equipment. One of the police officers held their hand up and prevented the paramedics from entering the room. The two officers split apart and circled the room in opposite directions, surveying the scene. Much of the room had been disturbed: chairs knocked over, a table tipped on end. Once satisfied that no one else hid in the office, they motioned the paramedics forward.

The male paramedic went to the man crumpled on the floor and felt for a pulse on his neck. Finding none, he pulled out a small flashlight and shone it into the staring eyes. He looked at the nearest officer and shook his head.

The female paramedic made for the figure in the chair. "This one's alive," she said and unpacked her gear. The male partner joined her, and they examined the unconscious man.

"What's this pile of junk on the floor? Is that a garbage can lid?" asked the female paramedic. "Look at the rest of the office. There's nothing here. Does this belong to him?"

"I don't know, but I need you to focus on him. Look at these burns," the male said. "I've never seen anything like them."

The female paramedic looked at the surrounding area. "Check out the floor to your right. See the fire poker and scorch marks? You don't suppose . . ." and her voice trailed off as she realized what must have happened.

"Will you stop! Hand me the gauze and tape and help me with this patient."

Both policemen approached the dead man on the floor. "I think that is Icabod Foe," said the taller one as the shorter officer knelt and carefully looked for a wallet. He found it in the back pocket and pulled it out, opened it, and removed the driver's license. "Man, it is Ichabod Foe. Do you realize what a political mess this is going to be? I better call the Captain and let him know."

Other police officers entered the room. A burly man wearing a black overcoat arrived and barked orders. Camera flashes lit up the room like lightning during a summer thunderstorm—little tents with numbers littered the floor.

The paramedics finished with the unconscious man and lifted him onto the gurney. They inserted an I.V. into his arm, attached a bottle of saline solution, and laid it on his chest. Then they gathered up the rest of their gear and wheeled him to the elevator and down to the ambulance.

As they wheeled the gurney past the police officer, the woman paramedic said, "Detective, there's a pile of odd items next to the chair. They don't fit with the rest of the room, and I think they may belong to this guy. I don't know if it is relevant or not, but I figured I'd let you know."

He grunted a "Thanks" and strolled over to the chair. He picked up each item and examined it. "Great, this case gets stranger by the minute."

Chapter 55

Caleb

Thursday, Early Morning

I bounced, and every inch of my body hurt. A moan rose from my throat.

Movement. I must be in an ambulance. I opened my eyes. The paramedic noticed I was awake.

"You're in an ambulance on the way to the hospital. What's your name?"

"Caleb Kincade."

"What caused your burns?"

"Fire . . . poker," I rasped.

"Many are severe. Some of the burns are very deep. I've never seen anything like it."

I passed out again.

Sometime later, I woke to a room with sterile walls and someone poking and prodding me. A doctor, assisted by a nurse, dressed my wounds. I closed my eyes as they continued their work.

"Mr. Kincade, the police want to talk to you," someone said.

I opened my eyes, and a cop hovered over me.

"I'm Detective Wright. Can you answer a few questions?"

I nodded.

"How did Mr. Foe die?"

"I don't know. Foe tortured me . . . burn me . . . drag'd a hot fire poker across my skin. Hit me. Asked . . . insane questions. Then he collapsed. I got out of my bindings and called 911. I must have passed out in the chair."

252

"Give it to me from the top," Detective Wright asked, clearly perturbed. "Please tell me in as much detail as possible. I am recording this conversation, so there is no misunderstanding."

Exhausted and drugged up with pain meds, I didn't feel like talking to the cop. With a hoarse voice, I explained how we had returned to Caroline's apartment and found Grace tied up. I told him almost everything except anything related to the Armor of God, demons, or spirits. *Where is the armor?*

When finished, I asked, "Do you know where my clothes are?"

"What's left of them are in a bag under the bed," the nurse offered.

"There was also a plastic tube and round garbage can lid, a knit cap, vest, and a couple of more things. Do you know where they are?"

"They're in my car. Why?" responded Detective Wright.

"They belong to me also. I know these items look like junk, but they have value to me. Can I have them?" I asked.

The Detective replied, "Any and all physical items found in the room are being treated as evidence. If they're proven not to be, then you can have them back. This whole thing is weird on a level I've never seen before. Is there anything else you can tell me?"

"No, I don't think so. I'm having a hard time thinking. Are we done?"

"There will be an investigation to see if charges are needed. Don't leave the area, Mr. Kincade. You'll be hearing from us very soon," He warned.

Detective Wright left, and the doctor re-entered. "Mr. Kincade, we want to observe you for at least eight hours. If you're okay at the end of that time, you can go home."

"Something happened tonight, and some friends of mine may have been hurt. Do you know anything about Caroline and Anna Sullivan, Bob Bennett, and Gloria Sanchez?"

"Yes, the little girl was in surgery. I don't know her condition. I patched up Pastor Bennett a while ago. I'll let them know you're here.

You need to get some rest." The doctor said as he closed the curtain, and I could hear his footfalls fade.

Tears pooled in my eyes, my throat constricted, and I choked a sob down. *Oh, Anna, I'm sorry I couldn't save you. The cost was too high.*

Chapter 56

Caroline

Thursday, Early Morning

Gloria sat next to me on the couch. Bob had pulled up a chair. We held hands, wept, and prayed while the TV droned in the background.

Anna and the angel had faded away. We didn't know which direction they went. It didn't matter. Whether she lived or died, I was at peace and would accept the outcome.

The clock on the wall showed it was 6:30 a.m. We had been here all night. I could tell the hospital awakened as more people and noise filled the hall. The night shift prepared to leave, and the day shift arrived.

A weary Dr. Daniels entered the waiting room. We stood and waited for him to speak. Those few seconds felt like hours.

"Anna is alive and in Intensive Care. You can see her in a few minutes. But she died on the operating table. We kept CPR and oxygen going for almost ten minutes. I declared her dead at 3:17. We had stripped off our surgical gowns, and I had left the operating room. One of the nurses was about to shut down the heart monitor when her heart began to beat on its own. She called us back, and we finished the surgery. She's been in the ICU for about an hour. I didn't dare leave her until she was stable."

"Ms. Sullivan, I've never seen nor believed in miracles until now," Dr. Daniels said. "Anna was dead for a long time. We won't know the extent of the brain damage until she wakes up."

"Brain damage?" panic crept into my voice.

"She was dead. Her brain had little or no oxygen for at least eight minutes. The longest the brain can usually survive without oxygen is about four minutes. If there is no brain damage, then this will truly be a miracle. A nurse will get you in a few moments. You may go up, but your friends will need to stay here. At this point in her recovery, only immediate family is allowed in ICU."

"Thank you, Doctor," I said as he left.

Bob and Gloria wrapped their arms around me. We wept, hugged, groaned in pain from our wounds, and praised God for several minutes.

Someone new entered the waiting area. Gloria said, "Uhm, hello, Steve."

"Hi, Gloria. I came to tell you that Caleb Kincade is in the Emergency Room and would like to see you when possible."

"That's great news, Steve. Which alcove is he in?" Gloria asked.

"He's in eighteen. He's in pretty bad shape, covered with these unusual burns. I've never seen anything like it?" Steve replied. "It's been a long night, and my shift is over. I need to get going. Goodbye." He turned and walked out of the waiting area.

Bob and Gloria followed him to the door. I had taken a couple of steps when Bob turned around and put his hand out.

"I understand why you want to see Caleb, but you need to stay here and go to Anna when the nurse comes."

Confused and torn, I stopped. I needed to be with Anna, but I wanted to see Caleb. No, I needed to see Caleb. It surprised me how strong that desire felt.

"I'll stay with Caroline," Gloria offered. "Bob, you check on him, and I'll be down after Caroline goes to ICU."

Resigned but happy, I sat down and waited for the nurse.

Chapter 57

Bob

Thursday Morning

I felt like cheering. All of us survived this horrible ordeal. Well, not all of us. Angelo died, but he was with Jesus and mentally whole. Previously, by faith, I believed the saved spirit went to heaven. Now I had witnessed it. I hope when it's my time, my death will be as noble as Angelo's.

I followed the red line on the ceiling leading me to the emergency room through the maze of hospital halls. It took longer than I expected to get there. Gloria had pushed me in a wheelchair to Caroline, and with my injuries, walking proved to be a more significant challenge than I expected. I found Caleb's alcove. A nurse took his blood pressure and punched information into a laptop. At least I thought it was Caleb. Bruising and bandages covered much of his face. His eyes were closed.

The ER nurse lifted her head at my approach. "I'm Bob B'nnett; I'm Mi'ter. Kincade's fwend and Pastor. How's he doin'?"

"There're burns under the facial bandages, plus he has severe burns on his arm and side. There are also multiple puncture wounds on his back and shoulder. I'm glad the beast that tortured him died."

"Foe's dead?" I asked incredulously.

The nurse replied, "You mean Ichabod Foe? Wow! I would've never guessed . . . I heard Mr. Kincade tell the officer that during the torture, Mr. Foe suddenly collapsed. Mr. Kincade untied himself and called 911."

Caleb's eyes fluttered open. The nurse noticed and said, "I'll give you some privacy," wandered off.

"We'come back," I grinned, or maybe it was more a grimace. It hurt to smile.

Tears welled up in Caleb's eyes, and a choking sob escaped his throat. "I c-couldn't say it . . . I couldn't . . .to save Anna. I'm so-so s-sorry." Another sob.

Confused, I asked, "What do you mean?"

"T-the demon said Anna d-died . . . if I w-worshipped him, he would s-save her. I couldn't d-do it. She's d-dead!" He turned his head, and the bandages on his cheek wicked the tears away.

Understanding dawned. "NO!" I shouted. "She's 'live."

"What?"

Lowering my voice, I said, "An'a's alive. She di' die on the op'rating table. Her sp'rit came to us as did an a'gel. D'en 'dey disapp'ared. We thou't she ha' gone to h'ven, but she came bac.' She's in ICU."

A coarse cry of delight erupted from the bandaged face. "Thank you, Lord. I . . . I thought she was dead. I thought Caroline would hate me for not saving her. Thank you . . . Thank you. How's Caroline?"

I proceeded to tell him about Caroline's injuries. My face hurt to talk, but I explained how Anna had been shot during the struggle and died but then came back. I spoke in low tones so that a passerby wouldn't hear our discussion.

Gloria arrived. It surprised me how I felt when I saw her. She gave me an all-too-brief hug and turned to Caleb.

"Caroline is with Anna. The nurse said Anna's still unconscious, and Caroline wants to be there when she wakes up."

Then I whispered, "What happened with Foe? Was there, a-you-know-what?"

"Dead, yes, and gone. Later," Caleb whispered back. I nodded.

Gloria said, "Caleb, I'm glad you're back and are alive, but I'm whipped. Things seem pretty calm for the moment. Does anyone mind if I go home for a shower, clean clothes, and some sleep? I've already called in and told them I'm not going to be there today."

"They want to keep me here until the afternoon, and it sounds like Caroline is going to be tied up for a while. I say go get some rest," Caleb said.

"Wou' it be too much tr'ble to give me a ride to C'ty M'ssion?" I asked Gloria. "I need to check in an' get some rest too." Gloria nodded. I turned to Caleb, "I'll be back l'ter t'is af'ernoon."

Caleb agreed, and we all said our good-byes. When we got outside, Gloria wore a big grin. She took my hand and squeezed it as we headed for the car.

Chapter 58

Caroline

Thursday Morning

I hobbled into the ICU behind my nurse escort. Soft beeps and whirrs filled the room. It took a moment for my eyes to adjust to the dim light. My breath caught in my throat. Anna lay bundled in blankets; I could only see her arms and pale little face surrounded by mountains of machines. An IV tube snaked from her arm to a bag hanging from a hook, and wires escaped under her gown, running to a heart monitor. A second tube trailed out of her nostril and over the far side of the bed.

"She'll probably sleep a couple of hours. Make yourself comfortable. Can I get you anything?" inquired the nurse. Speechless, I shook my head. "Get some rest and let me know if you need anything."

Oh, Anna, what have I done? Guilt sat in my abdomen like a heavy meal. I dragged a chair to the side of the bed. Maybe it would have been better if she had gone with the angel. "Brain damage," that's what the surgeon said. Her brain lacked oxygen for at least eight minutes, and we wouldn't know the extent of the damage until she woke. Another helping of guilt piled on top of the first.

I gently took her little hand in mine and kissed it. While my cheek rested on the back of Anna's hand, the tears and prayers flowed.

*****

Fingers ran through my hair. I heard a tiny, hoarse voice, "Mommy?" I had fallen asleep with my head on the edge of the bed.

Pain erupted from every part of my body as I sat up. I hurt like a giant bruise.

"Hi . . ." The words stalled, and I had to clear my throat. "Hi, Sweetie."

"Mommy, I feel fun'ee. My tum'ee hurts." She slurred the words.

"I know, Sweetie. The bad man's gun fired, and you were shot in your tummy. Do you remember the bad man?" She nodded her head. "The doctors had to cut your tummy to take the bullet out. They had to give you some medicine that makes you feel funny."

Anna pushed her covers back to look at her stomach. She ran her hand over her gown and winced.

"Those are the bandages that cover the cuts the doctor had to make," I said. My eyes moistened. "I'm so s-sorry, Sweetie." Tears threatened to escape. "Can you ever forgive me?"

She rasped, "Why?"

The damn burst. "B-because it's my fault you got shot. I fought with the man. I pulled the trigger. I shot you!" I buried my face in the blanket and sobbed. My shoulders shook, and I sucked in great gasps of air. Everything hurt, but I didn't care. I don't know how long this release of emotion went on. I felt a tapping of a small hand on the top of my head.

"Mommy, I forgive you. You're my Mommy," she cried and tried to wrap her little arms around my neck, but tubes and wires stopped her. We both cried for several more minutes. I reached for the facial tissue, blew my nose, and wiped my eyes. Then with a clean tissue, I dabbed her tears.

Anna's eye widened. "Mommy, what hap'ened to your face?" she whispered.

"The bad man hit me many times after I hit him," I explained. "What do you remember, Sweetie?"

Tears refilled her eyes. "I 'member Grace bein' hurt 'n the bad man hittin' me 'n taking me. I 'member you and Mr. Kincade. I saw you fightin' the bad man." She paused. "I also 'member Mr. Angel an' sunshine."

She remembers more than I thought. "You're going to be here a while, but I'll be here, and the nurses and doctors will take good care of you."

"A-hem," I turned and saw Caleb in a wheelchair. He looked pretty rough, but my heart leaped. "Are you willing to have a visitor?"

"Oh, Caleb . . ." I stiffly stood, walked over to him, and threw my arms around his neck. I cried into his shoulder for a while, even though every part of my body protested.

Pulling my head back, I said, "Wait . . . I thought only family members were allowed in here. How'd you get in?"

"I told them I was family. I hope I didn't lie." His battered face broke into a grin.

I wiped my eyes and nose with a tissue. Our eyes met, then our lips, and I gave Caleb a big, tear-soaked kiss. "No, I don't think you lied."

Chapter 59

Caleb

Friday Afternoon

The late afternoon sun streamed into the room and crawled up the wall like a slow-moving spotlight. Anna was released from the Intensive Care Unit and moved to the hospital's children's section. Flowers and butterflies decorated the wall. All the staff wore brightly colored scrubs.

Anna looked much better. A rosy blush painted her cheeks and her eyes bright with curiosity as she chatted quietly with her new stuffed animal friends. She still had an IV in her arm, but other tubes and wires had been removed when she was discharged from ICU. The doctors expected there to be some brain damage, but so far, we had seen none.

While Anna appeared better, I couldn't say the same for the rest of us. Except for Gloria, each of us displayed an assortment of bruises, bandages, and stitches. Bob's arm sported a sling.

We were a happy but apprehensive group, ecstatic we had survived. But Detective Wright called Bob this morning asking us to meet him at the hospital at 4:00 p.m. The detective wouldn't tell Bob why he wanted us together. Were we going to be arrested? What would happen to Anna?

Four o'clock arrived, and no Detective Wright. The butterflies in my stomach took flight. 4:15 . . . 4:23 . . . 4:37. The time crept by at a snail's pace. A knock at the door, and I jumped. Detective Wright entered the room, flanked by a patrolman. "Let's step into the hall," he ordered. We followed him out the door.

This doesn't look good. Without a lot of fanfare, the detective stated, "This case is filled with anomalies. I don't like it when things don't make complete sense. I spoke to each of you either the night of the incident or yesterday. Your stories don't exactly match, but they're consistent enough that I believe you. Angelo's death was not your fault. Somehow he just showed up. The state will be investigating St. Mary's security. He shouldn't have been able to escape unless he had help."

He paused. We waited. "The death of Matt Glockner, the gunman, is being ruled self-defense. His hand had gunpowder residue, as did Ms. Sullivan's. Pastor Bob, your hand only had a trace. This is consistent with your story. He was a dishonorably discharged ex-Marine. He was well-trained in hand-to-hand combat. He was an expert marksman. He is now the primary suspect in several unsolved cases."

Detective Wright paused again. He looked at each of us. I think he hoped for some spontaneous confession. "Regarding Mr. Foe, his death has been ruled 'natural causes.' The report says he died of a massive brain aneurysm. Off the record, the coroner said it looked like something liquefied his brain. Mr. Kincade, the medical examiner, assured me that you couldn't have caused Mr. Foe's death,"

He looked at each of us again. We remained silent. "I know you're not telling me everything. And on one level, that gnaws at me. On the other hand, I think it is in our best interest to let this go. You're officially cleared. There is no action pending on the state's part. However, I suspect there may be some legal action from Foe Financial Services," Detective Wright concluded.

He turned to the other officer who reached around the cart next to him and retrieved a black plastic bundle. He handed the bag to Detective Wright, who, in turn, gave it to me. "You said you wanted these back. Everything is here. Why you want this junk is beyond me." He looked at each of us one last time, did an about-face, and strode down the hall. The other policeman trotted to catch up.

Each of our faces bore a colossal smile. We returned to the room. Bob held his finger up as he stuck his head back into the hall to make sure Detective Wright was gone. He waited a few more moments, then dropped his hand, and like a gunshot to start a horse race, we all cheered. Moans and groans soon followed the spontaneous celebration as we had forgotten about our wounds. Then we gingerly hugged, laughed, and wept together.

I felt an immense sense of relief. "I thought for sure we were going to be arrested," I said. Then I had a revelation. I turned to Caroline and took her hands in mine. I looked into her eyes and said, "Do you realize only a week has passed since we woke in the Dream World? It seems like we've known each other forever. I feel like a new man."

"That's because you are a new man." I jumped and turned towards the voice. Ramiel appeared in our midst. He walked over to Anna and knelt next to the bed. Anna tried to wrap her arms around his neck, but the wound and tubes prevented her.

"Hello, Anna." Tears threatened to spill down her cheeks. She was speechless. The Ramiel took her outstretched hand in his. "You'll only be in the hospital a short while." He released her hand and gently placed it on her belly. A momentary glow surrounded it, which faded as he pulled his hand back. "That'll confuse the doctors." His laughter sounded like musical notes.

He stood and turned toward the rest of us and continued. "Rejoice! Your Lord and Savior is very pleased with you. You helped break evil's hold on this city. While Stanton won't be trouble-free, at least, it will be human trouble."

Thoughts and questions tumbled through my mind. We had been through a lot: the Dream World, demons, Foe, and Antiveritas.

"You look like you have something to say, Caleb," said the angel. "What is your question?"

"Why was I . . . I mean . . . why were we chosen for this task?"

"Do you remember the last answer you gave Antiveritas when he tried to tempt you?" Ramiel asked.

I thought a moment. So much had happened in Foe's massive office. I had a hard time recalling which scripture I had quoted. When I had the Armor of God on, questions like that were easy to answer. "I think I quoted Romans 8:28 about all things being good for those who love God. Are you telling me God needed me to suffer this trial so I could become what God wanted me to be?"

"That is correct," he replied. "Each of you needed this experience for different reasons. It has brought all of you closer to God and each other. If this test had been earlier in your lives, not every one of you would have been saved. If it had occurred later, one of you would be in Hell right now. The only way for all of you to come to Christ was for the trial to happen now. The defeat of the demons will trigger a spiritual revival in the city. Even more, souls will be saved because of your actions these last few days."

I smiled to myself. "Not bad for an old 'Dog,'" I said.

"What do you mean, Caleb?" questioned the angel.

"My father had a twisted sense of humor. He didn't want to have kids, but he had wanted a dog. He knew it would be socially unacceptable to name me 'Dog Kincade,' so instead, he named me 'Caleb,' which means 'Dog' in Hebrew.

"You are right, Caleb," Ramiel said. "But you are also wrong. Caleb can be defined as 'Dog.' The name conveys a dog's characteristics, such as 'faith, devotion, or whole-hearted.' Kincade means 'front or head of the battle.' So your name means 'God's faithful servant fighting wholeheartedly on the battlefront.' Also, the Biblical Caleb befriended Moses and Joshua and stood fearlessly against overwhelming odds. Caleb Kincade, your name describes you quite well."

My face warmed.

"There is one more message from your Lord," the angel said. "Keep the Armor of God. It will be needed again someday. Until then, your gifts will lie dormant, and you will not be able to see angels nor demons."

The angel faded from sight.

Caleb

One Year Later

Pastor Bob declared, "I now pronounce you husband and wife. What God has brought together, let no man put asunder. You may kiss your bride." Cheers and applause erupted from our church family in the pews. Bob had double duty being my Best Man and Pastor. Gloria was the Maid of Honor and Anna, the Flower Girl.

We turned to face the congregation. Bob said, "It is with great pleasure to introduce to you for the first time, Mr. and Mrs. Caleb Kincade." Additional applause and cheering filled the church sanctuary.

After the ceremony, just before noon, we relocated to the Missions Dining Room for the reception. We decided to have the party at the City Mission Soup Kitchen. That way, our church family and those homeless people we served and loved could share in our joy and a good meal. Bob and Gloria toasted our union with sparkling apple juice. A DJ played background music. Everybody had a great time.

Later, around 3:30 p.m., Bob walked over to me. "We gotta get to the airport. All the bags are in the car, and it's waiting for you out front. Gather your family. I'll meet you at the car."

Caroline stood nearby, chatting with some friends. Anna played with some girls at one of the tables. I walked over to her.

"Time to go to the airport, Sweetie." I held out a hand. She bounced off the chair and grabbed it. The next thing I knew, I was being dragged towards Mom. I got Caroline's attention and held out my free hand. Our fingers interlaced, and we headed for the front door. A host of guests waited for us outside to throw birdseed and cheer. Showered with seeds and love, we got in the back seat of the car. The girls brushed the birdseed out of their hair and giggled. Bob and Gloria drove us.

I felt exhausted and exhilarated. I had a chance to catch my breath. Caroline still held my hand, but Anna commanded her attention with a steady stream of Disney World questions. My eyes caressed my wife and daughter, and my thoughts went to the night before.

After the rehearsal dinner, we went to Caroline's apartment to put the little one to bed. Anna ran out of the bedroom, clad in bright pink jammies. She jumped into Bob's arms and gave him a big, good night hug and kiss on the cheek. Gloria received the same treatment. Then Anna turned to me and held her arms up to be picked up. I picked her up, and she wrapped her arms around my neck and said, "Night night Daddy."

"Daddy." I didn't know that a single word could melt a heart. She began calling "Daddy" about a month ago. Anna and Mom retired to the bedroom for prayers and snuggling.

A few minutes later, Caroline rejoined us in the living room. So much had happened during the last year. Anna's brain damage proved non-existent. Her mind got sharper every day.

After our ordeal, I quickly fell in love with Caroline. Six months later, I proposed. I was a nervous wreck and feared she might think it was too soon. My fears were unfounded.

Bob and Gloria started dating shortly after Caroline and me. They're engaged and intend to be married in a couple of months. I'll be the Best Man and Caroline, the Matron of Honor. Gloria works half-time at St. Mary's now. The other half of the time, she works with Bob as a counselor at the City Mission.

The Detective implied there might be a civil action against us for Ichabod Foe's death in the hospital. Lawyers representing Foe Financial Services contacted Caroline and me the next week, but it wasn't to sue us. Instead, they wanted to give us an "incentive" not to talk about the last day of Ichabod Foe's life. The incentive: five million dollars, job promotions, and raises for both of us. Of course, the government took a big chunk of that money. Another piece got socked away into a trust fund for Anna's college education. A lot of the money went for some much-needed improvements at the City Mission. We bought a minivan, paid for our honeymoon, and tucked the balance away for a rainy day.

The Armor of God lies hidden in a fire/water/bomb-proof case in my closet. After Caroline had accepted my marriage proposal, I found a new, two-bedroom apartment. We thought about living together to save money but decided we must remain pure before God and Anna.

It was one year ago today I woke in the Dream World. So much had happened. I thought about my life before Jesus took over. Just like it says in Second Corinthians 5:17, "This means that anyone who belongs to Christ has become a new person. The old life is gone; a new life has begun!"[23]

---

[23] 2 Corinthians 5:17

On November 13, 2009, I did experienced the nightmare in chapter one. Never had I encountered a dream so realistic with sight, sound, color, and touch. Yelling, "Jesus is my Savior," is how I exited the dream. I shot out of bed drenched in sweat, and my heart pounded hard in my chest. My first thought was, "I don't want to forget this dream" because I knew dreams fade with the light of day. At 2:00 a.m., I was handwriting notes on a piece of paper. I recorded the dream in as much detail as I could remember.

As I laid back down, I had two thoughts. The first was to thank Jesus for being my Savior.

The second was this could make an interesting story. If there was going to be a story, how might it go? And the plotline unfolded in my mind. You see, God literally inspired me to write this story.

The significant events in the first chapter happened in my dream in the order presented in this story. I did chop off a short section at the beginning that did not affect the overall dream. I added details to make it smoother to read, and I added details to describe elements better. But, the main events happened in the order presented.

I have never aspired to be a writer. I read many books, mostly mystery, science fiction, and fantasy. My strengths and aspirations in high school and my career have tended towards the sciences and technology.

About 6:00 a.m. on that day, I woke and went to my computer to record the dream. When I got to the end of the nightmare, I kept writing and what you have read is the result.

I try not to think of this as my story. This story is God's story, and He inspired me to tell it. As I wrote the book, I felt a solid connection to God. I suspect God placed this story in my heart to help me more than to help others. But I hope others, at some point, will read the story receiving encouragement and blessing from God.

Dear Reader: Thank you for taking the time to read this book. I never expected to write a book, but I did. I pray God blesses you as you read this. Perhaps you will be inspired to do something unexpected.

Gerald Thompson

Made in the USA
Middletown, DE
30 June 2021